PRAISE FOR TURF

'Lucas cleverly contrasts the banality of school life with the brutal code of the streets. An exhilarating, tragic tale and a terrific debut' *Financial Times*

'A powerful and unsettling novel, Turf's biggest success is its protagonist, a character as misunderstood, complex and terrifying as the world he must flee' *Observer*

'An unusual and original novel' *Independent on Sunday*

'This compelling story sheds light on the lives of a group of disaffected young people, for whom life is cheap and belonging to a gang is everything. An astounding and thought-provoking novel' *Booktrust*

'Turf is a fantastic, heartbreaking, emotional and gritty novel. Utterly realistic and completely devastating – one of the best novels I've read this year' *The Review Diaries*

'An exceptionally powerful debut novel; John Lucas is a writer to watch' *Books for Keeps*

'Jay makes for a lively, intelligent, wryly funny narrator. The fact he can see the hopelessness of his situation makes his tragic trajectory all the more poignant' *Metro*

'A harrowing but illuminating read' *Bookbag*

JOHN LUCAS was born in East London. The youngest of six boys, John comes from a large family of writers and artists, although he originally followed a different path by working in TV and video post-production for a number of years. John began to develop an interest in writing in his mid-twenties and studied a degree in Creative Writing at Middlesex University. *Turf* is his debut novel and the short story at the back of this book, *Trouble*, is a reimagining of the London riots through the eyes of characters from *Turf*.

TURF

JOHN LUCAS

CORGI

TURF

A CORGI BOOK 978 0 552 56612 4

First published in Great Britain by Bodley Head,
an imprint of Random House Children's Publishers UK
A Random House Group Company

Bodley Head edition published 2012
Corgi edition published 2013

1 3 5 7 9 10 8 6 4 2

Set in Bembo

Corgi Books are published by Random House Children's Publishers UK,
61–63 Uxbridge Road, London W5 5SA

For David

ONE

When you're fifteen, everything matters. I'm not just talk-ing about the obvious stuff: what music you like, who your crew is, whatever. I mean *everything*. All the little details. The way you carry your bag, the way you wear your jeans. The way you tie your shoes, the way you walk in your shoes, the kind of shoes you're wearing. The way you cut your hair, the way you wear your hat. Where you cross the road – *Traffic lights and zebra crossings are for pussies, bruv* – to where you sit on the bus. Your postcode, your estate, your school . . . You try living this life and see if it don't make you a little . . . tense.

Where you go for lunch, what you're eating for dinner. What crisps you like, what chocolate. Mars, Twix, Snickers: too mainstream. Toffee Crisp, Double Decker: too pikey.

Maltesers, Flake, Twirl: too girlie. Yorkie: too much to prove. Now, you would think a Galaxy would be too girlie, but actually a Galaxy is a good choice. It shows a certain class, like a man's got taste.

Personally, I'm sick of all this. What I really want is a Milky Way. A bar that's light and fluffy. A bar that takes me back to a time when life was simple, easy. A time when I could run around in shorts and a vest pretending I was a spaceship. A time when I could eat whatever chocolate bar I wanted.

Now life's not like that. Now I got to be serious. Now I got to be switched on every second. My phone goes. It's Shads. *Hurry the fuck up*, it says.

See what I mean?

The bass from his car stereo is shaking the shop windows: *Brum-brum brruuum. Brum brruuum.* I grab a bar from the rack and pay for that and the drinks.

Bill, the wise old dog of an owner, shakes his head at me, jowls wobbling.

'What, Bill?' I say.

He smiles. 'You always take so long to decide, Jaylon.'

'I know, I know.'

Shads's little black Corsa is half up on the kerb outside, hazard lights flashing, looking angry, impatient like a flea. I open the back door and get in, and before I've even got the door closed behind me, Muzza's slammed the car into gear and bounced us off the kerb.

'Careful with my door, bruv!' Shads shouts . . . at me.

Muzza swings the car round, seesaws back and forth until we've got just enough of an angle to avoid smashing into any parked cars, and we're gone.

Being in Shads's car feels like being in the smallest club in the world. Music's always blaring, so people are always shouting and it always feels crowded. That's without even mentioning all the illicit substances you can find inside. Shads should hire it out. It would be more exciting than those white limousines you see driving around the West End on stag do's and hen nights. Take Muzza's driving: he treats the streets of Hackney like a rally circuit. I can't believe he even manages to stay on the road most of the time, let alone not get pulled over. It might even be a tactic. If he was driving normally we probably would be pulled over. This way the cops barely even see us.

I hand Shads his Lucozade, and he grins at me, all eyes

and teeth. Diggy's in the front passenger seat and I pass him over a bottle of Sprite. I'm with the holy trinity of the Blake Street Boyz, and that means trouble.

'So, you banged that girl of yours yet?' says Shads, raising his voice above the stereo.

'No, not yet,' I say.

'You want to hurry up and bang her, bruv. She's fit. She's got a nice bit of meat on her. I like my black girls with a bit of meat on them. They carry it better than meaty white girls. Meaty white girls look fat. Meaty black girls just look like they got an *appetite*. You get me?'

'Yeah,' I say. 'Chocolate?'

'Mm – Galaxy Caramel, good choice.' Shads takes the bar and slides out a whole finger for himself. 'Bandy Man,' he says, passing it over to Diggy.

Diggy takes a chunk and passes it to Muzza. When I get it back I'm left with one piece. I hold it up. If this was a film, right now I'd be staring stonily at the camera.

Muzza tosses his piece up and manages to catch it in his mouth. He's Shads's main backup, the muscle, but I think he's taking his role a little too far. I've noticed he has trouble even bending his arms these days, his biceps sticking up and stopping them halfway. I've never spoken to Muzza that much, or at least, he's never spoken to me. He's a big Turkish guy of few words. Grunts and snarls, but as far as I can tell, few actual words. He arcs us across onto Lower Clapton Road without changing pace. A chorus of horns greet our arrival, but then we're forced to pull up violently behind a long line of buses and I nearly head-butt the back of Diggy's seat. Muzza starts kneading the steering wheel and muttering to himself, frustrated that his rally moves have been put on hold by the busy evening traffic.

This might be a good time to find out exactly where we're going but I don't want to seem worried. It's hard enough for me anyway. I always *look* worried. My eyes are too big. It's a problem when you're trying to be a gangster. It suited the Boyz when I was younger – I could get away with stuff un-suspected – but I got to keep close tabs on myself now I'm mixing it with the big boys . . . or at least squint a lot.

'So you're allowed out tonight then?' says Shads.

'Not exactly,' I say.

'That's what I like to see: a man with his priorities right. Still . . . I wouldn't mess with that aunt of yours. But then you'd never get me up there: too high.'

'Yeah, I think she was trying to get closer to God. You get me?'

To say my aunt Marsha is religious would be an understatement. She's even done her flat out like a Welcome Break for the soul; a handy stop-off on the trip up to heaven. I'm staying in her spare room and I share it with a metre-high plaster Sacred Heart Jesus and two pictures of the Holy Spirit – one dove, one ball of fire. There's a Moses holding the Ten Commandments and a life-size poster of another Jesus on the back of the door (when it's closed it looks like he's barging in the room). And the other day she added a small statue of St Jude – the patron saint of hopeless causes apparently – that she bought just for me.

Thanks . . . that really makes me feel good about myself, Marsh. Thanks a lot.

'That girl of yours, she's one of those churchy types too, innit?' says Shads.

'Yeah, well, she goes, yeah.'

Shads nods and rubs his jaw. 'I fucked this churchy girl the other day,' he says. 'Man, she was tough. I didn't know what it was. I was round at her place and I just couldn't give her an orgasm and I always like to pleasure a woman, but

man, it was like *she* was nailed to a cross she was that tense.'
Shads grins at me. It makes me nervous and I've realized it's
because all he does is draw his cheeks back and bare his
teeth. There's no real expression. It's like his skin's too tight
– like it's shrunk in the wash; tight over the muscles on his
arms, tight over his face and skull, showing up all the bumps
and ridges on his closely shaved head. It doesn't give him
much to work with. You'd get a more convincing smile
from a great white shark.

'That's the thing with these church girls,' he says.
'They're tough to crack. Now, if that girl of yours ain't
giving out, send her round to mine – I'll loosen her up.' He
pauses, must see the look on my face. He laughs and pushes
the side of my head. 'I'm not serious, bruv!' But I don't
know. I don't know if he can help being serious.

We pick up pace again and I look out at the passing
Clapton landscape – the beat-up shops and even more beat-
up people: an old guy in a wheelchair reading his paper in
a shop doorway; a woman down on her knees, begging
with her hands in the air, dressed up like some old gypsy
fortune teller. I've always wondered about people who beg
in a place like Clapton. I don't have much sympathy. You

7

want to go up West or something . . . at least to Islington, show a bit more ambition.

Shads laughs loudly. He's leaning forward with his arms up between the seats. I try and listen in, hoping I'll find out where we're going, but then I notice a suspicious-looking handle poking out the back of his jeans. I keep my eye on it, make sure I'm not imagining things, but he flops back and turns to me.

'I want to talk to you about your balls,' he says.

'What?' I say.

'Your balls. You got balls, yeah?'

'Well, yeah . . .'

He moves round so he's facing me, one leg folded under the other and his arm along the back of the seat, tapping his fingers close to my ear. 'Well, I ain't so sure, bruv. I heard what your buddy Milk did the other day in school – putting that kid's face in the Bunsen burner. I like that sort of positive action. Why don't I ever hear about you doing shit like that?'

'He didn't actually put his face in it; he just threatened him.'

Shads's eyebrows raise. 'That's not my point, bruv. He

would have done if required. That's the important thing. Now . . . would you?'

I lean forward, away from the tapping fingers. The car's feeling hot. 'I do it when I need to,' I say.

'Yeah, but you never find the need, do you?' He quickly changes position again, facing the front, both his arms out across the back. He opens his legs wide, bouncing on his toes. He sniffs, scratches and rubs at his jaw. All jerks and twitches. Shads is short, but he compensates by having body language that shouts in your face.

'The thing is, Jay,' he says, 'if you're going to join the Olders you got to have balls.' He pulls my shoulder so I'm sitting back again and turns towards me. 'I got to lay low. You boys have got to be my eyes and ears, and if you join the Olders you got to be my balls as well.' He pauses and looks past me through the window, maybe wondering if he could have put that a bit better.

If I'm honest, I knew this had to be about the Olders. I'm sixteen in a couple of weeks and that's graduation time. The test, the initiation, changes depending on who you are and what Shads wants from you and I know he isn't going to go easy. He's showing too much interest. The thing is, the

9

Boyz see it as a compliment if you have to do something big, something extreme, but the way I'm feeling I wouldn't mind being passed over altogether. Let me stay in the Youngers. I'll be the Blake Street Boyz' Peter Pan. Let me have my Milky Way. Leave all this grown-up stuff to people who want it.

'So tonight's about the Olders?' I say.

'Wait and see,' says Shads, his face cracking another grin. 'You'll enjoy it; it'll be fun.'

We drive through Homerton and on to Hackney Wick. Motorways loom over factories and car yards. It's the perfect place for a gangland execution. You can almost smell the undiscovered bodies, and I can't stop my mind from racing like Muzza's behind the wheel. That's another problem with the gangster life: the inside of your head ends up looking like the inside of a coffin. I can't get hold of a friend, I start thinking they might be dead. I see a group of kids I don't know, I think *I* might be dead. I'm driven to a wasteland with a man who looks like he's got a gun in the back of his jeans and I think . . . well, I think anything could happen.

We turn off the main road and onto a street parallel to

the overhanging motorway. Between the two are rows of car breakers and garages.

Diggy pokes his head in between the seats. 'It's just up here,' he says. Shads tells Muzza to pull over and he gives us all hits from an ornate little snuffbox full of coke. Shads holds a silver scoop out to the three of us, all delicately each time, like he's feeding a baby.

We move again, and further along turn off in front of a high, meshed gate. Sitting in front of the gate on a battered old school chair is a wiry white guy with slick-backed hair and stained blue overalls, sucking on a cigarette. He stands as we pull in, moves his palm across his head and bends down to Diggy's window.

'We're here for the action,' says Diggy.

'Name?' the man says, filling the car with the smell of tobacco. Shads waves his hands at it.

'Shadwell and associates,' says Diggy, slowly and deliberately like we're arriving for a business meeting.

The man nods, grimaces as he holds his cigarette between his lips, and steps back to open the gate. He bends down again as we drive through. 'Follow the track round to the left. They're almost ready to go.'

I'm feeling the hit already. Sergeant Sherbs has cracked his knuckles and is taking control. He's whipping my insides into shape, my muscles pulsing, my mind sharp and glassy. This is way better than the stuff me and Milk get to sell. That's cut with all sorts. I'm surprised we don't get more complaints. But then, most kids don't know any better. They're just happy they can get it at all, even if it means two weeks' lunch money. If their imaginations are good enough they'll persuade themselves they're on a nice buzz anyway.

We bump along a dirt track, car parts on either side in unsteady stacks. 'Easy, Muzz, easy!' shouts Shads as we hit a pothole. Muzza grunts. If Shads wasn't in the car he would probably love this terrain, but Shads isn't happy: he grabs at his door and the back of Muzza's seat like he's holding the car together himself.

We turn left and there's a garage in front of us. Three cars and a couple of vans are parked unevenly outside. The door's pulled low but there's a light on and I can make out a group of standing legs.

Muzza parks and we get out. I can hear voices inside the garage. Cars whoosh by on the motorway, hidden now by the towers of tangled, rusted metal, and somewhere in the distance there's the rhythmic pop of fireworks and the high-pitched whine of rockets.

'I love this time of year,' says Shads. 'You can get away with all sorts.' He opens his eyes wide and makes the sound of slow-motion explosions.

Muzza takes the lead and walks towards the garage, heaving up the door. The talking stops. I hang back and follow last. Sergeant Sherbs can't get all my brain cells on the front line and a big part of me is still feeling the novice. I loosen my neck and shoulders, disappear further into my coat and try and get into role as the silent, moody backup.

Strip lights on chains hang low from the roof and the air inside is thick with the smell of chemicals. The legs belong to a group of seven or eight men milling around a small plywood enclosure; all white and shifty. A skinny, ginger-haired guy breaks from the group and hops over, a gold rope chain swinging at his neck. 'Shadwell!' he says, and the talk starts up again.

'Terry!' says Shads, opening his arms wide but then backing off when Terry goes in for the hug. 'Handshake, mate, handshake!' And Terry has to make do with a clasp of hands and a pat on the back.

13

'Good to see you, mate!' says Terry, not noticing what could have been an awkward moment.

'This is Terry, boys,' says Shads, adjusting the back of his jeans, making sure everything's secure. 'He's been looking after an investment of mine, haven't you, Tezza?'

Terry rubs his hands together. 'That's right. I was about to get him out of the van. One of your boys want to give me a hand?'

Shads nods at Muzza, and both him and Terry pull the garage door up again and are gone. Diggy mumbles something about doing some business and begins skirting round the enclosure. Suddenly me and Shads are alone. Shads gets out his little box of tricks again. He moves in close and we both take quick hits. I sniff and gulp hard.

'Jaylon,' he says, taking the back of my neck with a clammy hand, 'I want you to do a job for me. I'm having trouble with the Yoot again. One little prick in particular is ruffling my feathers. A little prick *you* know. His name's Ram; he goes to your school.'

'Yeah, yeah, Ram, course I know him, yeah, yeah.' The words are tumbling out of me. I feel like I should be catching them, shoving them back in.

'Course you do. That's why I'm disappointed I'm the one telling *you* about it. If someone's causing trouble you should be coming to me, not the other way round. The Boyz own your school, the Boyz own the Downs, but the Yoot are getting ideas that they can muscle in. Now you got to be firm with these pricks.' Shads slides his hand from my neck and scoops out another hit. 'That's why you're going to kill Ram for me.' He says it all calm, flat, like it's nothing, and I can't respond because I've got another scoop of sherbs under my nose.

I'm not ready for it but I've got to take it. My nose stings and I have to pinch and rub at my sinuses. 'Kill him?' I say, through a mouth full of glue.

'Yeah . . . but I want you to use a shank, not a piece. Guns draw attention and I'd be worried you wouldn't have a clue what to do with one. Anyway, stabbing's more satisfying. It's more personal, you get me? More intimate.'

More intimate? Shads's attention is drawn by the garage door coming back up and I'm left hanging. Terry and Muzza shuffle in, carrying a big plastic crate with a grille on one end. Shads slides back towards me, slippery, slippery. 'Do it and you'll be in the Olders. Don't— What am I talking about? There ain't no *don't*, is there? *Don't* ain't in my vocabulary, bruv! Now come on, let's watch some sport!'

Diggy's done the rounds and must see my expression. No doubt my eyes are on full beam. He comes over, gives a sharp nod. 'Told you, yeah?'

I nod back.

'Don't worry about it. We've all got to do it some stage. We'll help you out.' He nods at me again, squeezes my shoulder. It's not much but it makes me feel a bit better. I like Diggy. He's tall, long arms and legs. That's why people call him Bandy Man. And even just having him at that angle is reassuring. It's like he's overseeing things, keeping us all in check. I wonder what Shads would be like if Diggy wasn't around to keep an eye on him. I'm about to ask what he knows about Ram when Shads calls us over to the crate.

'Meet Sugar Ray, boys!' he says, and through the grille I can see a dark brown pit bull sitting on its hind legs, a streak of white down its front. It looks calm, steely. 'Had him since he was a puppy,' says Shads. 'Named after Sugar Ray Robinson, obviously: best fighter of all time. Terry here's been training him up.'

16

'He's an athlete,' says Terry. 'Not left nuffin' to chance. He's gonna go far.'

The other group are talking, drinking cans of beer, some with their heads down, tucking into Diggy's goods, but one man with thick glasses and bushy sideburns breaks away. He leaves the garage. With him goes a big guy with a tattooed neck that's wider than the shiny bald head that's on top of it.

'That's the competition,' says Terry. 'Jo O'Dowd, guy in the glasses. He's been a trainer for about twenty years. His dog's been going nearly as long though, so we shouldn't have too much of a problem.'

'The dog's been going *how long*?' hisses Shads. 'You told me Sugar's first fight was going to be a walkover, Tezza! We were gonna ease him in gently!'

'Course, Shadwell, course.' Terry twitches. 'I mean . . . he was good in his day but he's on his last legs now. Even O'Dowd's getting ready to pay his respects.'

Maybe it's the effect of Diggy's goods, or the prospect of blood in the air, but by the time Jo O'Dowd comes back in with his dog, a sandy pit bull, muzzled and pulling at its leash, the garage is crackling. Shads is bouncing around, like he wants to get in the pit and join in the fighting. Even Muzza looks excited. But it all feels far away to me. The sherbs should help, but with all the new information I've been flooded with, I'm feeling numb, split in two; a passenger in my own body. I don't think this is going to be my idea of a fun evening.

The referee, middle-aged with combed-back wavy white hair and black darts shirt, gets into the pit and stands on the dirty red carpet that's spread inside. He claps and rubs his hands. 'It's time now, gents! Let's have a look at those dogs!'

The plywood is pulled apart at the corners and Terry shuffles Sugar Ray into the pit. O'Dowd brings his dog in through the opposite corner. Everyone's gathered tight around and shouting. One man in a suit is so charged he looks like he's about to explode. He's shouting, 'GOOORRRNTHEEEN, GOOORRRNTHEEEN,' like some prehistoric terror bird. Both Terry and Jo O'Dowd have tight hold of their dogs; they're both up on their hind legs now, clawing and gnashing.

The only thing I've got to compare this to is boxing, but in boxing the fighters shift and jerk and psych themselves up. They hop and bounce and hit their gloves together. You get a sense of what they're feeling. You're in the ring with them. Watching these dogs, I don't see anything behind their eyes. It's not even that they look like they *want* to kill each other. They're just doing it because it's the only thing they've ever done.

'Hold your dogs!' shouts the ref.

Terry pats Sugar Ray hard on the ribs. 'Rip his face off,' is his only advice.

The ref holds his arm up, leaves it for a few seconds, and swings it down. Both dogs are let go and immediately become a swirl of slavering, snarling flesh.

I joined the Blake Street Boyz when I was twelve. That's late compared to most of the Youngers, but then I didn't move to the estate until I was eleven. Milk lived three doors down from me and we became friends straight away. Our door was open, all our furniture being moved in, and Milk came and stood in the doorway and asked if I wanted to play on his PlayStation. Of course, he wasn't called Milk in those days, just plain old Chris, but that's how easy it is to make friends when you're young: you like playing, I like playing – let's go play!

19

The Boyz ruled the estate and I soon found out that if you weren't in the gang you weren't anybody. That didn't bother me that much at the time; I didn't even know what being in a gang meant, really – other than having a big group of friends on tap – but Milk was desperate to join and because he was my new best friend we helped each other. Milk was tough – tougher than me – but I had the brains. I was sharp. And black, which on the estate and in school means you don't have to prove so much. Milk wouldn't have got in without me, and I wouldn't have lasted without him. The Boyz saw we made a good team.

My mum always used to say: *To make it in the world you've got to understand the world.* What I don't think she realized is, you move to an estate like Blake Street and that *is* the world. It's hard to see more than that. Before secondary school and before the estate, understanding meant listening to my parents, doing my schoolwork, reading books. I didn't even question it. Once I did question it, I couldn't see the point in it any more. What was it meant to do for me? Get me a job some day? In Hackney – the kind of Hackney I know – getting your education on the street is what matters. You can use it there and then. And if you use it right it pays off.

The Boyz started us off slowly – running errands, storing stuff in our flats – but gradually we moved on to the occasional bit of dealing and stealing. Soon it began to feel like a proper job. The Boyz became our friends, family, teachers, employers, and the gang was like a business. In most businesses people talk about climbing the career ladder; in the gang it feels more like an assault course. And because it's all laid out like that, because you can see the territory, it's easy to get a taste for it. A taste for the money, the respect, the glamour.

The gang's everywhere, it affects everything. When you need them that's a good thing, but when you don't . . . It's like Shads said, there's no such thing as *don't*. No one tells you that in the beginning. Once you're in there's no out.

What made being in the Boyz exciting was that feeling of control. You don't have that as a kid. You're always getting told to do this, do that, you can't do this, you can't do that. With the Boyz there was freedom. At least that's what it felt like. Now I'm not so sure.

In school there's rules – uniforms, homework, exams – but no teacher's going to kill you if you turn up to the wrong class or wear trainers instead of shoes. I'm not saying it's like that on our estate, but you go outside and that's the level things are at. I'm not exaggerating. Shads says, *You got to be firm with these pricks.* That means killing someone. Being firm means killing someone. And I'm the one who's got to do it. Do I have a choice? I think I might have made my choice. I think I might have made it when I was too young to know it even *was* a choice.

Shads shouts and kicks the plywood. Sugar Ray's in trouble. The O'Dowd dog is dragging him backwards, his teeth clenched around Sugar's jaw. There's a nasty ripping sound. The O'Dowd corner goes up:

'Kill him!'

'Get in there!'

'GOOORRRRNTHEEEEN.'

Blood hits the pit wall. I can smell it, and it's mixing with the smell of oil and sweat and fur. I look up at the low hanging lights, the chains. Listen to the snarling, dog *and* human. I could be in some torture chamber.

Shads shouts again. Diggy tries to calm him down but Shads shrugs him off. Sugar Ray's on the ground and the O'Dowd dog has him by the neck, but gradually Sugar Ray stops fighting back and the other dog begins easing off until he's just standing there panting, not interested in a no-contest.

'I think we have a winner, gents!' calls the ref.

The O'Dowd corner go up again but are cut short by a loud 'FUCK OFF!' It's Shads and he climbs into the pit. I get the feeling this isn't in the rules but I don't think Shads cares. 'My dog's not dead,' he says, like it's the most obvious thing in the world. 'This is supposed to be a fight to the death, yeah? Well, my dog is not dead!'

'Sorry, son,' says the ref and I flinch at the word *son*. 'It's over. We've got a clear winner.'

Shads shakes his head, hands on hips, and turns to Jo O'Dowd. 'What the fuck is wrong with your dog? He's just sitting there like a pussy. Make him fight!'

'There's no point,' says O'Dowd. There's a general murmuring of agreement around the pit. 'He's trained to fight, and it's not a fight any more.'

Shads flings his arms about – he's in danger of looking stupid. Then, out of nowhere, he swings his leg back and kicks Sugar Ray hard in the ribs. But there's no time for anyone to react to that because Shads has pulled the gun out from the back of his jeans. 'I want this fight to end the way it's meant to end,' he says, turning to all corners. 'Otherwise I refuse to accept the decision.'

Sugar Ray lets out a wheezing noise and tries to move but his legs are too unsteady. There's silence around the pit, everyone frozen. I'm waiting for Muzza and Diggy to step in but they're as quiet as everyone else.

The ref, cautious, steps slowly towards Shads, his hands out. 'Look, son' – *I wish he'd stop saying that to him* – 'it's over; your dog's not going to survive this.' He stops himself from adding, 'Especially after you've just kicked him,' but shows wise restraint.

'Bullshit!' says Shads.

Jo O'Dowd leans into the pit and puts his hands on his dog, checking injuries. Shads turns towards him, and in one movement, all casually, he points the gun down and fires. The sound fills the garage and my head, and so much happens in the next few seconds that it takes a while to figure it all out. O'Dowd falls back at the shot, and his dog hits against the pit wall, which collapses. The fat-necked guy screams and goes down as well, and as he falls he takes two others with him.

As far as I can tell, Shads's bullet has passed straight through the dog, the plywood and hit the fat-necked guy's leg. He's crying out and his friends try to get him up. The ring of the bullet is still pounding around the garage or the inside of my head – I'm not sure which – and I duck away, thinking maybe the bullet itself is still rebounding. I feel something brush past behind me and it's Jo O'Dowd crawling across the floor. Shads spins around, waving the gun. The ref and a few others make a run for the door, pushing each other and bottlenecking up as they try and escape. Terry's turned into a statue, and Muzza and Diggy just look confused. Diggy stands with his hands on his head and Muzza is flexing and rubbing his arms.

The fat-necked guy is helped towards the door by his two friends, his arms across their shoulders. 'Trust you lot to bring a gun to a dog fight!' one of them shouts. I can tell he wants to add more but Shads's gun makes him think better of it.

Even so, Shads is spitting. 'You lot?' he says. 'What the fuck does *you lot* mean?!' and he's ready to fire again. He raises his arm, but at last Diggy steps in, grabbing hold of him, moving him backwards, and for a minute they're doing some kind of tango as Diggy keeps hold of Shads's out-stretched arm.

'Calm, calm, calm, calm,' he says. Shads's eyes are practically out of his head; he looks like he could take us all out. Diggy keeps tight hold of him, keeps repeating his 'calm's until they start to register and slowly Shads settles.

Apart from the four of us and Terry – and one dead, and one dying dog – the garage is empty now. I didn't even see O'Dowd leave and I wonder if he crawled all the way. I move for what feels like the first time in ages and I realize I've been clenching pretty much all my muscles because I feel stiff and awkward and out of it. I step over into the pit. I have to tread carefully to avoid all the mess and I get down on my haunches to look at Sugar Ray. His eye is wide and stands out against his torn, matted coat. I realize I've never seen anything look as scared in my life. It's as if all the energy, all the violence that's been bred into him his whole life has been drained and he's just left confused and suffering.

'Fucking useless piece of shit.' It's Shads, standing over my shoulder. 'Shoot it,' he says. I stand up, and for a second I want to shoot *him*.

He holds the gun out. 'Did you hear me?' I pause,

looking at it. 'You know what that is, yeah? You've seen one before, yeah? You fucking pussy! I said: shoot the dog!'

I take it and move it around my palm. It's heavy and slick with Shads's sweat. I flex my fingers around it. There's something in the feel of it, the weight of it, that clears my head. I look back at Shads, testing myself, testing him. Shads sniffs loudly. I sniff too. It's because of the coke, but we both know that a strong sniff with eye contact is body language for *Fuck you*. Neither of us moves. Shads's eyes narrow to slits. 'Shoot the dog,' he whispers.

I'm pushing against something, I know I am. I'm on the brink. The gun feels OK in my hand. I look down at Sugar Ray. He needs this to end and that's got to come first. His chest is pounding, his eye frantic. I shuffle the gun in my palm; make sure I've got it secure. I clench my muscles, clench my jaw and point the gun. The ringing in my head increases until it blocks out everything else. The world shrinks until it's just me and Sugar Ray, and I pull the trigger.

TWO

'I hope you all had a productive half term,' says Mr Wallace. 'I want to start by congratulating our Year Eleven football team, who beat all the odds *and* last year's champions in the first round of the Inner London Cup last week. Let's get a round of applause, please!'

I have to stop and grip my head. It's not much of an ovation, not very enthusiastic, but it's still like having Gatling guns whirring against my ears.

I should be at home in bed. If I had my way, I would be. But Marsha was getting up as I was getting in and she made sure she saw me, with uniform on and bag in hand, go back out the door again. It wasn't as late as it sounds; it's just Marsha gets up *early*. She calls morning what most people are still calling night. I tried to sleep for a couple of hours but I had the eyes of all my holy roommates on me, disapproving and passing judgement. I couldn't get comfortable, couldn't relax, and it wasn't long before Marsha was in my face again. I planned to walk around for an hour or so until she'd left for work, but being outside was so much effort I phoned Milk, met up with him and came into school.

Of course if I'd had my way last night I would have gone straight home after the dog fight. That was enough excitement for one evening, but Shads had other ideas. He said he was feeling stressed – surprisingly enough – and wanted us all to go back to his and unwind. He wanted to play chess.

'Chess?' says Milk.

'Yeah, chess,' I say. My back slides down the seat and I have to force myself up again. The smell of polish from the hall floor is raking at my raw sinuses. I wipe at the sweat on my forehead and pull at my school shirt, which is sticking to me like clingfilm. I'm hung over.

'Shads kept going on about his eighteen months inside and how good he got. All these stories about the money he made. So I'm thinking he's got to be pretty good. We're back at his, still doing the sherbs, and I'm not paying much attention to the chess. He plays Diggy – beats him. Plays Muzza – beats him. Then it's my turn and I start realizing . . . Shads is *rubbish*.'

'Rubbish?'

'Yeah . . . and the thing is, I'm quite good. I was in my primary school chess team.'

'Serious? I worry about you sometimes, bruv.'

'I didn't volunteer. They chose me and I got to get out of lessons. Anyway, I'm just playing my natural game, and out of nowhere I start winning. Of course, Shads doesn't like that and he starts getting all worked up, talking to himself, and I'm thinking, not again . . . and then he pulls his gun out and I'm thinking, I'm going to go the same way as the dogs.'

I told Milk about the first part of the evening on the way in, and no matter how bad I make it sound, he wishes he'd been there. He's even jealous I got to shoot a dog. I also told him about Ram and the initiation, which might have been a mistake, but I had to tell someone – and seeing as Milk and Marsha have been the only two people I've spoken to this morning I think I chose the better of the two options.

'You thought he was going to shoot you?' says Milk.

'Well, yeah ... if I won. I mean, he's using the gun to think with, like it's a comfort thing. Twirling it round his fingers, scratching his chin with it, but I didn't want to take my chances. So, from then on I try and lose, but trying to lose but trying not to look like I'm trying to, while I'm coked up and a gun's waving in my face? That was not my idea of relaxation, bruv. You get me?'

'So did you win?'

'No, I lost. But he made it fucking hard for me.'

Mrs Harris's face appears between our shoulders. 'Can you two stop talking and pay attention, please?'

We're sitting on the end of the back row, which has its benefits but it also means you're in the line of fire for any teacher on patrol at the back of the hall, and this morning it's Mrs Harris. She's short, Mrs Harris, and thin, but in the same way a blade is. I feel like she could cut you just by walking past you too quick.

I shrug and face the front but the sun's streaming in through the windows behind me and lighting up the stage, reflecting off Mr Wallace's mic stand, turning it into a Roman candle and making me squint. Mr Wallace is our head teacher and I always think he deliberately positions himself directly in the sun, like he wants to appear as some priest or prophet, the chosen one imparting words of wisdom to his flock.

I raise my hand to shield my eyes, but when I do I realize I should have worn a clean shirt this morning. These things can happen when you're not living at home. I just grabbed whatever one I could find. The effort of sitting upright is making me sweat from every pore and the sweat is rehydrating previously dried sweaty areas. It's the first day back after half term and I smell. That's not good. I need some air flow, and the air in the hall is stuffy and stale. I flap my blazer like wings, but that makes Milk and the two kids directly in front of me start sniffing the air and begin looking around. I sink into my chair and move slightly towards the empty seat on my left, but Milk nudges me and I realize the seat's not going to stay empty for long. Mrs Harris is letting some latecomers into the hall. The seat next to me is the nearest one available and the first kid is Carlton Ramsey. Ram. *Him*. I try and cover the seat. I stretch my arm out but quickly think better of it; it's no use, anyway: he's coming. I look at Milk and mouth, 'Be cool,' at him.

Ram sits down, a smile on his face. Ram's got one of those faces that looks permanently amused, like he's having this constant little joke with himself at your expense.

I face the front. I'm hoping Mr Wallace will say something so amazing, so interesting, so entertaining that I'll be carried away by his words for the rest of assembly and will forget Ram is even there. But Ram has other ideas. He leans towards me, the top of his head too close and the lines of his braided hair like some hypnotic swirly pattern. My stomach churns. Ram sniffs. 'You stink,' he says.

Before I can say anything, Milk leans in from the other side and I get hit by a strong whiff of his hair gel. 'That's 'cos he was fucking your mum all night,' he says.

Great . . . this is just what I need right now . . . really.

I'm almost passing out. Ram chuckles and seems content to leave it, but Milk shuffles in his seat. He doesn't want to let it go and I'm wishing I hadn't told him anything.

'How's business?' says Milk, leaning across me. I hold my breath and make a mental note to try and explain to him the concept of being cool.

'Business is good,' says Ram. 'Of course, it helps when you've got a decent product to sell; you should try it.'

'*You* should be careful. This ain't Yoot turf, bruv, and you know it.'

'You three settle down!' says Mrs Harris over my shoulder. Good one, Milk. Why don't you just tell him that I'm meant to be killing him in a couple of weeks too? Write a little note out for Mr Wallace to tell the whole school. Or just put your hand up and tell everyone the news yourself.

Both Milk and Ram are quiet for a few minutes and Mr Wallace moves on to the Halloween fancy dress competition this Friday. Not that I ever go in for these things, but the way I'm feeling now I could turn up like this and win first prize for my accurate portrayal of a moving corpse.

It's not long before Milk starts shuffling again. 'I saw you outside the school gates, Ram. Putting on that Jamaican accent. *Skonk, skonk.* You sounded like a fucking goose, bruv.'

'That sounds like the noise your mum makes when I fuck her in the ear.'

'How small is your dick that you can fit it in some-one's ear?'

'It's not my dick that's small; it's your mum's head that's big.' And Ram leans in, pulling on his ears and puffing out his cheeks.

'Right, that's it, you two: Carlton, Christopher – outside!' Mrs Harris grabs both of them and leads them noisily out of the hall, their protests making half the kids in front turn round to check out the dramatics. I'm practically horizontal now, trying to avoid all the nosy, curious eyes. And I'm thinking, That's him – the kid cussing Milk's mum and pulling faces. *That's him.* I run over what he's just said. *It's not my dick that's small; it's your mum's head that's big.* Suddenly they sounds like lyrics. I can see him singing them in a video, some slow ballad, on a beach, his open shirt blowing in the wind. I imagine Ram being spoken about in documentaries, his way with words, his imagination, his rare talents. What a waste, cut off in his prime. All because of me.

I get a flash of Shads, last night, in my face, all sweaty and twitchy, dishing out the sherbs: *Anyway, stabbing's more satisfying. It's more personal, you get me? More intimate.* More intimate? We're going to be linked for ever, me and Ram. I might feel closer to him than I ever do to anyone. His life is going to end because of me. Whoever Ram has been, whatever he's done, it's going to be hung on a wall framed by Jay with a knife in his hand. What do I do with that information? Where do I go? Home . . . that's where I go. I stand up, grab my bag and head out into the corridor, where Mrs Harris is leaning in close to Ram and Milk and jabbing her finger. 'See you later, bruv,' I say to Milk as I walk past.

'Jaylon, where do you think you're going?' says Mrs Harris.

'Doctor's appointment,' I say, not turning round. She hisses something at my back but I'm not listening. I'm breathing in the cool air of the corridor, feeling the weight of the school lift off my shoulders. I'm going to have a day off. I need one.

THREE

I'm close to a lot of benches. I got benches all over Hackney. Me and Milk have a bench in the school playground. Everyone knows not to sit on it. We got our bench by the row of shops near our school. Everyone knows not to sit on that, either. And me and Hannah have a bench. It's on the edge of a scruffy patch of green near her house. That's where I'm waiting for her now.

I wonder how long I'll be measuring success by the bench? If I ever make my millions, will I have a gold-plated bench in my bathroom? One covered in chinchilla fur in my bedroom? A motorized one with fat tyres on my own private golf course? I'm collecting benches the way billionaires collect houses. Monaco? Oh yeah ... got a two-metre bench down there by the harbour. New York?

Got a bench overlooking Central Park . . . actually it's *in* the park, bruv.

You got to start somewhere. The only reason me and Hannah have a bench is because private space is limited. She's not allowed in my bedroom and I'm not even allowed in her house. That's the problem being with someone when you're fifteen. You don't feel like kids but everyone's treating you like kids. You're stuck. Stuck with things like a bench.

While we're waiting, I'll tell you about Hannah. Hannah's something special. She's the sort of girl that can make going to church on a Sunday seem like an all right thing to do. That's not easy. Same goes with doing her homework and going to the library. She glides on through. She's the sort of girl who when she drinks through a straw never slurps.

She gave me a chance too. Bad girls tend to be *too* bad for me. You got to cut your way through this thick mass of attitude before you can even have a conversation. It's tiring. But then good girls make their minds up straight away and stay well clear like I'm some kind of criminal. The fact that technically I sometimes am is beside the point. Not breaking the law is pretty much impossible if you're living my kind of life. That's not *my* fault. All I'm doing is playing the hand I've been dealt. Anyway, Hannah was different.

We ended up meeting because my mum was losing the battle between the family and the Boyz. She brought out the big guns. Well . . . big Aunt Marsha to be precise: her older sister. Marsha lives on the estate as well, but the idea was that under her roof my bad ways would be corrected. I'd learn to walk the straight and narrow. Also, I'd be away from my little brother, Lloyd. If I was going down, they didn't want me taking him with me.

Part of my rehabilitation was to go to church every Sunday. I sat at the back, staring at the ground, arms folded tight. But the services went on for hours, and being that moody for that long takes a lot of effort. I started looking around, listening to the singing, and that's when I noticed Hannah. I guessed she knew who I was. They were a close-knit congregation and Marsha was an important part of the group. She helped organize events, the music, was always sitting up at the front. I could see her telling everyone: *That kid in the back's my nephew. I can't kick no sense into him so I'm going to let Jesus and the Holy Spirit have a go instead.* I'm being passed around . . . my mum, Marsha, now God. I wonder who's going to be next?

I couldn't believe I was even seeing Hannah to begin with. I blinked, rubbed my eyes, thought the boredom was making me hallucinate. She sang in the choir and I love watching a girl sing, even if it is religious songs. She got really into it, closing her eyes, following the music with her hands in the air. I needed a closer look. So after the service I went up to talk to her. She smiled straight away, her big friendly brown eyes shining like they were reflecting candles. The church didn't even *have* candles. Her hair curled and bounced around her shoulders; her skin reminded me of a Galaxy but looked softer and smoother than one could ever be; and she had a body too – the way her curves even managed to make church clothes look good.

I was all prepared for the worst but it turned out to be easy. We just talked. I realized I'd never had that with a girl before. I didn't need to pretend that I was a bad boy (if she was bad) or that I was good (if she was good). She took me as I was. Her head's kind of clear like that. She knows what she wants, what she likes. She's built on something solid.

It took three trips to the cinema and three walks home

before she let me kiss her.

'So you believe in all that?' I said. 'Jesus and stuff.'

'Yeah, of course.'

'Why? I mean . . . where's the proof?'

'I don't know; it's just a feeling. I feel it in church. It's not like Jesus has ever appeared to me and gone' – she put on a deep voice – ' "Hannah, I exist!" But there are little things. Sometimes things just have a way of working out.'

'Yeah . . . like what?'

'You're going to laugh.'

'Go on.'

'Well . . . I asked Jesus if he could make Marsha's sexy nephew actually be nice too.'

She was right. I laughed. 'And did he?'

'Yeah, I think so.'

I didn't mention that I didn't think *nice* was the word but I was happy to go along with it. I walked her to her gate and we stopped and kissed. Not for long, but it was one of those times you want to run through again because it happens and you can't believe it's happening, but while you're thinking that, you're not thinking about the actual event itself. 'We got to do that again,' I said. She smiled and

41

said goodnight. As she walked the short garden path I noticed a figure at an upstairs window. When I looked up, a curtain fell back into place.

That's as close as I've ever got to her house.

When she turns up I'm smoking a cigarette. She tuts and sits down at the opposite end of the bench. I take one long drag and flick it away. Then I shuffle along, swing my legs up and put my head in her lap, looking up at her. She sits there pulling a face, her hands up, like she's spilled something.

'My nose hurts,' I say. 'I think I'm getting a sinus infection. Can you rub it for me?'

'Is that why you left school early?'

'Yeah.' I take her fingers and guide them to the bridge of my nose. 'Just there.' I rub her fingers against my nose until she starts doing it herself. I close my eyes and begin drifting off.

'That better?' she says, after a couple of minutes.

'Yeah, getting there,' I say. 'I'm feeling stressed.'

'What is it?'

'Stuff with the Boyz.'

'What stuff? Actually I don't want to know.' She covers my mouth with her hand.

'Not everything I do is bad,' I try and say.

'What?' she says, taking her hand away.

'I said, not everything I do is bad.'

'No . . . not everything,' and she starts rubbing my nose again. 'Why don't you just leave?' she says after a while.

'Because I'm comfortable.'

'No . . . I mean the gang,' and she pinches my nose. 'You haven't signed anything, have you? They don't own you.'

'Not exactly. Look . . . I'm joining the Olders in a couple of weeks. Then I'll have more responsibility, more choice. It's not easy in the Youngers; everything you do has got to go through the big boys.'

Hannah shakes her head. I know to her it sounds stupid – all these rules and regulations.

'What if you get yourself into trouble? *More* trouble? What about school? Getting a job, having a career?'

'Say that word again?'

'What word?'

'That last word you said.'

'Career?'

'Yeah . . .'

'What about it?'

'You sound like a seagull. CAREER-CAREER.'

She pinches my nose. 'I'm serious. What are you going to be? A professional gangster? You can if you want, but I'm not interested.'

'I like you talking like that.'

'Like what?'

'Like . . . I don't know . . . like there's a future. I forget that sometimes.'

I close my eyes again. I feel her shuffle slightly and her arms wrap around my head. I feel her lips against mine. I've learned to concentrate on how they feel now and it's the best feeling in the world. It's so good there's no room for anything else at all.

FOUR

I don't have a key for my mum's any more; at least, not officially. I borrowed Lloyd's and got one cut but when my mum's in I have to pretend I haven't got one. Even so, I don't think it's fair that I'm not allowed a key to my own home. It is still my home; I don't count Marsha's. Most of my stuff's still here, and my bedroom – even though Lloyd's in there too – looks like my bedroom and not the inside of a church.

It's Lloyd who comes to the door, still wearing his school uniform even though it's gone six. I expect more of a welcome but I recognize that glazed-over look he has on his face. He opens the door slowly, squeaks, like Muzza on helium, and wanders back towards the bedroom. It's dark in the hall. I flick the light switch as I walk past. Nothing happens.

45

'Mum in?' I say to Lloyd's back. He raises his arm slowly, waving into the gloom in the direction of the living room. I follow behind, he turns left into the bedroom and in one easy movement flops into position up close to the TV screen, picks up his Xbox controller and restarts his game. He's clearly been like this for hours. The fast movement of his thumbs is the only evidence that he hasn't been lobotomized.

My mum bought him an Xbox after I moved out. It was bad timing. I feel like I've been replaced by a machine. There's silence apart from the sound of electronic grunts, kicks and punches.

Lloyd's got the same big eyes as me, but they're set a bit further apart, which manages to make him look more naturally happy. He takes after our dad in that sort of way, where as I take a bit more after our mum. He's got more weight on him than I do too. I could eat all the fast food in Hackney and still hide behind lampposts. That's why, when I'm with Milk, most of the time I do the talking and he does the Bunsen burner treatment.

Lloyd seems to have forgotten I'm there. 'How's school?' I say. I hate asking that question. I hate being *asked* that question. It's a sign you've got nothing else to say. It's a last conversational resort, mainly used by relatives and friends of relatives who don't know anything about you other than that you're at the age when you're probably going to school so you're on safe ground asking about it.

'It's all right,' he says.

I wait for more but he's not interested. I turn to the wardrobe. Inside I've got a shoebox of DVDs. Some of the cases are empty – well, empty of discs – and I take out five wraps of sherbs and four eighths of weed, all wrapped tightly in clingfilm. The sound of Lloyd's game has stopped and I can feel him watching me.

'You know if you ever touch my stuff I'll know about it, yeah?' I say over my shoulder, making sure my back's blocking his view. 'And I'll take you round to Marsha's and throw you off her balcony – but before that you'll get one of her fish curries as your last meal.'

'Eeeeeuuurrgh,' he says, and restarts his game.

I get up. 'Exactly,' I say. 'That's the noise you'll be making all the way down. Do you want a game, then?'

'Of what?'

'I don't know. Whatever you're playing.'

For the next ten minutes I get trounced at *Tekken 6*. I'm ashamed to say I'm better at chess than I am at computer games but I like doing my big brother bit. Even though Lloyd doesn't say much, I can tell he's pleased he can beat me for once instead of the Xbox. But it's not long before I've taken enough beats and I decide to leave him to it.

'You want to play a different game?' he says, perky now.

'No. I got to get back for dinner. Unless . . . you want to go for me? Marsh would love to see you.'

'No,' he says, pushing me.

'It's all right, Lloyd, really. I'll call her.' I get out my phone and pretend to call. Lloyd tries to grab it off me and I retreat to the doorway.

'Stop it!' he says.

'You sure? You really don't want to go?' My phone's at my ear. I mouth at him that it's ringing. 'I'll just tell her – what? You . . . you think her food tastes like shit and she can stick it up her— *Lloyd*, I'm shocked at you, bruv!' He grabs a pen from the desk in front of him and throws it at me. It hits the door as I make a quick dart into the hall.

My mum seems to have developed a hyper-sensitivity to light; that or she's trying to cut back on energy bills. But then saying that, she doesn't like the curtains open in the daytime either. The pot plants are starting to suffer, getting all sick and yellowy. It's only Lloyd's room that seems to get any light. I should probably move all the plants in there before they give up altogether. My mum's not going to do it. When she's in the flat she's glued to the sofa, her eyes glued to the TV. I think medically she'd be described as a cabbage.

I manage to find the living-room doorway, the ghostly glow from the TV giving me something to aim for, and I stand there watching her.

Shads has got a spare room in his flat where he lets his more needy customers hang out; the ones who find it hard to walk once they've parted with their funds and tried their goods. My mum wouldn't look out of place in there. The unnatural light from the TV makes her look ill and her face is tired and lined. She seems to be shrinking too, taking up less and less space on the sofa. I noticed the shrinking a while ago. I think it coincided with my dad leaving and it makes me wonder if she'll keep shrinking, turn slowly into a Brussels sprout, and one day we'll lose her down in between the cushions.

I think about turning the light on, giving her a shock, but she's concentrating so hard on the screen and looking so fragile it might push her over the edge. I notice her tense up but she doesn't turn her attention away from the screen. I walk into the room, into her eye-line, and wave my hand in between her and the TV.

'What are you doing?' she says. Her voice sticks, like she hasn't spoken in hours. She frowns and shifts in her seat.

'Just checking,' I say. I walk back to the chair near the door and sit on the arm; it's high-backed with curved arms, the sort of chair your granddad would sit on. It's got a brown cord cover and I make a loud scraping noise across it with my fingers.

'How's school?' she says, breathing out heavily, maybe realizing I'm not going to go quietly.

'It's all right,' I say, instinctively copying Lloyd. Then there's silence. That looks like the end of the conversation. I make the scraping sound again but it's not satisfying.

'Well, I don't want to interrupt you,' I say. 'I can see you're very busy.'

She shuffles again, pulls her legs up underneath her and folds her arms tight.

I sigh as loudly as I can, get up and flick the light switch as I leave the room. Nothing happens.

Out on the balcony I cling to the wall and fill my lungs with the cool evening air. There's a strong wind blowing. A Coke can rattles along the concrete below. Leaves and carrier bags swirl up high.

I feel like I've just escaped some airtight container. It makes me worry about Lloyd. I gave him a quick cuff round the head as a goodbye but he barely noticed it, all his attention on the Xbox. I know my mum's trying to keep him away from the Boyz, but seeing him like that makes me think he might be better off with us. At least he'd be experiencing real life.

My ears are still ringing from last night. I say ringing – it's more like a crackle, static interference, like I'm in between radio stations. I shake my head and rub at my ears, opening and closing my mouth, hoping to massage my eardrums better.

I cross the car park, the wind blowing hard against me. I can hear fireworks over on the Downs – pops, bangs, fizzes.

I look up, but I don't see anything above the grey blocks, only fast tumbling cloud that's all smoky yellows and murky purples.

Even though I'm stuck between two flats I don't want to live in, I'm glad of the estate, glad to be tucked away inside. When we were younger we used to treat it like a huge adventure playground. We got to know every corner, every hiding place. Every block was different, had a different feel. That's what mountain ranges are probably like, every peak with its own identity, own personality, and Blake Point's like Mount Everest. The wind hums around me as I walk up the raised gangway. The block's pale bricks stand out against the bruised-looking sky and I almost swirl with the wind, trying to see the top looming out over me.

Of course, piss on your way up a mountain, it's probably not that noticeable. Piss in the one working lift of a twenty-one-storey tower block and you create a problem, and that's exactly what someone's done. I contemplate taking the stairs but it really *is* like climbing a mountain getting up to Marsha's – I'd probably have to camp overnight, so I decide to brave it. What sort of person pisses in a lift? I can almost understand it on the stairwell: you might have a long way to go and you haven't got the limited amount of time you have in the lift. Maybe it broke down, but even then, there's got to be options. Either way, by the time I get to the eighteenth floor I'm as short of breath as I would've been if I'd taken the stairs. I take some big gulps of air when I step out onto the landing, but the relief is short-lived because I pick up the ominous whiff of industrial spices and cooking fish. It gets stronger the closer I get to Marsha's door. It makes me wonder if she's ever had complaints from the neighbours. I lean against the wall for a minute and compose myself. When I open the door the full force of the fish curry hits my nostrils and the edge of my vision starts going hazy.

I don't know whether it's because Marsha's never had kids, never even had a relationship as far as I know, but her cooking is definitely a sign that she's spent too much time alone. You could say it was an acquired taste but I don't think the word *taste* even comes into it. The only explanation can be that the obliteration of her taste buds over the years has led to the dishes getting stronger and stronger to compensate. I can see her in the future, standing there in one of those biohazard suits, the kitchen quarantined, still adding more spice, more zing, more *flavour*.

I hover in the hall and take off my coat and trainers. Marsha has a no-shoes policy, like you're about to walk on holy ground. I take deep breaths, shrug my shoulders, loosen my neck muscles and pump my fists. Believe me, it requires this kind of preparation.

Marsha has her back to me. She's wide and manages to block the view of the entire cooker. Her grey-streaked hair is tied back in a bun. She's wearing a turquoise cardigan that's stretched tight across her back and a big flowery skirt that hangs down like a giant lampshade, almost to the floor. She looks like the back end of Scooby Doo's mystery bus. Her wardrobe seems specifically chosen to make her look twenty years older than she actually is. She wears skirts like that so often I've given her the nickname Deadly Lampshade. I imagine her being some comic-book villain: the Deadly Lampshade, poisoning her victims with her toxic recipes and evil concoctions and managing to elude the authorities by disguising herself as the van of a crime-fighting Great Dane.

'That's good timing,' she says, without looking over her shoulder. 'You hungry?'

There are many ways to answer that question. Being a woman of God you'd think she'd appreciate honesty but I plump for a cautious 'Yeah . . .'

The table's already set. Besides the food, another problem is that Marsha insists on eating 'properly', which means sitting at the tiny kitchen table, with its sticky plastic cover, and no TV – not even any music or radio – to take the edge off; just a heavy atmosphere, the clink of cutlery and the torture of my taste buds.

'So, how's your mother?' she says, emptying the contents of a large pan onto two plates of gloopy rice.

I pour myself some water from the glass jug on the table. 'Same as always. I had to hold her wrist to make sure she still had a pulse.'

'She works hard. She's entitled to relax when she gets home.'

'Well, yeah, there's relaxing and then there's turning into a vegetable. Anyway, all she does is sit at a desk all day. I've seen her. How hard can that be?'

My mum works in the job centre, trying to help people get back into work. I remember an awkward moment when my parents were still together and my dad lost his job, and he had to go in there and apply for benefits. He didn't talk to any of us for days after that. It scarred him. I think it had a lot to do with them eventually splitting up. And I think that's part of the reason why he got so into gambling – the bookies was somewhere he *definitely* wouldn't bump into my mum, no matter how often he went.

'Your mother spends a lot of time and energy worrying about you and your brother,' says Marsha.

'Yeah, looks like it. She's shut Lloyd up by giving him an Xbox and she's got rid of me altogether. She should be celebrating. She can spend all her time with her feet up in front of the telly.'

Marsha shakes her head and puts the pan back on the hob. There are now two heaped plates of bright pink fish curry on the table; the pink of the curry is eerily similar to the pink plastic frames of Marsha's oversized glasses, almost as if they're made from the same chemical compounds. She then puts a small basket of home-made bread rolls down in the centre of the table. I say bread rolls – they're more like bread rocks. Anywhere else on the table and the basket would be in danger of flipping it up like a seesaw under the weight. Unlike her curries they taste OK but they can break your cutlery and your teeth in the process.

Marsha says a quick grace, and then the race is on to think of some topic of conversation before I start getting asked awkward questions. But the problem with trying to force conversation is that my mind goes blank. I'm scouring my brain, unloading my memory banks, but they're empty, I'm getting nothing.

'How's Hannah?' says Marsha, beating me to it.

'Yeah, good.' I force a forkful of curry into my mouth, immediately washing it down with a big gulp of water, and I swear I feel it fizz on contact.

'Yes, she is good,' says Marsha. 'She's a good girl. I just hope she's being a good influence on you and you're not being a bad influence on her.'

I make a huffy noise and manage to lift a bread roll out of the basket and lower it carefully onto my plate. If I dropped one of these off the balcony it could kill someone.

'You just make sure you treat her well, that's all I'm saying.'

She might have a point but it annoys me when she talks to me like this. I mean, I'm supposed to be here for rehabilitation purposes, not to be told how bad I am all the time. What's that supposed to do for my spirits? It doesn't help, and suddenly my mind has flipped and I've gone from searching for something to say and finding nothing to trying to ignore a hundred different ways of provoking her that are all hopping around pleading to be let out. I try to distract myself by sawing my bread roll in half. After about thirty seconds I've barely made a scratch and my resolve is weakening.

'I'm not sure I should be taking relationship advice from you, you get me?' I give up on the roll. I need a drill, a chainsaw. Marsha has her back straight, eyebrows arched, waiting for more, and I don't want to disappoint her. 'Well, have you ever had a boyfriend?'

I shouldn't be talking to the Deadly Lampshade like this but I can't help it. It's like when you've got toothache and you can't help fiddling with the tooth, digging your nails into the gum to alter the pain you're feeling, like it doesn't matter if it's worse, so long as it's different.

Marsha stays still, her hands resting on the table, knife and fork in her fists, giving me the green light.

'I guess you don't need one though, do you? You got Jesus. You should take some tips from him. I thought that's what this church thing was all about? At least he gave people bread and fish they could actually eat.'

I don't know where this is coming from. I'm impressed with myself but also confused as to why I'm only this quick when I'm saying bad stuff. 'Imagine if he gave five thousand people this?' I say. 'There'd be a riot, you get me?'

'Yes, I get you,' she says quietly. 'I get you loud and clear. You can be as cheeky as you want. Cheeky's never going to get you anywhere in life! You moan about your mother; at least your mother works. At least she's managed to raise a family! You're only good for raising hell! And you think she's done a bad job? On her own all this time? She tried to give you an education! She tried to give you a chance! You've been given a damn sight better chance than a lot of these kids. It's not her fault you're doing your best to throw it all away!'

'How did we get on to this?' I say. 'I'm just trying to eat my dinner. All I'm saying is, you don't make it easy, and maybe there's a link with *you* being on your own all this time as well.'

I can't help smiling, but it's not a Shads smile – it's too edgy. I'm pushing it, and you never know what you'll get back from the Deadly Lampshade. It's like poking a tiger with a stick.

'So much like your father,' she says under her breath. She looks down and begins eating again. That's a low blow. I expect more from Marsha than that. I at least expect her to play fair. But in a way it means I've won. It shows she's not up for a long, drawn-out battle. It also gives me a way out.

'I don't need to hear this,' I say. I bang my cutlery, scrape my chair back and leave the kitchen making as much noise as possible.

'What about your dinner?'

'I'll get something out. Something edible.'

Marsha gasps and bangs her own cutlery down.

The no-shoes policy means it's hard to make a quick, dramatic exit. I have to spend a valuable thirty seconds crouched down in the hall putting my trainers on, and this gives Marsha time to meet me there.

She stands over me as I squeeze my heel into my shoe, the lampshade in my eye-line. 'So you're going to run away, are you? That's your answer?'

'Leave me alone,' I say, getting up.

'Leave you alone? When are you going to stop playing

the victim? You think it's so hard for you? If you had any clue how hard life really was you wouldn't be acting like such a damned fool!'

I shake my head at her slowly, try and look unimpressed. I open the door but I have to squeeze past her to get out and she makes sure she slams the door shut behind me. I stumble out onto the landing. I hear a muffled cry inside, and there's a bang against the door. For a second I'm confused about how I've managed to find my way out here again so soon. I immediately want to go back in, but then I start going over what's just happened and I realize I'm better off out here – I'm better off out on the estate, I'm better off with my friends and I'm going to go and find them.

Raising hell? Who actually says that? It would be a lot easier to take what she said seriously if she didn't use such antique language.

I take the stairs down. I can't face the lift again. After a flight I start speeding up, running. I begin leaping down the last few steps of every floor, making the leaps bigger and bigger as I go until I'm nearly jumping entire flights. It starts getting hypnotic, the movements the same every time, the floors flying by. I begin to lose track of where I am in the building. I keep expecting to reach the bottom, but every corner there are more stairs and it goes on and on. I start wondering if it's ever going to end and think about being in a world that's just one long staircase. That's what Hell would really be like: no lakes of fire and screaming tormented souls, just one long staircase and you don't know whether you're meant to go up or down, but whatever way you go it never stops, never changes. That thought makes me speed up even more, and eventually I fly down the final flight, career into the main hallway and nearly slam into the opposite wall.

I stay there for a minute, panting, bending over and holding my knees; the ringing in my head louder, my pulse thumping.

When I get my breath back I call Diggy. It turns out most of the Boyz are over on the estate football pitch – a walled and fenced-in concrete rectangle a couple of blocks away.

I listen to the Boyz laughing and joking through the phone. Just hearing them sets me thinking about Ram. I'm not ready to joke about him yet. I think about the pitch with its fences as a high as a prison yard's. I'm not ready to be serious about him either.

I make my excuses, hang up, and start walking out of the estate. Marsha would be pleased: I'm going to go to church instead.

FIVE

I haven't told you about Leo. Leo's the reason I'm going to church. I met him my first Sunday. He was sitting on the low wall at the back of the car park that divides the church from the old, rundown community centre.

I could smell him before I saw him. At least, I could smell what he was smoking. I followed my nose and saw him puffing on a joint that was lit up big and bright as a streetlamp.

He was scruffy-looking, his light brown skin greasy, unwashed. He was wearing an oversized parka jacket and unlaced boots, loose jeans tucked inside, and he rocked backwards and forwards on the wall, puffing on the joint and humming, rumbling low like a didgeridoo.

'Greetings, brother,' he said as I wandered up, his eyes almost closed, the lids flickering.

'Yeah, er . . . greetings.'

'You come to join me in spiritual enlightenment?'

'I'm meant to be getting spiritual enlightenment in there,' I said, nodding towards the church, 'but if you're offering . . .' thinking he meant he was going to share the goods.

His eyes went wide and he locked them on me. 'I can offer you many things,' he said, 'but this is not one of them.'

He shook his head and brown flecks of leaf fell from his messy, overgrown hair. He settled back and put his hands together, one hand clasped over the other. He seemed to be waiting for me to go, but when I didn't move, and maybe noticing my disappointed eyes fixed on the joint, he got up.

He walked quickly between the parked cars, bending low to the ground like he'd lost something; then after a minute or so he found what he was looking for and brought it carefully back over. It was a leaf.

'Take this,' he said, all serious and ceremonial, cradling it in his hands.

'It's a leaf, bruv.'

He looked at me like I was stupid. 'Yes . . . yes, it is. Well spotted. It is also a gift. A precious one. I chose it specially;

treat it with care. And if anyone asks, say the wind gave it to you.'

I took it and rolled the stem between my fingers.

He sat back down. 'Where did you get it?' he said.

'You just gave it to me, bruv.'

'No!' he said angrily.

'All right, man. Sorry – the wind. It was the wind.'

'Yes.'

It looked like a kid's drawing of a fire – licking red and yellow flames. It was a good-looking leaf, I couldn't argue with that, but I would've preferred a smoke.

He started humming and rocking again, eyes low, hands together as before. I didn't move – he was entertaining to watch. The tone of the humming went up and down, changed to unknown words and back to humming again. Then he coughed and glanced out of the corner of his eye. When he saw I was still there he stood up and raised his arms.

'And I beheld the great and the marvellous!' he said. 'Those who walk to the rhythm of falling leaves! This trenchtown elixir, this Earth spirit! Under tarred firmament and mustard moon! My heart is a jumping bean! In a

Babylon, in a soul wilderness! Concrete and saccharine! Minds are glossy magazines!

'I am Mister Music! Play on with hasted felicity! I *am* Mister Music! I *am* the gate of the gods! I'll be your walk-in wardrobe, your binding comforter. Roast this bean with fire! Show me the blood of the saints!' He sat back down, flipped up the hood of his parka and shot me another quick glance.

'That normally scares them off,' he said.

'No, man . . . I liked it. *Babylon . . . blood of the saints . . .* Sounds like what I'll be getting in there in a minute, anyway.'

'You'll learn more from that,' he said, pointing the shrinking joint at the leaf. 'Put it to your ear.' I left it where it was. 'Do it!' he said, angry again. That time I did as I was told. '*Listen.*'

'Jaylon!' came a familiar booming voice. I jumped. It was Marsha. Not, as far as I could tell, speaking through the leaf, but from the other side of the car park. He chuckled.

I shrugged, tried to compose myself. 'I'm being summoned, bruv,' I said.

'Then you can hear them. That's a good sign, very good.

Fly, my brother. Fly . . . but first take my hand.' I did. It was rough, papery.

'Leo,' he said.

'Jaylon,' I said. 'See you later, Leo . . . Mister Music.'

I crossed the car park.

'I'm not having you escaping that easily,' said Marsha. 'Come on, the service is about to start. And why are you holding that to your head?'

'It's a leaf, Marsh. He— The wind gave it to me.'

Marsha arched her eyebrow. 'Did it really,' she said. 'I think we'd better get you inside quickly.'

Leo's been there every week. I try and talk to him, try and get a toke off him. Most of the time he talks, but sometimes it doesn't seem like he's even there, just gets on with his didgeridoo humming. And he's never let me have a smoke.

The car park's deserted. The church all shut up. There's a light coming from an upper window in the flat above the church where Pastor Burke lives, and an orange glow from the security lights on the scaffolding around the community centre. There's no sign of Leo. I've only seen him on Sundays. I'm not Marsha – I don't make a habit of going to church during the week; maybe Leo doesn't either.

I scout around the car park, make sure he's not hiding in any dark corners, and I sit down in his usual place on the wall. The wind is still up and I close my eyes and concentrate on the feel of it against my face.

Being an old tramp is suddenly looking like a good career option. I wonder if Hannah would prefer me doing that to me being in the Boyz. *Actually, baby, I've decided I'm going to take your advice and leave the gang . . . and I'm going to start living with this old tramp guy that I've been talking to outside church. What do you think? I think he sleeps in the old community centre; you can come round after the service on Sundays. Bring some soup and cigarettes, though, yeah?*

'Greetings, brother,' says a voice to my side, and I leap out of my skin.

'Where did you come from?' It's Leo, sitting on the wall away to my left.

'You seem troubled,' he says.

I raise my eyebrows. 'How do you know that?'

'I could smell it in your walk, see it in your thoughts, feel it in the curve of your spine.'

69

I rub my hands up my arms, straighten my back.

Leo takes a joint out of his parka pocket and lights it. 'You want to talk about it?' he says.

'No . . . yeah . . . I don't know . . . Actually, yeah, I *do* know. I want to shout about it, bruv. I want to broadcast it from the rooftops but I can't.'

'I see, yes. Well, just give me an idea. You don't have to tell me the details.'

'I can't, man. I'm in an impossible situation.'

'Nothing's impossible.'

'This is.'

'Is it about a woman? If it is, then I'd believe you. Women are impossible: impossible to please, impossible to understand.'

'It's not about a woman.'

'Then you've got nothing to worry about.'

'I have, bruv. I got *a lot* to worry about.'

'OK, then – give me a moment.' I turn my head away and I can feel his eyes on me. He hums like before, making noises, words, back to humming. Then he stands up, clears his throat and raises his arms, holding the joint like a burning torch. 'Impossible is a state of mind! Hold fast to the tabernacle and you will split the mountain! You will free the spirit and winnow the heart! Blessings have been scattered on the wind. In time they will bud! In time the way will open! Seven limes hang in the dark! But beware the fever! It will blur your vision when you most need to see! And you will see that it all matters! All of it!' He lands back down heavily. 'Does that help?'

'Not really, bruv, to be honest.'

'Disappointing,' he says.

'I was hoping for something more, like . . . concrete, you get me?'

'Concrete is man-made!' he says. 'Soulless! You are made of the Heaven and the Earth, the Alpha and the Omega. You are always and for ever amen. Don't talk to me about concrete.'

'Sorry, man. Look, I appreciate it. How about giving me a toke on that?' I say, nodding at the joint. 'That might help.'

Leo holds it up. 'Let me tell you about this. This herb grows where only I can harvest it. It's a potent plant – too potent for the uninitiated. I call it Burning Bush. You know why I call it Burning Bush? Because through it God *speaks*. And to the uninitiated God's voice is as unintelligible and as strong as a tornado, a whirlwind. You would be blown away. And that, my brother' – he points it at me – 'that would not help your situation.'

I shake my head and look up at the lit window above the church. 'Maybe I'll talk to Pastor Burke about it,' I say.

'Pasta bake is unintelligible also.'

'Pastor *Burke*, bruv.'

'Whatever. Whatever yourself.'

I turn to see him shuffle and put his hands together, one palm over the other. I can't help laughing. 'Is that it?' I say.

'Is that what? Where?' He looks around.

'Is that all you got to offer?'

'That not enough?' I shake my head. 'Then sing with me.' He holds out his hand, twitches his fingers. 'Many problems can be solved through song. Let Mr Music show you.' He starts humming again.

Hannah, home, Marsha, the Boyz, Leo . . . I feel like I'm pinballing around and quickly running out of bumpers.

I stand up. 'See you later, bruv.'

'Disappointing,' he says again. 'Go then, my brother. Go get your fill of pasta bake.'

'Pastor Burke, bruv.'

'Whatever. Whatever yourself.'

I start walking back across the car park.

'You should always take a hand when it is offered!' he calls after me. 'You never know when you might need one!'

I ignore him and keep walking.

'Wait!' he shouts. I stop this time and turn round. He trots across the car park. 'Take this,' he says, holding out a wide brown sycamore leaf.

'Thanks,' I say.

'You're welcome.' He bows, the hood of his parka flopping onto his head. It obscures his face as he stands up straight and he leaves it there. He turns and wanders back into the shadows, making shapes in the air with his hands and humming loudly.

Yeah, thanks, Leo. *Thanks a lot.*

SIX

At lunch time the row of shops near my school looks like one of those seabird nesting colonies you see on nature programmes. All these kids in black and white uniforms arrive for an hour, scream, shout, cackle, squawk, stuff their faces and leave behind a mess of food cartons, drink cans, chips and chicken bones. That's because at my school if you're anyone, you don't eat in school, you eat at one of the local restaurants: Hot Chick! or Chicken Ribs And Pizza.

Our school's in a residential area; it's too much of a trek to go anywhere else for lunch, so both restaurants have a captive clientele, despite their problems. The problems start with their logos. With Chicken Ribs And Pizza it's the capital A on And. The design of the lettering means that from a distance it looks like it's called CRAP. But then the

Hot Chick! logo is a chicken with long eyelashes and a lip-sticked, puckered beak. I don't like my food having that much personality. If the sexiness of a chicken was important to me I doubt I'd want to see that chicken fried in breadcrumbs.

You can tell most local people avoid the shops at lunch time, but even then I don't think they know the true politics of the situation. For years now there's been a dividing line between the two restaurants – the Westhall Yoot go to Hot Chick!; the Blake Street Boyz go to Chicken Ribs And Pizza – and from there everyone else makes their choice and shows their allegiance. Sometimes the tensions boil over – not surprising considering it's just the newsagent that divides the two – but if we don't keep an eye on our turf we could risk losing it altogether. That's why at lunch time you'll find me and Milk, sentries on duty, stationed on our bench outside Chicken Ribs And Pizza.

The way I'm feeling today, though, I wouldn't mind being in the library. For one, I'm not hungry, and two, I want the peace and quiet: the cool library air, nothing but the rustle of pages, the occasional nerdy cough. A bit of peace. There's too much going on out here. The Yoot crew standing in a tight circle away to our left, laughing, shouting so loud it's like they're trying to use it as a weapon, trying to hit us with it. They're shooting sly little glances over, all set up, always ready. It's tiring just watching them.

Since being told about Ram and the initiation, I'm seeing things different. I can't take any little word, any little action on its own. It all means something, it's all got significance. They could be joking about me; maybe they've got moles in the Boyz' camp and know all about the plan. They could be planning something themselves. Maybe my eyes are giving me away, flashing like twin lighthouses, sending out warning signs about the jagged rocks of my guilty conscience. *And I haven't even done anything yet.*

I wish Shads hadn't told me. I wish he'd just sprung it on me, a surprise birthday present. This waiting's going to make a mess of my head. Part of me wants to get it done now; just go over there, jook him while he's eating his lunch. Would that count? Probably . . . but then there's not much point being in the Olders if I'm in prison for the rest of my life. No . . . there's no point killing Ram until I can get away with it . . . actually, until there's a *chance* of getting away with it – that's closer to the truth. That kind of logic makes me feel ill and the smell of chicken is already turning my stomach. The only thing I can face for lunch is a Galaxy and I'm hoping the familiar, comforting taste of chocolate on my taste buds will soothe my over-active brain cells.

Thankfully, we've got more kids arriving to block the view of the Yoot. I've noticed if me and Milk sit still for long enough we become the centre of a mini solar system, other kids slowly getting drawn in by gravity. The ones closest are always the ones that should be there – other members of the Boyz: *Actual Boyz*. Then other kids with the right status level: *Honorary Boyz*. Then the further out, the weaker the connection: *Wannabe Boyz* – kids who drift by in these wide orbits, hoping to pick up some trace of gangster stardust, some faint ray of credibility (I should also point out that, despite the titles, the last two groups are also open to girls).

I don't mind the Actuals and the Honoraries; it's the Wannabes that get on my nerves. I'd hate to be one of those distant satellites. I wouldn't know what to do with myself. I think I'd admit defeat and head off to the library with my head down but my dignity intact.

Milk's already decimated a selection box of chicken, ribs and chips and is rooting around for any edible bits he might have missed. He probably could eat all the fast food in Hackney – and it's starting to show. His small dark eyes are slowly getting smaller, sinking further into his chubby face. The rest of him is filling out too. Part of me thinks it's deliberate – the bigger he gets the more of a presence he gets, the more intimidating. It's all part of the job for Milk.

'I tried one of those new pills last night,' he says.

'Yeah?' I say. 'What are they like?'

'I don't know. I fell asleep.'

'You what?'

'I was at home, yeah? I thought I'd just try one. You know I don't like selling anything I haven't tried myself: I feel like I'm being bad to my customers. But yeah, fell asleep. I mean, I had a good dream. I dreamed I was white-water rafting, which I reckon must've had something to do with it, but I want more from my pills than that, really.'

'Yeah . . . I know what you mean.'

'I'm going to have to get rid of 'em quick. When word gets round they're going to be a hard sell.'

Milk manages to scrape up the dregs into one messy

handful, cranks his head back and shovels it into his mouth.

'I'm still hungry,' he says when he's guzzled it down. He holds onto a chicken leg but tosses away the cardboard box, getting it close to but not quite in the nearby bin. He looks around.

'Eh, yo, Fuller!' he calls, and throws the chicken leg, hitting Mickey Fuller on the shoulder – a floppy-haired white kid with big nervous eyes, out on the very edge of our solar system. Mickey tries to ignore Milk and the chicken leg, and take cover behind his group of friends waiting outside Chicken Ribs And Pizza.

'Fuller, come here!' shouts Milk.

That draws a lot of attention and Fuller's got no choice but to find out what Milk wants. He ambles over. 'Hi, Milk,' he says, looking awkward and suspicious.

'It's not Milk to you, Fuller, you should know that. It's Chris. Only my friends call me Milk and I don't remember us ever being friends. Now, I see you're using our restaurant for lunch – what are you getting?'

'I was going to get some chicken.'

'Of course you were getting chicken, Fuller. What kind of chicken?'

'A selection box.'

Milk's in his element now, slipping into a well-rehearsed routine, very professional. 'A selection box?' he says. 'Which one's your favourite?'

'I like the deluxe one.'

'Whoa! You hear that, Jay? My man Fuller here likes the *deluxe boxes*! A bit of *deluxe* chicken for lunch. My man Fuller must be *flush*!'

There's a ripple round the gathering crowd, part amusement, part shock at the extent of Mickey Fuller's extravagance. Even the Yoot are looking over.

'How much is one of those deluxe chicken boxes then, Fuller?'

Milk knows exactly how much they are; it's our restaurant, but he wants everyone to know how much cash Mickey Fuller has to spare for lunch. Fuller mumbles something.

'What's that, Fuller? Speak up.'

'Four-eighty.'

'Four-eighty? My man spends four pounds eighty on his lunch! And it's only the start of the week. Wow . . . you must have money to *burn*, bruv!'

Milk hops off the bench and moves in close to Fuller, crowding him, his face barely a chip length away. Some of the crowd recognize this as a sign to move on – they could get involved, see too much, become culpable witnesses.

'I've got some new pills, Fuller – you want to buy some?'

'N-no.'

'Sorry, I'll rephrase; I'm not making myself clear. Buy some fucking pills off me, Fuller.'

'I'm hungry though, Milk – I mean – I mean, Chris.'

'Well, take a pill and you won't feel hungry, will you? Now give me your money before I get angry.'

Fuller shuffles again; he glances at the remaining spectators and his face burns. He quickly looks round at his friends, who have pushed their way into the safety of Chicken Ribs And Pizza. They do their best to avoid looking back.

'You're making me angry, Fuller. I don't think you're quite getting what I'm saying to you. Now buy a pill off me or I'll fucking shank you.'

'You'll – you'll what?'

'I'll shank you, you prick. Now give me your money.'

Fuller rummages in his blazer, his hands shaking;

he fumbles so much he can't even negotiate his pockets.

'That's right, Fuller. Look, I'm only making you buy one. I'm being kind to you. That's only five pounds.'

Conveniently it's a crumpled five-pound note that Fuller finally manages to put in Milk's hand. Milk flattens it out, holds it up to the light. Satisfied, he checks his own pocket and pops something into Fuller's hand. Fuller goes to look at it but Milk stops him.

'Not here, Fuller. Jesus . . . show some sense. Anyone would think you didn't trust me. You see,' says Milk, stepping back, playing to the crowd, 'I could have just taken your money, but no, I stick to my word. What do you say?'

'Thanks . . . thanks, Chris.' Fuller's so caught up in the situation he sounds genuinely grateful.

'That's right. Now, get the fuck out of my face.'

The crowd begins breaking up, but there's a buzz, conversation's heightened, everyone asking each other if they saw what happened, re-enacting it. Milk's beaming.

Fuller doesn't know what to do. He stands still for a minute, staring at his fist, too scared to open it. He begins to go towards his friends, but there's a big crowd waiting to be served and it doesn't look like he's capable of standing still, and after a couple of false starts he wanders back in the direction of the school building. After a short distance he breaks into a jog.

Milk tugs at the edges of the five-pound note.

'What the fuck was that?' I say.

'What?' says Milk.

'You can't say to someone, *Buy a pill off me or I'll shank you.*'

'Why not?'

'It's no way to run a business, that's why not.'

'I'm hungry,' he says, as if that's all the justification he needs. 'You want anything?'

'No, I'm good, bruv.'

Milk shrugs and heads into Chicken Ribs And Pizza, pushing his way to the front of the queue.

I hear the sound of a rumbling bass behind me and immediately tense up. There's a sharp screech of brakes followed by a couple of toots on a horn. There's a ripple in the Yoot crowd, all turning, suddenly up on their toes. But I don't need to look. I swear I can feel it, feel the vibes. It's like a haze, thickening the air. I hop off the bench. Muzza is sitting at the wheel of the Corsa. Shads is leaning out of the passenger-seat window. 'Get in!' he shouts.

'What about Milk?' I say, pointing him out as he orders lunch number two.

Shads mulls it over. 'I don't want him stinking out my car, getting his mucky hands on my upholstery. Get in. You can see your boyfriend back at school.'

Milk sees this and I try and mime that I'll see him back at school, and a look flashes across his face that reminds me of Mickey Fuller two minutes ago. He looks like he's just lost his appetite as well.

'Where we going?' I say when I'm in the car. Muzza does his customary getaway and my neck snaps back.

'Round the block a few times. We need to talk logistics.' Shads pokes his head out from between the front seats. 'We've managed to tap one of Ram's more loyal customers. Name's Shaky. Know him?'

'No.'

'Course you don't. Anyway, seems Rammy's been dealing rocks. Bet you didn't know that either? You know a crackhead's only loyal to the man holding the goods. And now I'm holding the goods. We're going to set up a deal on the Downs one evening next week – all you got to worry about is turning up, and when Ram shows: *blam*.

We're doing all the work for you; you should be grateful.'

'Yeah, thanks.'

'I'll have a little soiree round at mine that evening – see it as an early birthday party – that way we're all covered. You nip out, do the business, head back to mine a fully-fledged member of the Olders, bruv! That'll be a cause for genuine celebration. Ain't that right, Muzz?'

Muzza grunts. Shads says it all so quickly, so smoothly, I can barely take it all in. It's the verbal equivalent of being shoved on an ice rink. I'm slipping around trying to get some purchase, legs wobbling, about to end up on my face.

Shads has to turn round to face the front as Muzza swings the car left, then right, his stomach clearly not totally adjusted to the G-forces Muzza manages to create, and I use that as an opportunity to rest my head back on the seat. I close my eyes.

Sitting like this reminds me of being on a roller coaster. I always wanted to go on the roller coaster at theme parks and fairgrounds, but whenever I did, the only way I could get through it was by closing my eyes. Sounds lame, I know, but it was a reflex thing, I didn't feel like I had a choice. Now I want to keep my eyes closed, stay in the dark till this ride's over. Maybe I could negotiate the timing. Why does it have to be one evening next week? Why can't it be tonight? After school? Next year? A week and a half is a really annoying amount of time.

'Wake up,' says Shads and I realize we're outside the school gates. 'And don't worry,' he says, with a grin that tells me the exact opposite.

'I'm not worried,' I say, narrowing my eyes, turning them down. 'Thanks for the lift.'

SEVEN

I didn't get a chance before but I should probably tell you more about Marsha's flat. Even though it's turning more and more into a cave, my mum's flat is pretty normal. Milk's flat is normal. Shads's place – even though it's so sleek the air feels too thin to even breathe properly – is still normal enough, but Marsha's needs to be described. Mainly just so you know what I'm dealing with.

When she's not cooking, it smells of candle smoke and it seems to hang in the air for days because it's all too quiet, too still and too tidy. I never actually see her doing any housework either; it's like God does it for her while she's out. No one ever comes round but there are enough chairs in the living room to have a council meeting. It's the sort of place that makes you think you're never alone. It doesn't help having the beady eyes everywhere: the crucifixes, the little statues; then there are the framed prayers and Bible quotations in fancy writing on the wall. Everywhere I look there's something or someone telling me I'm doing wrong. Then there's the biggie – her pride and joy and the freakiest thing in the flat: the picture on the wall above the mantelpiece in the living room. In fact it's the freakiest thing I've ever seen. Actually, it's more than a picture, it's a hologram. If you stand on one side it's a picture of a smiling Jesus in robes, clean beard and hair. On the other it's a Jesus with a crown of thorns, bare shoulders, all bloodied and messy, his eyes rolled back in his head, mouth open. All of it in this ghostly green light.

I've started standing directly in front of it – him – and then hopping from left to right, getting him to change as quickly as I can. It's becoming a ritual, every morning and every time I get in from school, sometimes before I go to bed: stand in front of the hologram Jesus and get him to change. Life/death, life/death, life/death, life/death, life/death, life/death, life/death, life/death, life—

'What in Heaven's name are you doing?'

It's Marsha.

I shrug. 'Trying to see the join,' I say. I didn't hear her come in; the hologram gets hypnotic sometimes.

'I don't think it works that way,' she says, putting her bag down, unbuttoning her long navy mac and going to hang it up in the hall.

I look back at the picture. 'Why do you need all this stuff, Marsh?'

'Look around you,' she calls from the hallway. 'Everyone needs this stuff. Look at all the lost souls out there, crying for some kind of salvation. Flailing around not knowing what's what . . . not even knowing themselves.' She wanders back into the living room. 'You get to know the Lord, you'll realize that's all you'll ever need to know.'

'Doesn't sound like enough to me.'

'That's because you don't understand. You don't try to understand.'

'I don't understand having a picture like this up on the wall.'

'It reminds me of what Jesus gave up for us.'

It reminds *me* that all this religion stuff is a bit too crazy. Anyone that needs a dead person hung on every wall as a *reminder* has got problems.

'Don't you want salvation?' she says.

'I don't even know what the word means.'

'Then you should look it up.'

I feel like saying it's too late. But then I think, I'm only fifteen, it shouldn't be too late for anything, but that's what it feels like.

'Are you around for dinner?' she says.

'No, I'm meeting Milk.'

I'm expecting some kind of comeback to that but all she says is, 'Suit yourself,' and heads out of the room.

I look back at the happy Jesus, then switch again to the mashed-up one. Life/death, life/death, life/death, life/death, life/death, life/death, life/death.

EIGHT

I flick the blade out, I bend it back in. I flick the blade out, I bend it back in. I flick the blade out, I bend it back in. I flick the blade out, I bend it back in.

'Take a toke on that, bruv,' says Milk. 'It'll blow your fucking nuts off. And put that away, you're making me nervous.'

I flick the blade out, I bend it back in. I flick the blade out— and Milk grabs the shank off me and puts it down out of my reach. 'Seriously,' he says. 'Smoke that.'

I take the joint. I don't know whether I really want it but it doesn't matter; even if it doesn't make me feel good at least I'll feel *different*. I take a couple of deep drags, hold the smoke in, let it fill my insides, then sigh it out. I rest my arms on the wall, my chin on my arms, and look out through the bars.

Me and Milk are sitting up on the roof of Blake Point, looking out over Hackney and the sprawl of the city beyond. On our left is Hackney Downs and past that the Westhall estate. For those of you that don't know – and why would you, it's not exactly a tourist destination – Hackney Downs is a chunk of plain, square park – the Blake Street estate on one side, the Westhall estate on the other. Another side is bordered by the overground railway line, and opposite that is a street of old large houses – not posh or anything, they're all split into flats. It doesn't look much from up here; it doesn't look much from down there. It makes me wonder why it causes so much trouble.

Some fireworks are going off over on the Westhall side of the Downs. White rockets shooting off into the air, not getting that high before they fizzle out. I hand Milk back the joint. He chuckles. 'Even their fireworks are shit,' he says.

'How did it all start?' I say and I realize I'm a bit stoned already. I've lost that gap between thinking and talking.

'What?' he says.

'The beef with the Yoot.'

Milk mulls it over. 'Because they're pricks.'

'Yeah . . . I know that. But it must've started somehow. Something must've happened.'

Milk looks at me, puzzled. Not like he's confused about what I've said but confused I'm even thinking that way.

'They're our rivals, innit?' he says. 'Always have been. And look at it . . . they got all this attitude, they haven't even got a decent estate.' Milk waves his hand airily. 'All that outdated 1960s black and white Bobby Charlton shit.'

Milk's stoned already too, which is a relief. His joints are always too strong. He sneers and shakes his head, puffing on the joint and looking out over the Downs. 'They deserve what they get living somewhere like that,' he says.

That's not really answering my question. I don't remember us moving to the estate and being given a contract, a declaration that we'd joined some closed-off, special club. It was a place to live. It could've been any-where. It could've been *there*.

I lift my head off my arms and look over Milk's shoulder. In the distance I can see the maze of five-storey red-brick blocks that make up the Westhall estate. It's not like it's just us. They're the same. If I went over there now I probably wouldn't make it back out again. I could go over there and start planting flowers – it wouldn't make any difference. It's like when you're a kid and you build yourself a little den and shoot anyone who comes near. It's the same thing, but now the dens are real, the guns are real and the killings are real. *Bang, bang, you're dead* . . . and then . . . you actually are.

Some loud pops sound from a different place on the Downs, out of sight. 'I love fireworks,' says Milk. 'Makes me feel like I'm in a war zone.'

'What's so good about that?'

This time Milk looks at me like I'm stupid.

'You're lucky you live in Hackney, bruv,' he says. 'Imagine growing up in the country . . . even Zone Three. Think how boring it would be; think how hard it would be to be a gangster. We got it right here, on our doorstep. Take next Friday – I can't *wait* for next Friday.'

'What's happening next Friday?'

'The fireworks display on the Downs. After you've shanked Goosy Ganja some *serious* shit is gonna be happening! There's gonna be some *real* fucking fireworks.'

'What fireworks display?' I'm reaching now. 'How do you know?'

'I keep my ear to the ground. Plus there are signs up all round the place.'

'What signs?'

'About the *fireworks display*. It's all gonna go down at the fireworks. That's the idea.'

'How do you know?' I say again, not managing to stop the whine in my voice.

'I have my sources.' Milk nods, slow and cool. I'm starting to think Ram's impression of Milk's mum might have been more suited to Milk himself. Big ears, big mouth.

I don't like the idea of me killing Ram becoming an event for the whole of Hackney to get involved in. 'If I stab Ram, bruv . . .' I feel like I'm conjuring up some kind of demon just by saying the words, like it's a spell. 'If I stab Ram, there's not going to be any fireworks on the Downs. The place is gonna be a crime scene, you get me?'

Milk shrugs. 'Yeah . . . but if they happen it's gonna look like we're celebrating, innit? The Yoot are gonna be screwing!' He chuckles, all squeaky, his shoulders jabbing up and down. He hands back the joint and stops laughing, staring cold at me. 'You're sounding like you don't even want to do it,' he says.

Maybe it's the green but I'm feeling Milk's eyes right inside, scanning like an X-ray, and all he's seeing is black and white: you react, you're weak; you ask questions, you're looking for excuses. Do as you're told, somehow . . . somehow that's all right. Even talking about it's too much. I should stop pushing, stop picking. I can see a bit of Milk's faith in me crumble and blow away like dust. Where's all this coming from? I don't know. Picking, picking, picking. And if I pick too much it might all come apart. I draw the smoke in deep, hoping it'll stop me thinking, hoping it'll push it away, far enough away for it to look small and insignificant. But it's making me feel worse. It's growing instead. Getting urgent.

I test myself. I picture myself on the Downs next week: seeing Ram, trying to surprise him but being too loud. I see myself fumbling with the shank, it feeling too heavy. Ram standing there laughing. I get the blade out, it needs both hands. I step towards him – I'm in slow motion, Ram's moving normal speed. He moves away easily, runs away, laughing. Taking everything.

I shake my head hard, try and clear it, and listen to the pops and screams of the fireworks, and the police sirens in the distance, always, always there.

'My mum got in this new cereal the other day,' says Milk. 'It's like cornflakes but they're all chocolatey with marshmallows. It's almost too much sweetness for me – you'd like it though, bruv.'

'Sounds good,' I say, but it only comes out as a whisper.

Milk sucks his teeth. I think that was him trying to lighten the mood but I'm not ready for it. I give him back the joint. He finishes it off, picks the shank off the ground and gets up. He purses his lips, concentrating on the knife. He bends the blade in and flicks it out again, makes a couple of stabs in the air, bends it in and hands it to me. 'I'm hungry,' he says. 'Let's go up Dalston . . . get a Maccy D's.'

Walking feels good, just one foot in front of the other. All walking is, is losing your balance then regaining it. Losing your balance, regaining it. I'm good at walking. Been doing it for years. I'm a natural, got it down, and we walk up to Dalston, stoned, slow and spacey. I keep my head low, coat up, hands deep in my pockets, gripping the shank handle.

'What's wrong with you, man?' says Milk. 'I don't see why you're all depressed and shit. You got to start looking at the positives. Even if you get caught, so what? You go inside for a few years. Everyone will think you're a *bad boy*. No one will fuck with you after that. Look at Shads: he wouldn't be who he is if he hadn't been inside.'

'Yeah . . . I don't really see prison as a promotion, though, bruv.' I could say if I get caught for murder it might be slightly more than a few years but I keep quiet.

'I want to go inside one day,' says Milk, almost wistfully. I look at him and raise my eyebrows. 'Not for long,' he says, shrugging. 'Just so I can say I've been there, you get me?'

That's the thing with Milk – he's desperate to join the Olders. On his sixteenth birthday he'll be knocking on Shads's door on the stroke of midnight, birth certificate in hand, begging for his initiation. He'll want to do something big as well, he won't care. Firebombing a whole Westhall block, shooting, stabbing . . . give him a chainsaw, a tank – anything for that shiny, glinting, golden chance to be one of the big boys.

Milk's always been a good friend. He's generous, always shares stuff, and even though he can't keep his mouth shut, he's dependable, solid, there when you need him. The problem is he takes being in the Boyz too seriously. I mean, you need to take it seriously – it's a serious business. But Milk takes it to higher levels. He puts in overtime. He sleeps it, drinks it, eats it.

His family doesn't help. He only lives with his mum – he's got two older brothers but they both moved out a while ago. They come back a lot, though, and so does an endless stream of cousins and uncles, and they're all involved in something dodgy. And it's like he's grown up with this idea that the best way to get anywhere is by doing stuff you're not supposed to do. It's all short-cuts and easy money.

It's true. When I stay over at Milk's it's like being surrounded by treasure. There are games consoles and loads of games; there's huge TVs with new films to watch all the time. He even buys his green off one of his cousins, and when we're smoking in his flat his mum even makes sure we've got enough snacks! When I go back home (home-home, I'm not even counting Marsha's) it's like stepping back two hundred years. It's not surprising he wants to make the most of it; not surprising he laughs at all the people stuck in queues following the rules. That's what he's grown up with.

Maybe if his family were all bankers he'd be a really good banker. Maybe if they were all footballers he'd be a really good footballer. As it is he's on his way to being a really good criminal.

Dalston's busy and angry, everyone scowling, moving fast and in my direction. I'm fighting against the tide. There's a group of suited men outside the shopping centre trying to convert the masses; when one of them stops Milk he just laughs at him and we keep walking.

Why hasn't anyone else mentioned the fireworks to me? Maybe Milk's making it up, at least exaggerating. He does that all the time, filling in the gaps, trying to create some drama . . . but what if he isn't? A woman barges into me with her arms full of shopping bags. She seems angry at first, then sees my face and looks sorry, but when I don't react at all, just let her bounce off me, she looks confused and moves on. I'm feeling stuck solid, like a dam, keeping a whole ocean at bay, shut tight. Pressure's building.

We fight our way to McDonald's, order our burgers and take a seat in the window. After the walk it's good to sit down, watch other people do the battling, struggling on with their lives. I chew on the burger but it's tasteless. The dam's blocking the flavour. I'd probably need one of Marsha's specials; that's the sort of wrecking ball I'd need to break through. Taste, feeling, choice – they're all blocked up.

I give up on the burger and focus on my Coke. I drain it and chew on the ice, crunching it between my teeth. The ice feels good, the cold passing through my cheeks. Maybe I need extremes – hot, cold, life, death.

After we're done, Milk wants to get the bus back from the other side of the road. I'm waiting at the crossing when I notice him looking at me and shaking his head.

'What?' I say.

'You need beeps and the green man to help you across, bruv?'

I don't say anything and follow him a safe distance along to where we can cross freestyle. It takes a while for enough of a break in the traffic, and while we're waiting I watch the people at the crossing make it over, safe, unruffled, no harm done. And I'm wondering if it's really that bad, wondering what difference it really makes, wondering where we got all these rules from, who made them up. The Gangster Moses and his Ten Commandments. It's more than ten, though. It's so many I've lost count.

The bus stop is outside the bookmakers. Unlike a lot of bookmakers this one doesn't have anything in the window blocking the view inside. The lights are on bright too. For a second I worry I might see my dad in there but Dalston's a long way for him to travel. As it is there's only two men in there – one short, crooked-looking old black guy at the slot machine and an old white guy with long grey hair up at the counter.

The bookmakers is depressing, especially in the evening when it's empty and there's torn betting slips all over the floor. It's too functional somehow; not enough attention has been paid to make it a pleasant experience, as though the punters aren't important enough to be given a little comfort: the lighting's too bright, the chairs are badly designed. My dad spends hours in the bookmakers and I've always thought they could do more to make him comfortable. It says something about life, going a place like that to try and get your hands on luck and change your fate. You can almost see the dreams shivering in the corners.

The old white guy is taking a long time at the counter. I watch him, then realize why he's taking so long. He's collecting winnings, *a lot* of winnings. A big wodge of notes in an envelope that he slips inside his coat. I turn to nudge Milk but he's already watching and I know what he's thinking. The old guy shares some kind of a joke with the cashier, then with the old black guy as he walks past. He pushes the stiff, cracked glass door and stands in the entrance, breathing the outside air like he's standing on a mountain. Then he turns, not up the main road but down the narrow side-street beside the bookmakers. Me and Milk don't have to say anything; we wait a few seconds then follow behind. The man walks slowly, lightly, following the road round to the left behind the main road buildings, to where it's even darker, even quieter. It's like he's asking for it.

Milk quickens his pace. 'Oi, mate!' he says. The man turns his head slightly, slows down. 'Mate!' Milk says again.

This time the old guy stops, turns to us. 'Yes, my brothers?' he says, his voice low and syrupy. It doesn't suit him. He's scruffy, his hair lank, unwashed. Skin rough and pale. He smiles and his smile doesn't suit him either. It looks young somehow, sort of innocent.

'Yeah,' says Milk. 'Trick or treat, innit?'

'I'm sorry, my brother?' He's saying 'brother' like Leo. Maybe it's some new talk among old tramp types.

'Trick or treat . . . Halloween, innit?'

I move in closer, over Milk's shoulder, making us bigger.

'Halloween? It's a festival I no longer recognize. Another of your nourishing spiritual celebrations, flayed, neutered, diluted, polluted, shorn of worth by a people too poor of mind to appreciate the power of the ritual and how it weaves you tighter into the universal pattern. Besides,' he says, 'you're five days early.'

Me and Milk both stop. I'm trying to figure out what he's talking about, but when he begins to turn round Milk moves. 'I don't give a FUCK,' he shouts, and he's on the old guy, grabbing at his shoulders, trying to haul him down, get at his jacket. The old guy holds firm, his feet don't move; he sort of bends with Milk, like he knows some kind of martial art, ends up grabbing *him* and pushes him all lightly, effortlessly into the street, across the street, tumbling into the opposite gutter. It all happens so quick, I just stand there watching. Milk doesn't move and I look at the old guy, my mouth open. He smiles at me. It's a strange smile; before, I thought it made him look younger but it's more that it

104

makes him look *ageless*. It seems wrong. It doesn't fit; *he* doesn't fit. What's he doing here? What's he doing in the dark, alone, with all that cash on him? It's like he's just turned up uninvited.

And I hate him for that. He doesn't know – doesn't know the rules. He deserves it, and my hand's on the shank handle and it's flicking out the blade. His smile is cracking the dam and I don't care any more. It's cracking, bursting, flooding. I'm in a place that's quiet and dark and I need to know I can do this. I need the practice. I swing my arm back and lunge for him in the same movement. I expect him to move but he stands still. My arm swings up and the blade connects with his side, just under his arm. He lurches backwards, his breath heaving, taking me with him. There's a scream – not outside, inside, a break, the feel of bones cracking and jarring but I don't think it's him; it's in me, in my head. For a second I worry I've missed altogether, that the whole thing's in my head, but when I pull on the shank I know I haven't. I yank it out and hit him again, same place. He staggers back and I'm pulled with him and we're against the wall. His fingers dig into my shoulders, his breath in my face – alcohol, sweet. Once more I hit him, and it's easier this time, getting used to it already. His eyes are wide, an icy blue, and for a second they seem to be searching deep inside me, but then they blur, lose focus. He splutters something, gasps. His knees buckle and he slides down the wall. I stand there, my whole body moving with my breaths. My hand's wet, cold, but I don't want to look at it. His eyes are fading, going out. His neck loosens and his eyes droop, staring at nothing now, gone. There's a grab at my shoulder and I'm almost ready to use the shank again. It's Milk.

'Come on!' he shouts and I follow him, running up the street. I can't even feel my legs. I'm just floating, moving, making distance. Floating away.

NINE

Jesus points to his heart, a red blob on his chest. I don't know what it means, his heart on the outside of his body. His hands are scratched and bleeding too, his eyes down, avoiding me. I get down on my knees, try and get in his eye-line, but he seems to be looking past me, not seeing me. I get up, look at the Holy Spirit, the fire one, a ball of flame on the wall by the bookcase – that's better. I open my arms out, wait for it to take me, swallow me up, burn me up, but it doesn't move. I can't even feel the heat. The dove's no good either; I need more than pigeons. St Jude has a weird look on his face – either he's drunk or he's in pain; maybe he's been trying to save my soul but come back exhausted and traumatized. Moses looks serious, holding up a big slab of stone like he's about to hit me with it, remind me of the commandment I've just broken, the biggie. Then there's Jesus on the back of the door, shoving his way in, the enforcer, the muscle, come to take me away. I stand in front of him, eyeball to eyeball.

'What do you want?' I say. My voice sounds weird. It sounds strained, like it's breaking all over again. 'What do you want?' I say again. 'Come on!' Nothing. 'Come on!'

He keeps his mouth shut, happy to stand in the doorway, all his friends surrounding me. I lean against the door, my forehead resting against the Son of God. The breath's coming out of me in strong, sharp heaves. *Why did I come back here?* . . . I didn't have anywhere else to go. Milk was like a little yapping dog; he wouldn't shut up. Once we'd got a safe distance away he started going over it and over it, like I hadn't even been there, hadn't seen what happened, hadn't *done it.* Then he remembered the money – *I can't believe you didn't get his money, bruv!* No, I didn't . . . I just killed him. *You jooked him up and you didn't even get his money!* Milk thought it was *funny.*

I'm not prepared for this. That makes me laugh out loud. That *is* funny. *Not prepared?* That makes me sound like I've left the flat without a coat; gone to school without doing my homework – not trying to deal with the fact that I've just killed someone. This is crazy; we need training for this sort of shit. Proper training. It doesn't add up. It makes no sense. It's all a mess. I try and focus on my breathing, in – out, in – out. I step back and look at Jesus again. No help. I can't stay in this room. Then I think, What if Marsha's flat really *is* a Welcome Break for souls? What if the old guy passes through on his way up? I look around: every shadow, every shape's suddenly a ghost. Then the door vibrates and a thousand volts pass through my body.

'JAYLON?' It's Marsha.

'Yeah?' I say, sounding like I'm being strangled.

'What's going on in there?'

'Nothing.'

'It doesn't sound like nothing. I keep hearing strange noises . . . talking. Are you on your own?'

I look around. 'I don't know,' I say.

The door opens and Marsha's face appears, her forehead all scrunched up. 'What's going on? Are you OK? There's blood on the hand towel.'

'There is?'

'Yes. Are you hurt? Have you been fighting?'

'No.'

'You have, haven't you?' She squints. I don't think I can take a grilling from the Deadly Lampshade right now. 'Are you hurt?' she says again and begins to come in the room, and I instinctively step back, like she'll be able to smell it on me, pick up on my sins, sense the old guy in the room.

'I'm fine, Marsh.'

'Well, what about who you were fighting with?'

'What about them?' I say.

'Are they OK? Who was it? You look . . . *frantic*.'

'They're fine, Marsh. Look, I've got to go out.'

'Should I call the police?' she says.

I push past her into the hall and start fumbling with my shoes; despite everything I still remembered that. 'What do you want to call the police for?'

'I'm worried about you,' she says, standing over me, her hands on her hips. She's too close.

'I'll see you later, Marsh.'

'Wait!' she says, grabbing at my shoulder. I shake her off – too strong, but I don't want her to touch me; she'll feel it then, definitely. She keeps talking, nearly shouting, but I'm ignoring it and I'm out the door. She follows me along the

110

landing but then I'm down the stairs, leaving her voice bouncing off the walls, echoing, distorting until it's just noise. I take the stairs even quicker than the last time but I've got so much adrenaline in my system I could run a marathon, two of them, just *keep* running.

She won't call the police. What would she say – *My nephew's acting crazy and he's left blood on a towel?* They're not going to waste their time on that. They'll be more worried about a dead body in Dalston for one thing. But I need to be somewhere . . . somewhere safe, somewhere different. I can't see the Boyz, can't see family.

I call Hannah.

'No, you can't come round,' she says.

'Please.'

'No.'

'Why?'

'Because you can't. You *know* that.'

'Look . . . I have to. I ain't got anywhere else to go.'

'What have you done?'

I think for a second. 'There's some kids after me. It's the Yoot. I got to get out of the estate. I need to go somewhere they won't find me.'

There's silence. A long silence, almost as if we're having some telepathic conversation. 'OK,' she says finally. 'But not now. You have to wait until everyone's asleep. I could be killed for this.'

That makes me laugh again. *It's not funny, Jay.* 'Thanks,' I say. 'I appreciate it.'

'You'd better. I'll text you when the coast is clear, OK?'

'OK,' I say, and she hangs up.

There's nothing I can do but walk. I can't stay still. My hood's up, pulled low. I want to disappear inside it. Maybe if I concentrate hard enough I'll actually become invisible, blend in so much I just become air. But even then I can't stop hearing the sirens. Every one of them's calling my name: JAAAAAAAAAAAYYYYYY-LOOOOOOOONNN. I'm not even scared of getting caught . . . I don't know what it is. Marsha was right. I'm feeling frantic. I'm like a loose electricity cable – sparking, twisting, whipping. JAAAAAAAAAAAYYYYYY

LOOOOOOOOOONNN, JAAAAAAAAAA
YYYYYYLOOOOOOOOOONNN, JAAAAAA

AAAAAYYYYYYLOOOOOOOOOOONNN. They sound like they're right inside me.

I don't get a text but I head to Hannah's estate anyway. Her parents are God people, like Marsha – they've got to go to bed early, up at dawn for prayers. I normally don't like Hannah's estate. It's one of those complexes of tightly packed beige maisonettes; the same colour as a desert and with about as much going on. But tonight I'm glad of it. I can disappear inside. It's quiet and anonymous. I do two circuits, drifting in and out of its neat replica streets. It feels like being on a huge stage set, and that lets a little bit of calm seep in. Hackney feels far away. I perch on a wall for a while, check my phone, chain-smoke three cigarettes. It's a cold night, the air is thin and sharp. I can smell smoke on the air, bonfires. And there's the fireworks, fireworks, fireworks. I think about calling Hannah but I don't want her to think I'm in too much trouble, ask too many questions.

Hannah's parents obviously aren't as devout as I thought because it's nearly one a.m. when I finally get a text that I can go round. But I'm not cold, not tired. Every time I feel myself relaxing, my mind runs over what happened in the side-street behind the bookmakers and I'm alert, but weirdly numb at the same time, shot through with chemicals.

Hannah's family mainly use the back of the house to go in and out but Hannah tells me to go to the front – I'm guessing because her parents' bedroom is above the back door. I text her, saying I'm outside, and I wait another five minutes before the door opens, slowly. Hannah pokes her head round. 'Quiet!' she mouths at me, her eyes wide. I step up into the hallway. Then before she closes the door she mouths, 'Shoes,' and I pull them off and hold them. There's thick, soft carpet on the floor.

It's not totally dark inside. There's some light coming from the kitchen to the right of the door, the window's near the security light outside and there's also a dim light coming from upstairs. The house smells of air freshener and clean washing. In fact it's probably the cleanest-smelling house I've ever been in. It makes me feel dirty – *more* dirty. I feel like I'm going to leave bloody footprints on the shag pile.

Hannah grabs my hand like I'm a kid in trouble and leads me in slow motion to the stairs. Despite everything that's happened already tonight, the idea of seeing her mum or dad appear at the top of the stairs would cap it all. Forget the mugging, forget the stabbing, the really bad bit is visiting your girlfriend at one in the morning.

I edge up the stairs. The house is new, it feels solid. No real creaks or noises, but all it would take is for someone to get up and that would be it. I don't think Hannah could explain that one. One small flight, a landing, then another few steps and we're on the first floor. The bathroom is to the right, door open, then there are two closed doors and Hannah leads me to the door round to the left of them and opens it carefully. She grabs both my arms and manoeuvres me into the centre of the room and makes me stand there. Part of me is enjoying being moved around like this. I'd like to be fed, watered, stuck in a pot in the corner. Just stay there and forget everything.

Hannah takes a dressing gown off the hook on the back of her door and pads it down on the floor to cover the gap. Then she goes and turns the lamp on by her bed. I get a first proper look at her room. This really does feel like holy ground. I take it in – the posters and photos on the wall, the cuddly panda on the end of her bed, the clothes, the pots of make-up and cream and perfume on the little white dress-ing table, the smell: it's her, it's all her. But then she's in front of me. She stands there, arms folded, lips pursed, eyebrow raised. She's wearing pink pyjamas dotted with little birth-day cakes; each one brown with thick icing and a single lit candle. It's an all-in-one thing like a giant babygro. The contrast between the look on her face and her pyjamas makes me smile. She looks grumpy, tired, amazing.

I don't know if it's safe to speak so I just put my arms out wide, as if to say there was nothing else I could do. She leans in close to me, cups her hand round my ear and whispers, 'If anyone finds you here, I'm dead. You know that? Dead.' *I wish she'd stop saying that.*

'I know,' I start to say as she backs away, but then she waves her arms at me to be quiet. I mime a sorry and then move in and whisper in her ear, 'I didn't have anywhere else to go.' For a second I feel the soft skin of her cheek against me and it sends a warm pulse straight to my heart. That's all I needed. That's all. Why didn't I just persuade her to let me come round straight after school? Miss out everything else? That's all I needed. I just needed to feel her, and I let out a long unsteady breath.

She folds her arms and then goes to my ear again. 'You didn't have anywhere else to go? What have you been doing? Actually I don't want to know.' She steps away again and covers her ears.

'That's good,' I whisper, pulling her hands away.

'That's good?' she says into my ear. 'Then I *do* want to know. Tell me. How can we be together if you don't tell me stuff?'

I don't say anything.

'I've let you come to my house. I deserve an explanation.'

'OK, I'll explain . . . but not now. I need to be able to talk for a start.'

'You'd better explain,' she says.

'I will,' I say. This time I keep my cheek next to hers and breathe her in deep. 'I promise.' I don't move away and she stays close, then moves round and looks into my eyes. Her eyes so close they're all I can see.

'You'd better,' she says, moving her mouth across my cheek and nuzzling my neck.

I go to say something back but instead just kiss her ear and her cheek and round to her lips. 'I will,' I say, and then we're kissing and I feel like I'm disappearing again but properly this time.

'I need to turn the light off,' she says, putting her hand to her head.

'OK,' I say.

Get into bed, she mimes at me, turns down the duvet and switches the light off. I take my coat off and let it drop to the floor. 'Put it under the bed,' she says, her voice barely audible, her gestures exaggerated to compensate. 'In case anyone comes in.'

I think me being in Hannah's bed would be more serious than my coat being on the floor, but I don't argue. I get into bed next to her and lie there not moving, not sure what to do. Then she moves in close and for a few minutes we just hold each other. She pulls the duvet up over both our heads.

'I don't want anything bad to happen to you,' she says from the darkness.

'Neither do I,' I say. 'To either of us.'

'Promise it won't,' she says.

I don't say anything. My chest feels like it's been clamped.

'Promise,' she says again. 'Or you can get out of this bed and out of this house.'

'OK, I promise,' I say, thanking God for the dark. And I realize that's the first time I've done that. The first time, and now it's too late. I feel Hannah looking at me. I find her lips and kiss her, but when I stop she finds mine again and we keep kissing.

I want to stay where there's nothing except touch. Get rid of all my other senses, let touch be the only thing that matters. I touch her cheek, her lips, her neck. I force myself to forget everything else, block it all out, no matter how bad. Nothing but touch. We keep kissing. In the dark I can concentrate, I can taste, feel, softly bite her lips, her tongue, her neck, her face.

My hands explore, find the poppers on the back of her pyjamas. I expect her to stop me but she doesn't; she moves in, our legs wrap together, her hand under my T-shirt. Her fingers conducting electricity under my skin, working deep, lighting it up, making it alive. Just touch, nothing but touch. That's all there is.

'Take this off,' she says, pulling at my T-shirt. I pull it up over my head, drop it on the floor. I take off my jeans as well and soon I can feel all of her. We're wrapped up together; we shift and move, hands exploring, places I've never been. I can't look back, I can't see . . . just feel — and I feel like I'm weightless, drifting, wrapped in a soft, shifting cloud. We speed up; I want to become a part of her, move into her until we're the same. Touch, feeling and nothing else.

TEN

And he said, What hast thou done? the voice of thy brother's blood crieth unto me from the ground.

And now art thou cursed from the earth, which hath opened her mouth to receive thy brother's blood from thy hand.

It's the third page and already people are being killed.

And Cain said unto the LORD, My punishment is greater than I can bear. Behold, thou hast driven me out this day from the face of the earth; and from thy face shall I be hid; and I shall be a fugitive and a vagabond in the earth; and it shall come to pass, that every one that findeth me shall slay me.

I'm feeling sick . . .

And the LORD said unto him, Therefore whosoever slayeth Cain, vengeance shall be taken on him sevenfold. And the LORD set a mark upon Cain, lest any finding him should kill him.

I close the book. It bangs louder than I was expecting and my eyes dart around the room to see if I've disturbed anyone. No one's moved; everyone's still in place. Jesus is still stuck to the back of the door. St Jude is still standing on his plinth. The Holy Spirit isn't flying around the room. Moses hasn't got down to beat me over the head with his stone tablet. Quiet and still.

I have to keep checking. During the day my roommates seem more relaxed; at night they get agitated. Now of course they've got good reason to be agitated, which means I got to be extra careful, extra vigilant. They've got a killer in their midst.

You might think reading the Bible would only make matters worse, but there's nothing else to read and I can't sleep. I need something else to think about, even if that something else is eternal damnation.

I managed to get out of Hannah's today, after sitting in her wardrobe for an hour and a half till her parents had gone to work and her sister had gone to school. I did it without getting caught. I'm hoping that's a trend that continues.

I felt bad saying goodbye to Hannah. I felt like I'd tricked her, used her somehow, made her an accomplice, and she doesn't even know. She's been texting me all day. She's suddenly making plans. She wants me to meet her parents properly; I mean, I've met them in church, in passing, but she wants to introduce me as a *real* boyfriend. She's old-fashioned that way. Proper. She's going to be picking out white dresses and looking at honeymoon brochures next. And what am I going to tell her? *Yeah . . . er, sorry, babes, you go for the white dress but I'll have to wear this jumpsuit and stay behind this Perspex screen.*

The fact is, the way I feel about her now, I probably would want to marry her, but I can't separate what happened last night. I think about Hannah, I think about that old guy. They're connected; like Siamese twins. I look at one, I look at the other. I feel sick, sick, sick.

I'm getting up.

I head to the kitchen, get a glass of milk and go and sit in the living room, turning on the main light and putting the dimmer switch low. I slump onto the sofa. For a minute I stare up at the hologram Jesus. Luckily I'm on the alive side. Even though I know it's just a matter of where I sit on the sofa, it still feels like I've tossed a coin and it's landed the right way up.

I turn on the TV and put it on the lowest volume possible. I'm impressed Marsha's got a TV at all. She's the sort of person I can imagine denouncing technology as the Devil's work; she'd be happier sitting around some old 1940s radio, or just reading the news from scrolls.

The only thing on is the twenty-four-hour news but it makes me feel like I might as well walk myself up to the police station and hand myself in, like it's going to be a two-way screen and they'll see me – an insomniac who can't sleep because of the guilt. I imagine the newsreaders stopping the autocue, standing up, walking round the desk to the camera and going: '*It's you!*'

I turn it off and stare at the blank screen.

I didn't go to school today, and Milk's been texting all day too. I think I've managed to persuade him not to tell anyone, but with Milk you can never be sure. He's acting so excited about it he seems to think it's a waste not telling anyone, like if we don't tell anyone it didn't actually happen. I'd be happy with that but I know, can feel it in my bones, that it isn't true. And this is it, the way I see it; I can't pretend it didn't happen. I can still feel the old guy's fingers on my shoulders but they've changed, distorted, and now it feels like the claws of some monster digging into me and I can't shake it off. And if I do pretend it didn't happen? If I try and get used to it . . . what's going to happen to me then? I feel like . . . I feel like I'd be killing *myself*.

I lean forward, rub my hands over my head and groan. It's a good groan, therapeutic. I listen to myself and it sounds a bit like Leo's humming. I'd like to see Leo now; even if he was just talking rubbish, giving me leaves, it would help.

There's a shuffling in the hallway and the *clunk-clunk* of the bathroom light going on. For a second I think about disappearing back into the shrine, but then I realize I'm glad Marsha's actually around. I'd even take one of her lectures right now.

I hear the toilet flush and then the light clunks again and Marsha pokes her head round the door. She's squinting without her glasses, looks like a different person. You wouldn't think pink-framed glasses could make someone more intimidating but that's the case with Marsha. Maybe that's where the Deadly Lampshade has all her power stored. Take away the pink glasses and she's helpless.

'What are you doing up?' she says.

'Can't sleep.'

'I'm not surprised, the hours you keep. Your body clock's probably all over the place. Do you want a drink?'

I raise my glass of milk. She nods and disappears again. Then I hear the sound of the kettle filling, followed shortly by the sound of it heating up.

I look up at the Jesus. I wonder if he was real . . . or how much of him was real. That's the problem with all this religion stuff – you got to take so much of it on board, so much of it that doesn't seem to add up, it makes the whole thing look shaky.

A few minutes later Marsha comes in, steaming cup in hand, pink glasses restored to face. She sits down in the armchair.

'Well, that hand towel cleaned up nicely,' she says. 'I wasn't sure if those stains would come out. Blood's normally a lot tougher than that. You're lucky. I don't like to throw them away, but then I don't like them stained either, especially with blood.'

Normally I'd think that was Marsha starting, but I don't have the energy to rise to it.

'What's wrong?' she says.

'Nothing,' I say.

'Sure?'

I sit there in silence. 'I was thinking about my dad,' I say eventually. I don't know where that came from but it makes me wish for a day when I can tell the truth. I swear all these little lies aren't good for me; I feel like they're blocking up my insides like cholesterol.

'I got a text from him the other day,' I say. That bit is true. 'All it said was, *Why haven't you been in touch?* I mean, what's that about? Sending a text asking why you haven't been in touch? He could just say a normal hello or something, you get me? I could ask him the same question and he's my *dad.*'

'Yes . . . that sounds like him. What did you do?'

'I didn't do anything. I just ignored it.' I gulp down my milk and bang the glass down harder than I mean to on the glass coffee table.

'Coaster please . . . Yes . . . you might be right but I

wouldn't hold your breath. The thing with your dad is, he's a coward. As long as he's got you on the back foot it means he doesn't have to take responsibility. He spent twelve years married to your mum and didn't take responsibility for anything, ever. I'd have more respect for him if he was actually a bad man. He's not a bad man, but to my mind it's better to be a brave bad man than a cowardly good man. Not that you should be bad – I'm not saying that – but a good coward is just a waste.'

I don't like Marsha talking about my dad like he's a waste – he is still my dad after all – but then I can't expect her to go easy. Going easy isn't her style. And my mum's her sister. She's got her own issues to deal with.

It's true, though. I do feel like there's a hole where he should be; where he should've taken some responsibility. I'm trying to make these decisions off my own back. Is it surprising if I make mistakes? Even mistakes as big as killing someone?

'You tired at all?'

'No . . . yeah . . . I don't know. I don't think I'd be able to sleep, though, whatever.'

'You want to watch a film?'

'Yeah, all right. Have you got any good ones, though?'

'They're all good. Whether *you'll* think they're good or not is another matter. Why don't you have a look?'

I get up and go to the cabinet under the TV. Marsha's got about twenty DVDs to choose from and even some old VHSs. Most of them are either black-and-white films or religious ones. They all look rubbish, but mine are back at my mum's.

'How old are you, Marsh?'

'What's that got to do with anything?'

'It's these films. You weren't actually alive when these came out, were you?'

'You're lucky,' she says, peering over her glasses. 'I'll assume you don't mean that the way it sounds. Just because they're old it doesn't mean they're not good. Often it means they *are* good. You used to get proper stories. Nowadays it's all effects.'

'Yeah . . . I like effects, though.'

'Well, why they can't fit both in I don't know. Anyway, how about that one?'

'What one?'

'The one on the left there. *It's a Wonderful Life*. It's

old and sentimental and cheesy but it might cheer you up.'

'Yeah . . . all right, then. I'll give it a go.'

Well, that confirms it: Marsha is officially stuck in a time warp. And it turns out *It's a Wonderful Life* doesn't have any colour in more ways than one. In fact it's the whitest thing I've ever seen. It could be from another planet. I don't know what Marsha could ever see in it. But then, there is an angel. I'd like to see him try and do something with my life. He wouldn't stand a chance. Take away this tower block, take away Blake Street, take away the Boyz and Hackney, then maybe. As it is, the odds are stacked too high. Life's not like that; you don't get second chances. If no one shows you the way first time around, you're on your own. And if you don't deal with it right you get blamed. But then I can't use that as an excuse for killing someone, can I? *Yeah, sorry, your honour, I realize killing an old man because I was feeling stressed was a mistake but I won't do it again. I needed to learn somehow and now I have. Thank you.*

The fact is, I *am* going to do it again. I'm going to do it again in a few days' time. And it'll be easier and I'll get over it quicker and I'll be different and I'll keep on dying myself.

'What did you think?' says Marsha.

'I didn't get it,' I say. 'You're not telling me you actually like that film, Marsh?'

'No, I hate it. I like nothing more than spending the early hours tormenting myself with awful films. Of course I like it!'

'Why? Was it even in English?'

'It's heart-warming.' Marsha sighs. 'Well, you sat through the whole thing. You couldn't have thought it was that bad.'

I don't mention the choices I had available.

'Well, do you want some breakfast? How about an omelette?'

'You serious? It's five in the morning.'

'Too early? If you stay up now, maybe you'll get back in sync and you won't have to sit up with me and watch old-fashioned films.'

'No . . . thanks, though, yeah?'

Marsha goes through to the kitchen, and I'm confused. I've got this weird feeling, like I'm exploring new ground; there's been a lot of that over the last few days. But spending three hours with Marsha and not arguing . . . that's an achievement, at least.

ELEVEN

I've decided to go and see my dad this morning. It's not a trip that takes much planning. He spends pretty much all his time moving between the points of a neat little pentagon on the Upper Clapton Road. There's his flat, set back off the road on the second floor of one of those big converted, crumbling-down houses. Either side of that are the two takeaway joints he eats at, and on the other side of the road are the Brown Cow pub and the bookmakers. If he's not in any of these five, you'll probably be able to catch him on his way in between. As far as I can tell his flat is the one he visits least.

If my mum's shrunk since my parents split up, my dad's grown . . . and keeps growing. He's got red-rimmed eyes that bulge out of puffy cheeks. His belly's become big and spongy. His personality too has got louder, rougher, more messy. He makes me think of a giant water balloon that could burst at any time. I don't know how much of that is him or the alcohol but these days he spends so much of his time drinking it's hard to tell.

I think what finally drove my mum and dad apart was when he won big at the bookies. I know that sounds weird, but stick with me. I don't think my mum minded him gambling before that. He'd lost his job with the council, and I think she was glad he was doing *something*. I'm sure she would have preferred it if he was working, but in the meantime he had a hobby, and as long as he was careful about how much he spent, she didn't see it as anything serious. She only realized it was serious when he won. My mum's main hobby was me and Lloyd; that's where she wanted her money to go, and I think she thought my dad felt the same way – it was just, while he was out of work, he had a different way of going about getting the money. But when my dad won over a thousand one time, my mum saw the truth of it. She thought that's what he had been waiting for, and now he'd won, got it out of his system, he'd share the rewards with the rest of the family. But instead of using the money, even just celebrating, he saw it as some kind of seal of approval for the whole gambling process. Like he was right all along, he was right to keep doing it, so he ploughed the money straight back in. He never won big again, and as far as I can tell he hasn't since.

It wasn't just that; it changed him too. Maybe he realized he should've got out at the top, and then when it was too late he couldn't deal with it. He could handle the losing but he couldn't handle the winning. And after he had won, he couldn't handle the winning *or* the losing.

I never really minded my dad's gambling either. To me it showed he had a bit of ambition. He wanted something from life. It showed that even while he was out of work he wanted to think big, aim high. He always put in the hours, and I thought that amount of effort deserved to get rewards.

After that win he started to spend more and more time away from home. While he was out I'd overhear conversations, my mum talking to Marsha, blaming my dad for fleecing their joint account. And really I don't remember much of him after that. Only flashes, like a storm blowing through the flat, grey, miserable – and sometimes there'd be thunder and lightning. I stayed out of his way and tried to make sure Lloyd did as well.

When he moved out we still had to see him. It was all planned, all regimented. We had a schedule. But then he stopped keeping to that and we only saw him when *we* made the effort. Now, like that text I got from him, he makes out that he's the one getting treated badly.

He's in the Brown Cow already, even though it's only eleven o'clock. I told him on the phone I was in my school uniform. He said it didn't matter – the Cow doesn't have a dress code. It's the sort of place that's open day and night to anyone desperate enough or brave enough to step inside. It looks like it hasn't changed since the Victorian times – and hasn't been cleaned since then either. I think its carpet was dark red originally but it's now mainly just dark, all stained and worn. The sofas round the edge of the pub are the same, with sticky black stuff along the edges of the seats like old gum. And the air inside is thick and stale and seems to have this yellowy fog about it.

The drinkers suit the surroundings. Most of them look like they live there, or it's their last stop anywhere. They all seem to walk lower to the ground than they do outside; more crooked, more weighed-down, like they're wrestling with their own private gravity.

It's busy considering it's not even midday. There's a small group of youngish men at the bar, talking football like their lives depended on it and their teams depended on them and their opinions. There's a few older guys dotted around, staring off into the distance or into their drinks. An old Rasta sits on a sofa tucked into a dark corner. When I look at him closer I realize his bulging mass of dreads is all tied up messily in a bin bag. He looks familiar, and while I'm trying to place him he raises his head and looks directly at me, stares at me. I look away quickly, feeling caught out.

My dad's sitting at a rectangular table on the far side of the bar with two of his friends: one a black guy who looks a few years older than my dad, and the other a white guy who looks a few years younger.

'Here's my boy,' my dad says. 'My big boy!'

'All right, Dad?' I say, giving a quick nod.

He comes and stands next to me and puts his arm round my shoulders. 'This is James and Tony.' He doesn't point out which one's which. 'I'll get you a drink,' he says, and he wanders off to the bar.

I ask his back for a lemonade and I sit down. It turns out James is the older black guy, Tony the younger white guy.

'Lloyd, is it?' says James. 'I remember you when you were that high.' He holds out an unsteady hand level with the table. 'They grow up so fast these days,' he says to Tony, his eyes suddenly glistening.

'Actually, it's Jaylon. Lloyd's my little brother.'

James frowns, looks at me like I'm trying to trick him. 'It's Jaylon,' I say again.

'That's right,' says James, clearing his throat. 'Two good boys he's got. Two good boys.' He nods as he says it, his mouth downturned, like he's imparting some deep piece of wisdom. I manage to stretch my mouth into a smile. This time it's one Shads would be proud of.

James points a finger. 'It's good to smile,' he says. 'Don't ever lose that smile.'

Again he nods, turns his mouth down even further. Tony nods too, and I wonder if they're both about to start hugging or crying. Luckily my dad gets back from the bar with the drinks and distracts their attention: three pints of lager for them and a lemonade for me. A big one because it's my birthday. He doesn't actually mention the date, and I wonder if he's been trying to remember at the bar and decided he'd play safe and go for something vague.

'So how's your mum?' my dad says, taking a large gulp of his drink. That's the same sort of question that would normally annoy me, but this is my dad – he doesn't play by the same rules as everyone else. That wouldn't be fair on him.

'I don't know,' I say. 'We don't have many conversations.'

'Why not?' he says, sitting forward, eyes bulging.

'Well, I don't see her much.'

'Why not?' he says, bristling, and I get a flash of what he used to be like before he moved out. Angry but sort of confused at the same time; like you couldn't take him totally seriously, but somehow that made me want stay out of his way even more.

'Well, I don't live there any more, do I?' I say.

'What do you mean?' And I'm worried his eyes might pop out of his head. Tony and James lean in closer.

'I'm at Marsha's, innit? I told you this, Dad.'

Even though I have told him a few times, he can't seem

to remember. 'What are you doing there?' he says. 'Why didn't you come and stay with me? And why did you move out? She got a new man in?'

'It was Marsha's idea,' I say.

I could say a lot more than that. I could tell my dad that I'm not sure even rats would consider spending a night in his flat. I could tell him that since he left the only way my mum's going to meet a new man is if he was beamed magically onto the sofa next to her and managed to wake her up out of her coma like in some fairy tale. But the mention of Marsha has got my dad excited and playing to his friends.

'It was always her. Me and his mum . . .' he says, pointing at me. 'Me and his mum would probably still be together if it wasn't for that sister of hers. She never liked me from day one. Never gave me a chance, and of course his mum listened to her more than she ever listened to me. Jealousy – that's what it was. She couldn't never find a man and didn't want her sister to have one neither. Petty. More than petty, it's psychotic.'

James and Tony murmur their agreement. It looks like they've heard all this before, but maybe having me there gives the story an extra edge. I feel like I'm seeing my dad through Marsha's eyes, through thick pink-rimmed glasses, and it's weird finding myself on the side of the Deadly Lampshade. I don't know what's happened to my allegiances. It's filling my brain with confusing information. I've only been sitting down for five minutes but I need some air already. I get up, say I'm going for a cigarette, hoping that when I get back the conversation's moved on.

'I don't like you smoking,' my dad says loudly as I get up.

I don't know what to say to that. My dad has one arm back on his seat, making himself wider, showing off maybe, trying to show he's still got authority, trying to show he can still set his son on the straight and narrow. He's drinking first thing in the morning and he's getting annoyed about me smoking – his argument's got big holes, but Tony and James both seem to agree with him, judging by the looks on their faces and so much nodding that their heads are in danger of coming loose.

Without even meaning to I mumble a 'Sorry, Dad' and head outside, my face burning, for a second wishing it *had* been him in the Dalston bookmakers the other night.

* * *

I light my cigarette and look back in through the pub window. I do remember him being a proper dad once – playing football with me, teaching me how to play chess. He'd be into telling me about stuff too: history, science, the stars and planets; and when it comes from your dad it's interesting, exciting, and you want to learn because you want to make him proud. I don't think he ever realized that. I don't think he ever realized how I saw him, how Lloyd saw him. It's just once things started to change between him and my mum he started to change towards us; like we were more on her side or something. He started to drift away, until one day he left altogether.

It must be weird suddenly leaving your wife and kids behind and going back to being this separate person without a family there all the time to fill in the gaps. I suppose now he's filled in those gaps with the points of his pentagon and maybe I don't fit into that shape any more. Maybe he's trying to fit me in; maybe him telling me about the smoking is him trying, but he can't quite get me in there, doesn't know how to get me in there. I don't know . . . I don't want to make excuses for him – he's my dad, he should be making excuses for me. Maybe we'll see . . . maybe he will do – if it's important enough.

The door to the pub opens and the Rasta with the bin liner covering his dreads comes out.

'You got a light, brother?' he says, his voice scratchy and deep, and I'm thinking *brother* must really be a new term among the Hackney down-and-outs.

'Yeah, bruv,' I say, giving it to him.

He lights his cigarette, hands the lighter back and moves a short distance away, leaning against the dusty green window ledge of the pub, looking out at the street.

Coming here feels like a mistake. I thought it would help clear things up; now I'm just feeling more confused. I want to listen to my dad but he doesn't say anything I want to hear . . . or even need to hear. I feel like I'm better off listening to Shads – at least Shads knows me. At least he knows that out of all the things I do, I'm about to do or I've done, smoking cigarettes is pretty low down on the list of seriousness.

I sense something and look up. The bin-bag Rasta is staring at me. He looks old, his face dark and lined, like burned bark. In fact he looks a bit like a tree, with his tangled hair, and he carries himself strong somehow, solid, like you couldn't move him.

'You see them?' he says slowly, nodding towards the window.

'What?'

'Look at them . . . fast . . . asleep.'

I turn back to the window.

'Look,' he says.

I *am* looking – he's got me too worried to do anything else – but I don't know what I'm meant to be looking at.

'You see? Fast asleep.'

My eyes search the inside of the pub. Everyone in there looks awake to me. I put my cigarette to my lips, but realize I haven't flicked the ash and it's hanging from the tip in a long curve. I go to flick it but it drops down onto my shirt. I rub at it, only managing to create a smear of ash on my front.

The Rasta laughs – a slow, deep, rhythmic laugh. 'You got a mark on you,' he says.

'Yeah,' I say. 'But you got a bin bag on you, bruv.'

He chuckles. 'Not just the ash; a mark . . . a stain . . . on your sooooooul.' He says 'soul' long, like a plane in descent, his eyes wide. 'You know what I speak about,' he says.

My guts feel like they've been dragged out of me, let go and have sprung back inside. I try and tell him I don't. My mouth moves but no sound comes out. He gets up and comes over, standing in close. I turn to face him, haven't got a choice. I didn't realize before how tall he was but I have to crane my neck to see his face.

'You got a mark on you,' he says again, looking deep into me. 'But marks can be remoooooved.'

He smells of tobacco and beer and sweet coconut incense. I can smell the plastic of the bin bag, see how it's tucked into and through his dreads – they're grey, thick like roots.

'You want to know how you remove stains?'

'Yeah . . .' I mumble.

'Sacrifice,' he says. His eyes are wide and bloodshot but bright as stars in the gaps. 'Sacrifice,' he says, drawing it out. His eyes go even wider, swallowing me up.

'What . . . what kind?'

'There are many ways. Many roads to the same destination, and that destination is truth. But sacrifice sets you on your journey. You understand?'

I nod, but only because I don't feel like I've got any

choice. All I can see are his eyes. He steps back, opens his palm and stubs his cigarette into it.

'Let the world see the mark.' He throws the cigarette away. He puts one hand behind my head and the other palm against my forehead and rubs it in hard. He pulls me in close. 'Sacrifice,' he says.

He steps back and waves his arms around my head, my shoulders, like he's trying to swat away some bees. A chill jolts through me, my whole body shivers.

'Better,' he says. Then he's gone, down the street. 'Wake them up!' he shouts back, light now, almost happy. He's bouncing, slow and easy, swinging his arms.

I rub my hands down my arms; I feel like I've been hit by a bus. My forehead's tight with the ash, but I don't rub it off and I wander back into the pub in a daze.

'What's that?' my dad says, squinting as I slump down in my seat and drain the rest of my drink.

'That old Rasta just rubbed his cigarette ash into my forehead.'

All three of them laugh, almost hysterical. Everyone else looks round and the ones who can see my head keep looking.

'Yeah ... he's a funny one,' my dad says when they calm down and get their breaths back. 'Only spoken to him once. Up at the bar. He just says to me – just comes out and says, no introduction or nothing – just comes out and says, "You take care of your son." I mean, what kind of an opening to a conversation is that? I'm thinking he thinks he's being clever, so I say, "Which one?" He says, "You'll see which one." Crazy man . . .'

My dad shakes his head and sips at his pint. Tony and James chuckle into their drinks.

I'm sitting there opposite my dad with a palm full of ash rubbed into my forehead, my eyes wide. *Which one?*

Dad, I think to myself. *Look at me, Dad.*

TWELVE

'There's nothing in here, bruv,' says Milk.

'What do you expect?' I say. 'It's the *Hackney Gazette*.'

'No . . . I mean about us. About the old guy.'

'Well, that's good, innit?'

'Yeah, suppose.'

Milk sounds disappointed, like he wants the recognition; maybe a cutting to stick in his own gangster scrapbook. The decision not to tell the Boyz, not to tell anyone, seems to be getting to him. He needs more evidence that it actually happened, needs it for his criminal credentials. I don't mention that he was only a bystander, he didn't do all that much, but then . . . I think he knows. He's begun changing his tone towards me, being a little more respectful, and the fact is, I've used a gun and stabbed someone in

147

the last few days; in Milk's eyes that's a couple of gold stars.

I'm surprised there's nothing in the paper at all, though. But then, maybe another stabbing just isn't news any more. You see it all the time these days. In some parts of London you get flowers in hanging baskets on the lampposts; in Hackney you get flowers on the lampposts too, but they're just for memorials.

Milk closes the paper. 'No . . . nothing,' he says. He goes to hand it to me but I don't want it.

'I can't believe we didn't even get his money,' he says, putting down the paper and picking a chicken wing out of his box.

'Can you stop saying that, bruv!'

'What? It's true, innit! That was the whole point! Getting his money. And you killed him . . . I mean . . . fair play and shit, but he had a lot of cash on him, bruv.'

'Can you shut up!'

We're on our lunch-time bench. It's still early — we haven't attracted any satellites yet — but still, I don't want it being broadcast around the place. Who knows where that bin-bag Rasta is? Or what sort of radio antennae he's got wedged into that hair, tuned to Guilty

Murderer kHz. The thought of him sets me shivering again.

By the time I got to school the bell was about to go for lunch so I came straight to the bench. I walked the whole way from the pub with lead in my veins, checking for the Rasta everywhere, feeling like he was just over my shoulder the whole time. I went over and over what he said to me . . . all that biblical talk, like he knew I'd been reading it . . . I don't know what to think about all that, I really don't. Maybe he was psychic, maybe he just knew I had something to hide – he could see it in my eyes . . . I don't know.

Milk nudges me.

'What?'

'All right, bruv. No need to shout. You've got ash on your head, that's all.'

'Where?'

Milk points it out and I rub at it hard with my cuff. I thought I'd got it all off. I kept it on my head until I got to the school gates, felt like I had to, but I've got enough to think about without being stared and laughed at by the whole school. If the Rasta shows I'll just have to try and explain that to him.

149

My phone goes and my heart flings itself at the inside of my ribcage.

'What's wrong with you, man?' shouts Milk as I nearly knock his chicken wing flying.

It's a text from Hannah, telling me I'm booked in for dinner with her parents on Sunday night. Straight away I'm thinking about an excuse. Maybe I could hand myself in to the police. That would get me out of it. I weigh it up: life sentence for murder or dinner with Hannah's parents . . . it's not an easy choice, believe me.

'Who's that?' says Milk.

'Hannah. I've got to meet her parents. Go round hers for dinner. Do it all properly, you get me?'

Milk laughs. 'You gonna tell them you fucked her?'

'I didn't fuck her, bruv. It was more like . . . more like we made love.'

'You *made love*? You're fucking gay, bruv!'

So much for Milk changing his tone.

'How can that be gay?' I say. 'How can making love to my *girlfriend* be gay?'

'Sounds gay,' he says.

I don't know how else to put it. That's what it felt like. I felt like there was love there and we were making it, making more and more of it. I'm not going to say I fucked her, I banged her; it wasn't like that; it was nicer than that – more gentle or something, more loving. I don't know . . . shit, man, I know that sounds lame but that's what it was like. I don't think I can say that to Milk, though.

Some of the Yoot are arriving at Hot Chick!, laughing and cackling. They're always noisier than the Boyz, like they've got to over-compensate; like deep down they know they're the poor relation. Ram's there, and just seeing him turns my stomach over. I expect to see the bin-bag Rasta appear and start pointing him out to me, waving his arms, doing a spooky dance.

'Look at those pricks,' says Milk, shuffling along the bench, suddenly attacking his lunch with more attitude. 'You getting any lunch, bruv?'

'Nah, man.'

'I never see you eat these days.'

'That's 'cos I'm not hungry. I think I'm gonna go for a walk.'

'A *walk*? What you going for a *walk* for?' Milk spits it out.

'I don't know. I need some space.'

I get off the bench, leave Milk shaking his head. Unless I want to do a big circuit round the block, or cross the road and make it obvious I'm avoiding them, I've got to walk past the Yoot. I flip the hood of my coat up, put my head down, hoping that'll be enough to help me pass under their radar. But I hear them stop as I go by, feel their eyes on me. 'What's wrong with the BSBs?' someone says.

'Yeah, man . . . fucking Bull Shit Boyz, blud!'

'Having a little falling out, blud?' says Ram. 'The fucking Bum Spear Boyz having a little tiff?'

I turn to see Ram thrusting his hips in and out, making pained noises.

'Gnack, gnack, gnack, gnack, Bum Spear Boyz, gnack, gnack, gnack.'

'Yack, yack, yack.'

I shake my head at them, not that that's going to do anything, especially when it's covered by my hood, but it's all I've got. The Yoot keep on cackling behind me. I worry about Milk, leaving him on his own, protecting the bench all by himself. He won't be happy with me. But I've got more important concerns and I can't deal with them in public. I think about going home but I don't want to deal with them there either. I head back to school, think about finding a cubicle in the toilets or an empty classroom. In the end I settle on the library – at least there I might be able to get away with pretending I'm doing work rather than just hiding.

The last time I went to the library was a couple of years ago, and for a second I'm worried they might not let me in, might have some system I don't understand, and all the geeks and nerds are going to laugh at me. But I'm desperate. I'm willing to risk it.

The moment I step through the doors my legs are ready to give way. The air's warm, stuffy, feels thick. You can almost see it, lit up by the beams coming in through the windows. The main desk is just to the left of the double doors. Miss Guney the librarian is sitting there, singing quietly to herself. She's knitting, working away at a heap of pink wool with oversized needles.

'All right, miss?' I say.

'Jaylon!' she says happily, like I'm an old friend. I'm surprised she even remembers my name. I've never seen her outside the library, which means I haven't seen her since Year Nine. I always think librarians should be thin and quiet and unhealthy, but Miss Guney's big and smiley, with frizzy brown hair and golden skin, and loud for someone who works in a library. She doesn't look like she's changed at all.

'It's been some time, Jaylon. What brings you here? Anything important?'

'Er, yeah, you could say that. I was . . . I was feeling stressed. I wanted some peace and quiet, you get me?'

'Well, you've come to the right place. I do hope you've come to broaden your mind as well?'

'Well, yeah, that as well.'

'Good . . . good.'

'What are you doing, miss?' I say, nodding at her knitting, her hands rapidly shifting the needles backwards and forwards.

'It's a scarf. It will be cold soon. You should try it if you're feeling stressed, it's very therapeutic.'

'Yeah . . . maybe, miss. I don't know how that would go down, though. I got a reputation to think about, you get me?'

'Of course,' she says, smiling. 'Feel free to take a book and sit down, Jaylon. Make yourself at home.'

'Thanks . . . thanks, miss.'

I don't know what to do at first. I straighten my back,

loosen my neck, make sure I look serious. There's a scattering of kids at the centre tables – four tables pushed together to make a large square. A few of them glance cautiously up from their books. They look like the sort of people who should be in a library – like ghosts, old-fashioned and pale. Outside they'd have to skulk around in the shadows, avoid kids like me, but in here they look more confident, in their element, and it flashes through my head that they might turn the tables and all rush me, grab their sharpened pencils and take out their frustrations.

But they don't. There's a few double-takes, maybe a bit of tensing up, but mainly they're too engrossed in their work. I walk through the open space in the centre of the library and begin exploring the narrow aisles.

I don't know whether it's the library atmosphere or all the books and the words and how they make me think of homework and revising, but it's hard to even stay upright. There are single desks at the end of each aisle, facing the wall; most of them are occupied but I see an empty one and head straight for it, grabbing a book off the shelf on the way. I don't even check to see what it is and I slump down in the seat.

I don't like facing the wall like this, the Rasta could be inching his way along the aisle towards me, but I'm too tired to do anything about it. I rub my hands over my head, over my face. It's so quiet the silence almost feels solid, like I could lean up against it. I open the book, and the first sentence is enough to start making my eyes close. I try and fight it but soon it's too much effort to keep my eyes open at all, too much effort to even sit up, and I push the book forward and put my head down on my arms.

The knitting needle's the size of a javelin; there's no way I can fit it inside my coat. It was a bad idea Shads giving it to me. Very impractical. All the kids are giving me strange looks. I felt self-conscious enough before.

The Yoot are all standing in a tight circle outside Hot Chick! Milk throws chicken wings at them but they don't respond, keeping their backs turned, and the wings are just bouncing off.

I'm holding the knitting needle in both hands, like a spear. I jab at the backs of the Yoot. One of them turns, puts his hood down – it's the old guy. He smiles at me, goading me, testing me. I jab at him with the knitting needle. He

156

doesn't fight back. I jab him again and again, and the needle snags in the old guy's coat, gets caught up. I pull at it, and the material of his coat starts to unravel and becomes wrapped around the needle. I pull it away, moving back with it, and the whole coat begins to come apart – and it's not just the coat, it's the old guy himself – made of wool and unravelling. I start running with the needle, holding it above my head like a flagpole, pulling a mass of untangling wool with me. The old guy has disappeared into the mass of wool, which is now the street, the buildings, everything. I'm pulling it all apart, and I've got to run faster and faster because the wool is stacking up behind me like a huge wave. The needle starts getting heavy, my arms aching, and I need to lower it, stop and rest, but when I do the wool bunches up and towers above me and begins to tumble and fall over me and I'm swamped, drowning in it. It's all over me, I get it in my mouth. I gasp for air, cough and jump. It goes completely black. I pull at the wool, manage to find a gap and get it up and over my head. And down. Down onto the desk. It's Miss Guney's scarf.

It's dark in the library. I thought I'd just closed my eyes, but then I've also got that weird sense of knowing, in my muscles, that I've been here for hours. I shift around. There's light coming from somewhere, a faint glow in between the bookshelves. I scrape my chair back, flinching at the noise. I stand up, my legs stiff. I grab my bag and the scarf and edge my way through the gloom, down to the end of the aisle and back towards the main desk. That, as it turns out, is where the light is coming from – a lamp pointing down onto the pages of a book that Miss Guney is reading.

'What time is it, miss?'

'A little after six. Did you have a good rest?'

'Yeah . . . yeah . . . Is this yours?' I hold out the scarf.

'Yes it is. I decided to finish it as it was. You looked like you needed a pillow. You appeared quite snug in the end.'

'Thanks,' I say. 'Why didn't you wake me up? I missed all my lessons.'

'You needed the rest. Sleep is so much more enjoyable when the rest of the world is awake,' she says.

I fold the scarf together, go to put it on the desk.

'Keep it if you want,' she says. 'A gift.'

'Thanks, miss, but I don't think it'll go down too well.'

'Your reputation, is it?'

'Yeah, something like that.'

'OK,' she says. She sounds disappointed. She takes it and bundles it up on the table next to her.

'You going home at all, miss?'

'Yes . . . soon. I've got a lot of books to get through first.'

'OK, then. See you later and . . . thanks, yeah?'

'No problem. You come and see me again soon.'

'Yeah, will do, miss.'

I leave the library; the rest of the school is deserted. I check my phone: there are seven missed calls and some texts – Marsha, Milk, Hannah, Shads. Somehow my phone's gone on silent; it wasn't earlier.

THIRTEEN

The first person I called on the way home was Marsha, and now I'm doing something I haven't ever done before: I'm having a night in . . . with *her*. Yep, that's right. I'm having a night in with the Deadly Lampshade. We're going to have a takeaway and watch DVDs. Can you believe it? What a turnaround. It was her idea – get some DVDs and a Chinese, and you know what? I'm looking forward to it.

When I get back she's out hiring the films and getting the takeaway. I check the flat for any sign of the bin-bag Rasta, any sign of the old guy, check my roommates haven't moved, do my dance in front of the hologram Jesus, then dump my bag and change out of my uniform.

I'm putting my jeans on when my phone rings. It's Marsha.

'Hello?' I say.

'Jaylon?'

'Yeah?'

'I'm in the Golden Mountain . . . anything in particular you want?'

'Yeah . . . chicken with black bean sauce and special fried rice and maybe some prawn crackers.'

'That's fine, fine. OK, I'll see you soon.'

'Cool, Marsh, thanks.'

Ten seconds later my phone goes again. I answer. 'Hello?'

'What are you doing?' It's Shads. I can't believe it. I didn't even check. I don't say anything. I should've checked the display – why didn't I check the display?

'I *said*, what are you doing?' He sounds offended.

'Sorry, bruv. I'm at home.'

'Yeah . . . you see my calls?'

'Yeah, yeah . . . I was going to call you. I've just got in from school.'

'What the fuck you at school for till this time?'

'I was in the library.'

161

'*You were what?*'

'Never mind.'

'Look, I'm taking you out tonight. We're going to pick you up in thirty minutes . . . and dress smart.'

'I don't think I can do it, bruv.'

'What do you mean, *don't*? What did I tell you about that word? Thirty minutes.' He hangs up.

I sit there, on the edge of the bed, mouth opening and closing like a fish. Shads asked me the other day if I've got balls; he should know: he's holding me by them. What am I supposed to do now? And dress smart? I turn to Jesus on the back of the door and hold my arms out. 'Stop looking all smug! Why don't you try helping for once?'

By the time Marsha gets back I've had a shower, a nervous shower, getting shampoo in my eyes because I don't want to keep them closed, don't want to let my guard down. I've covered myself in about half a can of deodorant and I'm in a black shirt and back in my jeans.

'You look stylish for an evening of films,' she says, grimacing at the air around me. I might have overdone it with the deodorant.

'I'm going out, Marsh.'

'What do you mean you're going out?' There's a quick flash of Deadly Lampshade. 'Are you planning on being long?'

I shrug. 'I don't know.'

She pauses, deflates a bit. 'We had an arrangement,' she says, but it's quiet, awkward.

'I've got to.'

'Got to nothing!' She pushes past me and bangs the bulging brown paper bag down on the kitchen table, grabs one of the prawn crackers that's poking out and bites down hard. 'What about all this food?' she says, white crumbs flying off. 'And I only got these films for a night. Films *you* wanted!'

'Save me some. I like cold Chinese anyway.'

She turns away.

'I'll watch the films when I get in,' I say.

'That's not the point!'

She keeps her back to me. Sighs. Then her shoulders shake, like her foot's on the clutch of the Mystery Machine. At first I think she's laughing, but then she sniffs and gets a tissue from her sleeve; blows her nose on it. I don't know what to do. And I get the feeling she doesn't either, which makes it all worse. Normally she'd be harder on me, maybe order me to stay in, but then forcing me to have an evening in with her would probably be missing the point.

'Well, go on if you're going!' she says, not turning round; breathing deeply, gathering herself up.

I think maybe I should give her a hug, but I can't hug the Deadly Lampshade; we haven't come that far yet. I want to explain myself, even though I know she's not going to understand, and that means it'll turn into an argument – but my phone goes anyway and it's Shads again.

'We're outside the block. Get your arse down here.' He hangs up, and I think, one of these days we're going to have to discuss his phone manner. Every time he hangs up it's like a slap in the face.

I mumble a sorry, but Marsha ignores it, and I go and put my coat and school shoes on and head out. The lift's been cleaned up so I'm down quickly and leaving the block.

The Corsa's got its back to me, red tail lights on. Bass pounding like a monster's heartbeat. Shads is in the back, even though it's just him and Muzza. He's wearing too much aftershave, a fresh, fruity one, filling the whole car . . . or at least it's trying to; it's battling with Muzza's aftershave, which is harsher, more industrial. The car's developing its own alien atmosphere, and mixed with my deodorant it's barely breathable. My nose starts itching and it's making my shampooed eyes even sorer.

'You stoned?' says Shads, looking in close.

'No . . . shampoo.'

He shakes his head. 'You been keeping a low profile,' he says.

'Yeah,' I say. 'Just trying to prepare myself for next week, you get me?' I have to say it all quickly, not breathing – there's a sneeze building.

'Yeah . . . Milk tells me you been busy.'

'*What?*' I let go of the sneeze, all over the back of Muzza's seat, and I'm hoping I haven't hit the dome of his head poking out over the top.

'He says you jooked some old white guy.'

'Yeah,' I say, rubbing my nose and feeling my chest turn in on itself.

I know Shads isn't going to report me to the authorities, but it going further than me and Milk makes it more real, makes the odds on getting caught shorter, makes it even more out of my control. I can't believe Milk's blabbed about it already . . . I can't believe I was stupid enough to think he wouldn't.

'I'm impressed,' says Shads. 'Milk says you didn't even take his money. Just did it for the buzz . . . That's what I've been saying to you: *balls*, bruv. That's what I'm after.'

That's what he's after? Well, at least I'm starting to fit Shads's criteria. Maybe that means he'll let me off; maybe that can be my initiation done with; maybe tonight I'll join the Olders officially and we can forget all about Ram, even forget about the old guy, consign him to history, the Dark Ages.

I have to hold tight to that thought because Muzza's reversing, swinging left, lurching forward. I grab at my seat belt, get it secure quick. But my guts have jumped out of the car and are waving goodbye.

'I'm taking you somewhere special tonight,' says Shads. We turn left out of the estate. I'm pressed against the window, Shads pressed up against me.

'Where?' I say. We straighten up and both flop forward.

'You'll see . . . it's a friend. A friend and business associate.' We move the other way, this time I'm leaning in to Shads. 'It'll be fun,' he says, gently elbowing me away. 'Educational too. You're a lucky boy.'

'Thanks.'

I manage to get up straight again and adjust my seat belt. I go to open the window, get some air circulating, but Shads stops me and holds up his magic box. I sigh; a deep sigh – a sigh that travels from my shoulders all the way down to my toes and back again. I picture my chicken with black bean sauce; picture mixing it in with the special fried rice; the cubes of sweet chicken, prawns, egg, peas . . . using prawn crackers to scoop it all up – but instead I look down and there's a scoop of white powder in front of my nose and it looks like I'm going to have to settle for a dinner of Class As.

'I've got plans for you, Jay,' says Shads. 'And hearing what you did the other night, I know I'm doing the right thing.'

'Does that mean I'm in the Olders, then?'

He smirks, splutters. 'Not yet, bruv! You hear that, Muzz? Muzz?' He breaks into a full-on laugh, waves the scoop around. 'My boy thinks he's in the fucking Olders already! Fucking hell, mate, if it was that easy I'd have half of Hackney knocking on my door! No . . .' His tone drops. 'You done it once – that deserves respect. But who was that? An old loser down some alley? Fuck that. Anyone can do that. I want you to do someone that *matters*. You're sending out a message, bruv. You take care of Ram, you're flicking a switch, starting something. Some old prick down an alleyway don't mean nothing. Especially if you don't get his money. It's a good sign, that's all I'm saying.

'You got a chance to be one of my main boys. I need brains in my organization, but you got to have a balance. You got to show that you got control. Over your brains *and* your balls. You get me? I had the balls before the brains, always had them. With you it's the other way round – even if you are shit at chess – but you got potential.'

The scoop finds its way back under my nose but it's a moving target and I have to grip Shads's wrist to keep it steady. I sniff it up and Shads shakes me off so he can give himself a hit. Part of me didn't want to let go. I need stabilizing. We get to the lights at the corner of the Downs. Muzza brakes, we both pitch forward and a scoopful of sherbs sprays over Shads's shoulder and the back seat. The lights change and Muzza's accelerating again, swinging right.

'Muzz!' shouts Shads, kicking the back of his seat. 'I want to get there in one piece, blud!'

Muzza grunts; it could be a sorry but then maybe not, because he's going even faster down the next straight, like he's trying to beat the all-time Hackney Downs lap record.

Shads quickly digs up another scoop, bending over the box and almost shovelling it in. He does it again, making the most of being in an upright position. He leans back, breathes deep and points the scoop at Muzza. 'He needs to go easy,' he says, tapping his nose. He's not the only one, and I have to tell him he's managed to get white haloes round both his nostrils.

We barely brake taking the next corner, and now we've got the Westhall estate to our left. The first feel from the sherbs is a jittery one – not helped, of course, by Muzza's driving – and just being this close to Westhall gets my heart rate up and my skin prickling. But it's a blur at this pace, and soon we're under the railway bridge and at the lights joining Amhurst Road. They're turning red as we get there but Muzza doesn't slow – he pulls a hard left, sending me and Shads veering right again. We might well arrive in one piece, but at this rate it's going to be a crushed and mangled one.

Amhurst Road is quiet and wide and its long gentle

curve gives Muzza no reason to slow down, but at least the contours of the road mean the pace isn't so noticeable and I can sit up, make sure my limbs are screwed in, adjust my internal organs and straighten out my spine. Shads fiddles with his box again. It makes me worry about where we're going if he needs Sergeant Sherbs to be on such high alert and I wonder if Shads has got a weapon on him tonight. I don't. I haven't touched the shank since I stuck it in the old guy. Took it home, washed it, hid it. I wanted to bury it, destroy it, but it's not going to go quietly. We're going to get reacquainted soon. It's going to rise again.

We come up to the busy junction with Dalston Lane; roads going off in a star shape. Lots of traffic backed up. Our set of lights is green and Muzza keeps his pace steady. As we get closer the lights change. Muzza accelerates to beat them but he's left it too late. Traffic begins to move, coming in from a diagonal right. Muzza speeds up, but a white van, first in the queue, is now right in our path. All we can do is brake but it's like Muzza won't accept it. The van's got time if it keeps moving, but it doesn't; it brakes right in front of us. Now Muzza does brake, but he's got to slam them hard and it's too late. Me and Shads fly forward, my right hand managing to grab Muzza's seat, and that pushes me in between the two front seats, the seat belt carving into my neck. I feel like I'm being forced into a closer look, and all I can see is the white of the van lit up by our lights. White, white, white. I grit my teeth, narrow my eyes, grip onto the seat, like that's going to help somehow, going to lessen the impact. A million thoughts rush through my head. I'm meant to see my life flash before my eyes, but it doesn't and I wonder what that even means; what I do see is how soft and weak I am compared to a heavy chunk of twisted metal and glass, and I'm trapped inside a chunk of twisted metal and glass and it's all going to come together and I'll be lost in the middle of it. I close my eyes, waiting for the impact, waiting for I don't know what.

But there's nothing.

I don't open my eyes, thinking maybe I'm frozen in time and when I do open them we'll still be crashing. But then I hear car horns, shouts, heavy breathing, time moving again. I can hear Shads muttering. I look around. He's dusting himself down, more coke down his front. Muzza's hunched over the wheel, shoulders going up and down, his breath rasping.

The side of the van is directly in front of us, a white metal curtain, bright in the beam of our lights. And untouched. There's movement. The driver of the van is getting out; a big, burly white guy in white overalls – the angled headlights all around us lighting him up. He walks slowly round the Corsa and comes round to mine and Muzza's side. He stops, bends down and peers in through my window. He meets my eyes; his are a sharp, patterned grey. His pupils contract and they make me think of round black rocks plunging into a rough sea. I feel like I'm following, being sucked in, but then he's up, moving to Muzza's window, and I rebound back. He taps at Muzza's window. Muzza lowers it down.

'Out you get, sunshine,' the man says, his voice deep and thick, like it's coming up from a well. It's a tone difficult to refuse and Muzza gets out without reply. Not even a grunt.

'What are you doing?' says Shads, grabbing my arm, and I realize I've got my door open and I've started to get out as well. He pulls me back in.

I try and listen in, but the conversation outside is muffled and I can't see above their chests, so I sit back and rub my hands over my face. I'm actually glad to be stationary, even if it is in the middle of a junction with horns blaring and in a car decorated with illegal substances. But I'm wondering how long it's going to be before the police show and if I should make a run for it.

I press myself up against the window to get a look at their faces. Unsurprisingly, the van guy seems to be doing most of the talking, his hand on Muzza's shoulder. He's so big he's making Muzza look small by comparison. The van guy points something out behind him. Muzza has to go on tiptoes to see what he means. At first Muzza seems to be protesting, but slowly the van guy wears him down. Muzza starts to nod. He looks down at his feet, the van guy lecturing him like he's a kid. Muzza doesn't seem to mind, though – he's taking it on board.

The van guy holds his arms out wide. Muzza shuffles in and does the same. And they hug. In the middle of the junction. And they stay like that, holding onto each other. A proper clench. Muzza has to raise his arms and bend backwards a little and pats the van guy's back. His eyes closed – he looks happy there, comfortable.

Shads leans over me to get a better look. 'What the fuck?' he says.

'I – I – I don't know, bruv,' I mutter.

The horns have died down – maybe everyone in all the other cars is as transfixed as we are. Then they break, pat each other some more, and a dazed-looking Muzza gets back in the car. He clicks his seat belt and starts the engine. The van guy sounds a couple of toots when he's back in the van, and he's gone. Muzza responds with the same and gently accelerates away.

'What the fuck was that?' says Shads. 'I can do without that kind of attention; and I can do without the whole inside of my car being covered in FUCKING WHITE, MUZZ. You get me?'

Muzza doesn't say anything, and on the other side of the junction he pulls in to the kerb and stops.

'Yes?' says Shads, after the three of us have sat for a minute in silence.

'I can't do it, boss,' says Muzza, and I'm surprised to hear him say a whole sentence.

'Can't do what, exactly?' says Shads.

'Drive,' says Muzza, patting at the wheel and then running his palms along his thighs. 'I can't drive.' He undoes his seat belt, gets out of the car and walks round to the pavement.

Shads mumbles something under his breath, grabs the seat in front of him and tries to strangle it. Satisfied he's broken the neck of the passenger seat, he scrambles forward and gets out too. I follow after him.

'What did that prick say to you?' says Shads, when we're all standing out on the pavement.

'He said I should slow down,' says Muzza.

'And you're going to listen to him?' says Shads.

'He knew what he was talking about,' says Muzza.

'I don't fucking believe it,' says Shads, turning back and forth, hands on his hips. 'He said slow down? All right, fine: slow the fuck down. I can see his point. He didn't say stop altogether, though, yeah?'

'No, but . . . I don't know . . . he didn't have to. It was in his eyes or something. I can't, like, concentrate.' Muzza shakes his head, puts his hands to his face, looking out through his fingers.

'My God,' says Shads, his voice going high-pitched. 'I was always suspicious of you gym freaks.'

'It's not that, man! I just . . . I can't explain it. I'm feeling ill, boss. I need . . . I need to lie down.'

To be fair to Muzza, I'm not surprised he can't explain

it. I'd have trouble if someone asked me for my rundown of events and I use a lot more words than he does.

'You need to lie down?' says Shads. 'What is this? You're supposed to be working! For *me*! Here, take a sniff, that'll straighten you up. No pun intended, bruv.'

'I don't want any more of that, man!' Muzza waves his arm and begins walking back towards the junction.

'Muzz!' Shads shouts, but Muzza just keeps walking, shaking his head. 'Muzz!' Nothing.

Shads turns to me. 'Now what?' he says.

Over Shads's shoulder I see a black cab coming this way, its light on. 'We could get a taxi,' I say, pointing it out.

Shads spins and steps towards the kerb, his hand raised. 'Taxi!' he shouts, but the cab doesn't slow, the driver with a blank expression on his face as he passes, trying hard not to see us.

'Fucking prick!' shouts Shads, and for a second I'm worried he's going to start taking shots at its rear end. 'Now you see why I need my own motor. It's misleading having those things black. They should paint them white. At least then we'd know where we stand.'

Next we find a minicab office but Shads wants to know

what cars they have before committing himself. At the moment they've only got a choice between a Ford Mondeo, a Volvo estate and some kind of Honda.

'No Mercs?' says Shads.

'No,' says the bored controller behind the Perspex screen.

'BMW?'

'I told you what we got.'

Shads turns to me. 'We can't turn up in one of those. I got a reputation to think about.'

I think about reminding him that a Vauxhall Corsa isn't that much better but I decide I'm better off keeping it to myself. 'I don't even know where we're going, bruv,' I say.

'Course not,' says Shads, shaking his head and rolling his eyes, like that's entirely my fault.

'Well?' I say.

'Limehouse,' he says. 'We're going to Limehouse to meet some important business associates of mine.' Shads shoots a glance at the controller, who seems slightly less bored now he's listening in to our conversation. 'That's why I can't turn up in some old piece of junk from the 1970s.'

'Why don't we get the bus?' I say. 'We can get a bus

straight to Limehouse. The 277. Then, you know, like, walk to where we're going. If that's better.'

Shads looks at me like I've just spat in his face. 'The *bus*?' he says. 'Get the *bus*? I haven't got the bus in about five years.' But then he softens. 'All right then!' he says, and pats my side. 'Lead the way to the bus stop!' and he ushers me out of the cab office.

We have to wait about ten minutes for the 277. This gives Shads time to replenish the sherbs in his bloodstream and make some phone calls. When the bus comes Shads gets on ahead of me and waits.

'You're going to have to pay for me,' he says.

'What? Why?' I say, stronger than I mean to, but I'm surprised that someone who tries whenever possible to broadcast his wealth to the world can't afford a bus fare.

'I don't carry change. I only carry proper money, Jay, *serious* money, you get me?'

I have to pay in cash for myself too, and I search all my pockets before I find enough change for both of us. Shads tuts and sighs, tells me he hasn't got all night, but eventually I find the right amount and we go up to the top deck and sit down at the back.

There aren't many people on the bus and we have the back row to ourselves. Shads stretches out, puts his feet up on the seat in front that faces us. There's a man sitting on the next seat after that and another four or five people spaced out along the deck.

Despite making himself comfortable, Shads doesn't look happy that he's had to resort to such a low-class level of transport. He looks around like he doesn't want to be spotted, like it might damage his reputation. He slides down the seat, kicks the back of the seat in front. That makes the guy sitting there turn and glance behind.

'What?' says Shads, but the guy doesn't reply. He turns back and leans towards the window.

With all the passengers safely facing the front, Shads dishes out a couple more scoops. I don't know how his body can process all this powder. My heart's already using my ribcage as a punch bag.

'I don't know what's wrong with Muzz,' he says, sighing loudly and settling back against the seat. 'It must be the steroids. I tell you, that shit ain't healthy.'

I want to turn him down, put him on mute. I'm not used to seeing him out in public like this, just *loose*. He looks me over, rubs the side of my head and pushes it away. 'You always look so worried,' he says. 'Like I scare you or some shit.'

'No,' I say. 'No . . . it ain't that, bruv.' I scan the deck, checking for any heads turned our way.

'What you got to understand, Jay,' says Shads, stretching out his arms along the back of the seats, crossing his legs over and managing to kick the seat in front again. 'What you got to understand is, I'm at war with the *world*, bruv. In my business, you got to get what you can when you can. No one's gonna give me nothing. No one's *ever* given me nothing. I've had to take it. And you know what? I'm glad. I'm glad it's been that way. I ain't ever sat around waiting. Waiting's for pussies.'

He pauses to sniff and rub at his nose. Sweat glistens on his forehead. His fingers tap, form a fist and punch down hard.

'I don't believe in laws, I don't believe in authorities. You know why? Because people like us, Jay . . . people like us . . . people like all the fucking Boyz, bruv – we're born with handcuffs on. You can ask nicely for a key but no one's gonna give you a key. You have to find your own key, and most of the time you got to steal a fucking key.'

He turns to me, his gaze going quickly from one of my eyes to the other. 'You want to spend your life in handcuffs . . . or do you want to take your chances?'

'Take my chances,' I say, flat, wanting to swallow but stopping myself.

'Yes, man!' he says. He flops back. 'You see . . . I'm free. I'm *alive*. If one day I get caught, I get caught, but I'm gonna make sure I enjoy the ride in the meantime. The whole idea, the whole *idea* that anyone can tell me what to do, it makes me sick. Who are these pricks who think they know better than me? No one knows better than me. You know why? Because I'm me. This is *my* life. You know what a lot of people forget?'

'What?'

'It's about survival; it's not about jobs and pensions and mortgages and all that shit. It's not about *school*. It's about survival. That's *all* it's about. You know what else people forget?'

'What?'

'That we're animals, bruv. That's what it comes down to. We dress it up, we got all these different names, different definitions, but basically . . . we're animals. Food, sex, shelter: we have those – we survive. And you're telling me, when life's that simple, that I need someone to tell me how to live? Fuck that shit! WHAT THE FUCK DO YOU WANT?'

I jump. Shads is looking at the guy in front again. The guy shuffles in his seat and turns back towards the window.

Shads hops onto the seat facing us, leans over to the guy. 'Is something funny?' he says. 'Oi, I'm talking to you. I said: is something funny?'

The guy gives a quick turn of his head. 'No,' he says.

'So why you smiling? Why you turning round to me and smiling?'

'I wasn't . . . I mean, you were talking loudly, that's all.'

'Right . . . so . . . what? We in a library, are we? At a fucking funeral? What?'

'No, it's nothing. I'm sorry . . . forget about it.'

Shads gets up, turns and slides onto the guy's seat, up close. My guts feel loose, my bladder full, and I have to grip tight. I wish I could grip Shads tight. Where's Diggy when you need him? Where's Muzza? I feel like I need a leash.

Shads puts his left arm along the back of the guy's seat, taps his fingers. 'You want me to forget about it now, yeah? What if I don't want to forget about it?' he says.

The man mumbles a sorry and goes to stand up but Shads grabs his shoulder and forces him back down again. 'You ain't going anywhere until we've sorted out our little problem.'

'I don't have a problem,' the guy says, his voice shaky. 'I just want to get off.'

'You don't have a problem; but *I* do. With *you.*' Shads looks at me. 'Sit here,' he says, nodding at the seat directly behind the guy.

I'm up and doing it straight away, thinking maybe if I do what he says it'll calm him down. I sit side on, my left leg up, and from here I see a glint in Shads's right hand.

'Cover his mouth,' says Shads. 'Do it!'

The 'Do it' blanks my mind and controls my muscles, and I swear there's no gap between me sitting there and me leaning over, both hands over the guy's mouth. He struggles, grabs at my wrists, and I pull hard. Following orders. Shads swings, there's a flash of metal, and he connects with the guy's chest. I feel the impact, like he's being hit with electricity, those pads in hospitals. I grip tighter. Why, I don't know. Just practical. I feel condensation

183

against my fingers. His arms reach out, flail. Another jolt, and another. I'm scared to scan the deck again but I do it. Whether they don't know what's happening or they don't want to know, no one's facing our way. Another jolt, and I feel teeth against my fingers but there's no pressure and his head is suddenly heavy and I'm holding it up.

Shads stands, puts his right arm deep inside his jacket. 'I think this is our stop, bruv,' he says, out of breath. He starts walking along the aisle towards the stairs.

I take my hands away. The guy slumps and I manoeuvre him to the side, against the window. 'Yeah, yeah,' I mumble. I realize I let go of those muscles I was holding and there's wetness down my legs, the sherbs making it hard to tense them again, and I try and cover myself with my coat, pull it down, but I want to cover my face at the same time and I make my way down the stairs in a sort of bending, crouching position. This only draws Shads's attention and he notices the front of my jeans. He looks at me and my face burns.

We wait at the doors for what feels like ages. I'm expecting shouts, screams. I don't see myself ever getting off the bus. But it carries on as normal, and when it finally stops and the doors open, I don't believe it at first, don't believe I can just step out onto the pavement and into the air.

Shads is moving fast. I keep my head down and follow. I hear the bus drive away, a purring sound. I don't turn to see what we've left behind.

FOURTEEN

Shads turns off the main road, going so quick I've got to jog every few steps to keep up, like a little kid. There's a square on our right; public gardens behind black railings. On our left there's a block of flats, the first in a sprawling estate.

After the old guy, I ran. I *had* to run. This feels different. This time every step's jarring my bones.

Shads crosses over, heading for the gap between the first block and the next. But I can't follow. I've got to stop and cling to the railings.

Shads looks for me as the estate's about to swallow him up, and does a double-take when I'm not there. He stops on the edge, faces me and holds his arms out. 'What?' he mouths.

I turn away and rest my head on the arm that holds the

railings; it sways a bit, unsteady, like a hammock that's too narrow for the weight. My skin's prickling, sweat everywhere. I feel like I'm going to faint.

I hear Shads's footsteps. I roll my head, keeping the weight on my arm, and I see his legs stop about a metre away. 'What's wrong with you?' he says.

'You killed him,' I say. 'You just *killed* him, bruv.'

'That's right, Jay. And what is your problem? Apart from the fact that you've pissed yourself.'

'I'm going to be sick.'

Shads steps closer. 'I want to get off the street, Jay. I got friends on this estate. I want you to get cleaned up, and I want us to get to this business meeting some time before midnight. Fucking get it together, bruv.'

I try and lift my head up, but that sends a nasty rush through me and I am sick, down on the pavement between us. Not much – I haven't been eating enough, but it stings anyway.

Shads takes a step back and turns away. 'Jesus Christ!' he says. 'Maybe I'm losing my touch. I thought I could spot talent, you get me? *Ability*. First Muzza, now you.'

I'm bent over. I spit, pull at the stringy acid in my nose,

wipe my mouth on my sleeve and spit again. 'I can't believe you just killed him,' I say.

'You should be used to it by now.'

'I don't want to get used to it.' I sound winded.

'It's too late for that, Jay. You get me? It's too *fucking* late.' He pauses. I know he doesn't want to look at me. I wouldn't want to look either. 'You're on your own tonight. I don't want you around me. You're an embarrassment. A *mess*.'

Shads starts walking away. I reach for the railings again and try and pull myself upright. And he's back over. He grabs my face hard, but quickly thinks better of it and wipes his hand on his coat. Instead, he points a finger close to my face. 'I don't like my boys letting me down,' he says. 'I got certain standards. None of my Olders piss themselves, bruv. You get me? What kind of shit is that?'

There are sirens in the distance. Shads raises his head and gives me a look that loads me with the blame, like, *I hope you're proud of yourself*; if we'd walked casually off the bus and away, it would've all been forgotten about. Instead my insides have betrayed us both. They've confessed all over the front of my jeans and the pavement.

Shads grabs at my coat and pushes me. 'Get gone!' he says. He spins, crosses back over the street and vanishes fast into the estate. The sirens increase, sounding everywhere; it might not even be about the bus, but I know that doesn't matter. I've got to disappear too. I follow in the same direction; head in between the blocks and into the car park beyond.

I wouldn't even think about going into an estate like this normally, it would be too dangerous, but I don't have much choice – don't have *any* choice. And I can't help thinking that's the way Shads wants it.

On the far side of the car park there's a children's play-ground and a basketball court, both empty. I don't see Shads anywhere, don't see anyone, and I hope it stays that way.

Cover his mouth. Why did I hold onto him? Because Shads told me to. Why did I even go out? Because Shads told me to. You try going against that. It's like going against gravity. It's like me saying to you: *Why don't you try floating in the air? Go on, it's easy.* No . . . No it's not. Is it? *Cover his mouth.* I didn't even think about it, didn't think I *could* think about it – just had to obey orders, do as I'm told, and look where it gets me. *Cover his mouth.*

What would've happened if I'd said to Shads, *Actually, bruv, I got plans tonight. Me and my aunt are having a night in watching films and eating a Chinese. Thanks for the offer, though, yeah?*

I didn't have a choice. Or maybe there was a choice . . . but if there was it was talking in some language I don't understand; dressed up in some clothes I don't recognize. Can you point it out to me next time, please? Before it's too late.

Maybe the CCTV wasn't working. Maybe no one looked at us; maybe they didn't want to, like that cab driver. No one looks at anyone any more, especially people like us; you never know what we might do. Look at us for too long, we might become real. We might hurt you. *A lot.*

But that's not even what's important. The details. I don't care about the details. I'm a part of it and that's never going to change. The mark's spreading, getting bigger and dirtier. What would the bin-bag Rasta say to me now? I wanted to listen to him, wanted to believe him, and I've let him down already. What do you do when you're up to your neck in blood? You put your head under, that's what you do.

I follow the estate as far as it goes, staying close to the

shadows. When that one ends, another begins. I cross borders I'm not allowed to cross, borders that are dangerous and under surveillance, but I don't care, and maybe it's the not caring that keeps me safe. I keep my hood up, my head down, make myself invisible. I keep walking – walking in a way that's becoming all too familiar.

I find my way to Dalston; back to the bookmakers. There's no police sign outside, no photo or poster in the window; no incident board at the entrance to the side-street. No sign it even happened.

There's a fine drizzle falling, so fine it just feels like the air's wet. You can only see it in the streetlamps and head-lights. I light a cigarette, draw the smoke in deep and stand close to the window, my breath steaming circles against it. It's busier than it was last time. A group of men dotted about, craning their necks to watch football on the wall-mounted screens. It could've been any one of them. *If they'd won enough.* And I don't like the way it makes life look: too much chance, too much luck.

I could've missed Shads's phone call. We could've hit the van. We could've got a different bus. I could be at home right now, eating my chicken and black bean; not innocent,

but still, like . . . still with *some* hope. All these little details
. . . you put them together and it seems more than me or
anyone else can deal with. I'm starting to see now why
Marsha believes in God: it's too big for us, there's too much
responsibility on our shoulders. Again I feel sick thinking
about it, and I take another long drag on the cigarette to
keep me grounded, keep me weighed down. We could've
got a different bus. Anything could've happened.

There's a short, unhealthy white guy hanging at the
back, frizzy greying hair and bushy beard, squinting up at
the screen. I picture him winning big. I picture him walking up a side-street that turns into a dead end. I picture
him getting on a bus that he never gets off. And it'll be the
end that people remember. It'll colour everything; everything he ever did. It doesn't matter what came before. If it
ends bad, your life's bad. If it ends tragic, your life's tragic.
Full stop.

I drop the cigarette, grind it into the pavement and light
another. I move away from the window and turn the
corner into the side-street. It's darker than I remember it.
When I've run over it in my mind it's always been brighter,
lit up in this harsh light. It's been longer too, like we were

trailing him, tracking him down, disappearing, getting lost. It's not like that. Not as dramatic. I guess it all happened quicker than I thought.

I move along slowly, change to the other side of the road. It feels safer somehow. Even so, every step is like a crashing cymbal. There's still no signs up, no boards. That worries me. I don't know why; you'd think I'd be pleased about that . . . well . . . maybe not pleased. Relieved maybe. But I want more proof, more evidence that it happened, that I've been feeling like I have for a reason. I don't want it all to slip away and become part . . . part of the background. Not even another statistic – it wouldn't even be that.

But maybe there is proof – and I feel ice in my veins. There's someone scuttling about just round the corner where it happened. I say *someone* – from here it looks more like an animal, brown and scruffy, crouching low to the ground, tending to plants and flowers. It looks like a memorial. But the flowers aren't lying there in bunches; they're stuck into the wall, into the ground, like they're actually growing, and I can smell them, strong in the air.

It's a woman. To her side is a small wooden wheelbarrow piled with loose plants, soil hanging off the roots, and she's wedging them into gaps in the brickwork, right where the old guy hit the wall and slid down. I walk slowly, move further in to the right and keep going to the end of the street, all the time watching. I get to the end and double back.

She's wearing a torn, dirty brown dress. Her hair is a dark, tangled mess, the drizzle beading up on it like spiders' webs. She hasn't got any tools – just using her hands, clawing, digging in, patting down soil – and she's frantic; grunting, panting, talking to herself.

It could be his daughter, his granddaughter. *Anyone.* And I think, I've heard about killers doing this before: they can't help it, introducing themselves to their victim's relatives. And I wonder why . . . but I can sort of see why. You're both connected to them, both connected to each other, in totally opposite ways, but in the middle there's a join.

'Hello?' I say.

She stops. I wait for her to turn round, but she stays still.

'What are you doing?' I say.

'Gardening,' she says, and she moves again. Her voice seems to bounce off the walls, sounds like music; fizzes through the air, catching the drizzle, turning it to steam.

'Why?' I say, cautious, not even wanting to hear the answer.

'Lots of life here,' she says, and I get a shiver across my skin. 'It's good ground. Good for growing.'

She sniffs at the air and turns her head. Her face is grubby, smeared with dirt, but her eyes are wide and shiny.

'Spare cigarette?' she says. I notice her feet are bare, but just as I do, she stands up, and the bottom of her dress covers them. She's short, just up to my chest.

'Yeah . . . yeah,' I say. I take out the pack and point it towards her. She takes one and I light it. She steadies my hand as she leans in to the flame. I don't want her to touch me, but her hands are warm and feel OK there. Petals unfurl on the wall behind her and an orange flower opens out. I stare at it, not sure I've even seen it.

'Thank you,' she says, taking rapid tokes. 'Thank you,' she says again, deeper this time, rougher. She coughs. 'THANK YOU,' she roars, and I have to take a step back. She giggles, satisfied. The smell of flowers pulses out from the wall.

'Why are you gardening?' I say, my mouth hardly opening.

'I told you,' she says, her voice like before, almost singing.

She coughs. 'I told you,' she says, rougher again. 'What are *you* doing?'

'Going for a walk,' I say. It sounds weak but it's all I've got.

'Seems an odd place to be walking.'

'Seems an odd place to be gardening.'

'I told you: good ground. Where you find an end you find a beginning.'

'What do you mean?' I say, but I don't think I even manage to say it out loud.

'I think you know what I mean.' She steps forward, her eyes darting across my face, examining me. She holds the cigarette between her teeth and puts her hands to my cheeks, moves my head slightly from side to side like she's checking I'm clean. Then she smiles and turns back to the wall, crouching low again.

The feel of her hands doesn't fade. It's like pins and needles.

'Were you related?' I say, blinking hard.

She springs up. 'Related to who?'

I give a sharp nod at the wall, at the memorial.

'Yes,' she says. 'Very close.'

I don't know why I'm asking; don't know why I'm even here. She sucks on the cigarette, blows the smoke towards me. 'I've got to get back to work,' she says. 'It won't last long.'

I should say sorry, own up somehow, but it doesn't feel right. I feel like I could make the flowers wilt just by standing too close. 'You want to take more cigarettes?'

'Yes!' she says. She takes three. 'Is that OK?'

'Yeah . . . help yourself.'

'Thank you. It needs work, doesn't it?'

'What does?'

'The voice. It's good for the plants but it's often a one-way conversation. It's easy to think they're not listening at all.'

She turns to them and shakes her head, drizzle spraying off. On the wall another flower opens out, fat pink petals standing out bright. I definitely see that one, and the smell is fresh and strong in the air.

'Very clever,' she says. 'I'm sure that was just for your benefit.'

She takes another plant from the wheelbarrow, crouches down and squeezes it in between the bricks. 'Goodbye,' she

197

says, through teeth clenched on the cigarette. She's back at work now. I feel like I've been dismissed. Maybe that was as much conversation as she needed.

I walk back to Marsha's in a daze, the feel of the woman's hands still on my face, the smell of the flowers in my nose, on my clothes, and the sound of her voice in my ears. And I can't think of anything else – there's not enough room in my head. My senses are all bunged up, overloaded. And I'm glad – glad I can't think, glad the whole night is being drowned out. But the closer I get to Marsha's door, the more it's diluted by reality. I couldn't handle a grilling or an argument.

But when I get in, the lights are off, Marsha's bedroom door closed. I didn't want her to be up, but now I'm on my own, I wish she was.

It doesn't look like the Chinese has moved since I left. The brown bag is still on the kitchen table, the containers inside and full. The bag of prawn crackers resting on top. Marsha tried tonight. She really tried.

I sit down, position the bag in front of me on the table and pick up the bag of prawn crackers. I take out a cracker and bite it. It sticks to my tongue and I try to spit it out. I let the crumbs fall out of my mouth and down my front, gathering up on the folds of my coat. I bite the whole cracker to bits and let it all fall out of my mouth and gather up on my chest and in my lap. I do it with another cracker and another. I get sick of the taste, so I pick up the bag and start crushing it in my fingers. I smack the bag into my face and crush it there. And I bang it down onto the table and slam my face into it. When the whole bag is completely broken up, I rip it apart and there's an explosion of white crumbs.

I sit back, covered; they're all over the table, on the floor. I put my arm out straight, rest it on the table next to the brown bag. My palm's vertical, my fingers out straight. I sit there, calm as a black belt, and sweep my arm to the side. The bag flies across the kitchen and slams against the fridge. The containers overturn and lose their contents on the floor. Black bean sauce oozes out and begins spreading across the lino.

FIFTEEN

'Galaxy is not for sale.'

'What are you talking about, Bill?' I say.

'I haven't just got Galaxies, you know. There's Planets, Mars, Star Bars, Milky Ways, Twirls. I've got the whole universe inside this shop. You can choose whatever you want.'

'You don't get Twirls in space, man.'

'Really? How do you know that?'

'I ain't ever heard of a Twirl in space.'

'Space is a big place, my friend. There's a lot there you haven't heard of. Look,' he says, and he takes a Twirl out of the rack, and a pack of Orbit chewing gum. He holds the Twirl up and moves the pack of chewing gum around it like it's – yeah . . . you get the idea.

'You see? If I had more hands I could show you properly.'

I don't have the energy for this. 'I want a Galaxy.'

'Galaxy is not for sale. I told you.'

'Then why have you got it in the rack?'

'It's not for sale to *you*.'

'Why not?'

'Because you don't want it.'

'I do want it!'

'No you don't.'

The bell dings. It's Milk poking his head round the door.
'Hurry up, man!' he says.

Bill puts down his interplanetary objects, rests his elbows
on the counter and puts his hands together. 'Go on,' he says.
'Choose.'

*Picnic, Star Bar, Drifter, Munchies, Yorkie, Lion, Flake, Toffee
Crisp, Snack, Kit-Kat, Topic, Double Decker, Wispa, Boost.*

*Dairy Milk, Fruit and Nut Dairy Milk, Whole Nut Dairy
Milk, Caramel Dairy Milk, Crunchie Dairy Milk, Crispy
Dairy Milk, Bubbly Dairy Milk, Turkish Dairy Milk,
Biscuit Dairy Milk.*

Every bar a different breakfast, but every bar could be a
different path; every bar a different future. I'm back where

201

I was last night. But last night I didn't feel like I had a choice; now there's too much of it.

You might be wondering how I can go to school after a night like last night – I have trouble spending a day there as it is – but this is the only way I'm going to keep my sanity. There was a conference going on in the shrine all night. They didn't let me sleep at all. During the day I've got a chance to redress the balance, hold it steady. Well, as steady as possible. But I don't even know what that is any more. I don't even know what chocolate bar I want. But a voice is telling me I do, really. And I can just about see it, even though I'm avoiding it deliberately, and I swear it's glowing brighter than the rest. Calling my name, almost. And I'm reaching for it, not stopping myself, even though I'm telling myself it's too much of a risk. Maybe it's tiredness, maybe it's all the death and the dying; and thinking how bad can it really be? How can it be worse? I pick it up – it's light, I can lift it – and I slam it on the counter. A Milky Way. Fuck you, gravity.

'Good,' says Bill. 'That's sixty p.'

I leave the shop shaking, feeling tremors and aftershocks.

'What is *that*?' says Milk, like he's just seen me come out wearing a dress.

'It's a Milky Way, bruv.'

'Yeah . . . I can see that. What you buying baby chocolate for?'

'Because I want it,' I say.

Milk shakes his head and sucks his teeth. 'You shouldn't be buying baby chocolate.'

'Why not?'

'You know why not, bruv! We got a reputation to think about. What are the Yoot gonna think when they see you with that? Put it away, man.'

'It's my breakfast.'

'Well, fucking eat it quick, then!'

I feel like telling him it's more than breakfast; it's my future now too. I breathe deep, hold the Milky Way like it's the hilt of a sword. I want to hold it high above me, make it conduct lightning, and bring it down on the head of the Devil, just like St Michael, my new roommate. That's right, I got another. *Thanks, Marsh.* I cleaned the Chinese takeaway up in a daze, not thinking. It was actually kind of therapeutic. I went through to the shrine, and there he was.

I tried talking to him, but I think he was too busy. He's dressed as a Roman soldier, wings spread out from his back. He's got his foot on the head of a beardy man with horns who's lying on the ground, and he's pointing a sword at him, like he's about to stab him right through the head. His name's on the plinth: ST MICHAEL. I told you, it's like a conference where you get those nametags. Tonight there'll probably be refreshments of little round wafers and goblets of wine.

So I lay there in bed, looking at the silhouettes of the statues in the dark. My head started to go over the bus guy, remembering his breath on my fingers, his weak teeth. He was mixing in with the old guy, the bin-bag Rasta, the eyes of the van man, the voice of the weird plant woman, the smell of the flowers. But in the dark I felt like I lost the joins, like my thoughts were clear to see. And I was outnumbered; I didn't know what they could pull. I tried not to think, tried not to even move. I didn't want the light on, didn't want to see all the faces, but instead I watched shadows come alive – saw faces anyway. I had to open the wardrobe doors in case anything was hiding in there. But then I saw faces in the clothes. I saw them in the curtains, in the bedding, on the wall. There *are* faces on the wall. I listened to the workings and rumblings of Blake Point; listened to the creaks and the bangs, the distant whir and clunk of the lift, the chattering pipes; listened to the wind howling past the outside of the block, clawing at the gaps in the windows, trying to get at me with its wispy fingers and razor-sharp nails, groaning – groaning like the old guy, like the guy on the bus.

I waited for morning, clung onto the thought of it like a rubber ring in a rough sea. But time does strange things at night. It stretches, warps, doubles back on itself. I don't think it's a side of the world we're meant to see. It's like trespassing backstage; catching reality with its pants down. I nearly went under, and by the time I got out of bed I was exhausted and soaking.

Apart from a few crumbs of prawn cracker, I haven't eaten anything for over a day now. But now I've got the Milky Way, I want to save it. I'm going to let it guide me. I put it in the front breast pocket of my blazer; leave it poking out the top. Milk looks disappointed, maybe even a bit embarrassed, and he walks ahead.

'So you gonna tell me about last night?' he says over his shoulder.

I follow behind. 'There's nothing to tell, bruv.'

'That's not what I heard.'

'What? What did you hear?' How does he do it? I swear he must have his own surveillance equipment, his own spy satellite.

'I heard you was out with Shads.'

'So? So what?'

'So something must've happened.'

'I don't want to talk about it.'

'I don't know why you're getting all this preferential treatment, bruv.'

I'm about to tell Milk that it didn't turn out to be preferential treatment when I hear a siren close by. A police van comes into view, heading towards us quick, lights flashing. We both stop. I can't help the look on my face, can't help freezing solid.

It doesn't slow as it approaches, and the ice starts to thaw, but it makes me realize how thin this surface layer is. I'm on borrowed time. Not even on borrowed time – it's stolen time; it's wanted-man-fugitive time.

The van passes. I breathe deep and pat the Milky Way in my pocket. Milk looks back at the van, leans over and spits on the pavement, a stringy mouthful of saliva, making his feelings clear.

The first two lessons are tough – tough to stay awake in as much as anything – and at morning break I manage to get a quarter of an hour's sleep in a cubicle in the mainly unused toilets on the lower-ground level near the changing rooms. I'm so tired I don't even need any support; the toilet lid down, just sitting upright, head lolling, mouth open.

Milk phones to wake me up, but it takes a few goes before I hear it and it means we're late getting to English.

Me and Milk have got a designated seat in English, which is important because Ram and Chacks, another of the Yoot, are in the same class. It was agreed – without any words actually being spoken, from what I remember – that me and Milk would get one of the tables in the corner at the back of the class and Ram and Chacks the one on the far side. These rivalries get complicated when you have to move in such tight circles.

When we get to class most of the kids are settled. The teacher, Mr Thompson, in beige cord trousers and jacket, with greasy hair, is standing up and leaning against the front of his desk, leafing through a thick wodge of papers.

We start heading to our table, but there's a problem: Ram and Chacks are sitting there. I do a double-take. At their table is a serious-looking man with a Dracula hairline, wearing a dark suit, his arms folded tight.

'What's going on?' says Milk. 'Who's this new kid?'

'We're not here out of choice,' says Ram, a big smile on his face. 'Believe me, it stinks here, bruv. Smells like your estate. I swear I can even smell your mum here, man.' He scans the area around his seat and waves his hand in front of his nose.

There's a ripple of snorts and nose-laughing, but it's all kept quiet – they don't want to risk any Milk-Bunsen-burner treatment.

Mr Thompson looks up from his papers. 'Settle down, you lot!' he says. 'Jaylon, Christopher: you can sit at the front. This is Mr Simmons, part of the inspection team. Kindly show a bit of respect. He's sitting in with us today.'

In a fluid motion, Mr Simmons unfolds his arms, jots something down in a black notebook and refolds them again.

'But that's our table!' says Milk.

'It's not *your* table, Christopher. It's a table you sit at. Anyway, you might find it easier to concentrate at the front.'

'I don't want to sit at the front, man!' says Milk.

'Sit down!' shouts Mr Thompson. It's unusual to hear him raise his voice and the shock is enough to make us both move to the empty table directly opposite his desk. Milk bangs his bag down loudly, grumbles as he opens it and rummages around. He turns round and glares at Ram. Ram sniffs at the air, grimaces, and waves his hand in front of his nose again.

Milk shakes his head and sucks his teeth. He turns to me. 'Why don't you ever say anything? Why's it always me who's got to stick up for our turf?'

'Quiet, you two!' says Mr Thompson. 'Give me that chocolate bar, please, Jaylon.'

'What?' I say, realizing I've only been half there.

'That chocolate bar,' he says. 'I don't want any food visible in class. I'll give it back to you afterwards.'

That wakes me up. 'You don't want any food visible in class? What, is that a rule or something?' I put my hand across my chest, like I'm standing in line for the national anthem. 'There you go, sir: it's gone.' And I'm pleased that despite everything I can still raise a few laughs of my own.

'Don't try and be smart, Jaylon. Give it to me. You can have it back at lunch time.'

'What difference does it make?' I say. 'I'll just keep it in my pocket.'

'It makes a difference because I am asking you to give it to me.' Mr Thompson beckons with his hand like he's directing traffic. He's definitely trying to be more strict than usual, and you can tell he's not used to it because he's picked the wrong topic. Or in this case, the wrong Milky Way. I doubt Mr Simmons is going to be impressed.

'You're not having it,' I say. 'Just forget it's there, you get me? Get on with the lesson, innit?'

'Don't tell me what to do!' Mr Thompson slams his hands down on our desk and leans over. He smells of solvents and tobacco. 'Give me the chocolate bar!'

My hand hasn't moved. 'You're not having it,' I say.

Mr Thompson's eyes shoot towards Mr Simmons. 'Then get out of the class,' he says. 'Wait outside Mr Wallace's office. I'll see you down there after my lesson. I'm sure Mr Wallace will be very interested to hear how you value snacks more highly than your education.'

I stand up, grab my bag. There's a murmur around the class, and clear above it all Ram laughing. Milk turns. 'What you laughing about, you prick?'

'Shut up!' shouts Mr Thompson, his voice straining.

I'm at the door and out into the cool air of the corridor. I've never understood getting thrown out of class for bad behaviour. To most kids getting thrown out is a bonus, a reward. And Mr Thompson's got it all wrong. Calling my Milky Way a snack is like telling Marsha a cross is just two bits of wood. It's more than a snack: it's a sign, a symbol, a beacon. It's hope. It's *hope* . . . and he can't take that away.

When Milk arrives, I've already been on the lunch-time bench for twenty minutes. I tried sleeping in the toilets again, but I couldn't get comfortable. The fifteen minutes I had there before was enough to make me a bit fussier and in need of more comfort than a smelly toilet cubicle can really offer.

I tried the library but Miss Guney wasn't there. The assistant librarian started asking too many questions: why wasn't I in class? What books did I want to read? Where was

I going to sit? It was clear she didn't trust me, and I knew she wouldn't let me get away with shutting my eyes for an hour. I was stuck. I didn't go anywhere near Mr Wallace's office.

'I told you you should've eaten that chocolate,' says Milk, stuffing a handful of chips in his mouth. 'The Yoot didn't need to see that, man.'

'See what?' I say.

'See you getting all, like . . . all protective over a piece of chocolate. It's weird. It's only a bar of chocolate, bruv.'

'What about them sitting at our table? That's *only* a table, innit?'

'That was different. That was about the principle.'

'So? So was this!'

Milk shakes his head and crams in more chips. The satellites are starting to settle into their usual orbits around the bench and we give our greetings: nods and touches of fists for the boys; nods and smiles for the girls. The Yoot are arriving at Hot Chick!, dragging their own satellites along in a long tail like a comet. They stop at the doors, bunch up and then take a left into the restaurant.

'You gonna eat anything, bruv?' says Milk.

I don't answer him. I'm watching the Yoot get settled and I'm getting ideas. The Milky Way's giving me wanderlust, the desire for new frontiers. I watch the Yoot lean against the windows, against the counter; sit up on the tables. I'm feeling the Milky Way in my pocket, next to my heart. I'm thinking about rules, boundaries, dos and don'ts. Thinking about how far I can take this. Thinking about how far it'll go.

'Yeah, I'm getting some lunch,' I say, standing up. 'I'm gonna get a *feast*, bruv.'

I take a route away from the bench that gets noticed straight away. I can feel the eyes, hear the change in conversation, feel the change in the air, the expectation.

By the time I get to the door of the restaurant I know I've got the spotlight focused on me, and stepping inside feels like walking onto a stage. I've spent so long looking at Hot Chick! from the outside, it doesn't feel real inside. I'm expecting it to be all props and painted boards.

'I think you must be lost, blud,' says Chacks, coming straight over and standing in close, leaning his head like a buffalo. 'Crap's next door, you get me?'

'I ain't lost,' I say. 'I thought I'd sample some of the goods in here; vary my diet.'

'You ain't gonna be sampling shit.'

Inside, there's the same hierarchy as the Boyz have. We got members of the actual Yoot, honorary Yoot and wannabe Yoot. Together they're enough to fill the restaurant, but it's only Ram, Chacks and two others – K2 and Dollar – that are actual Yoot, and the four of them are now standing in front of me. The others won't get involved – they wouldn't want to risk it – but it's still four against one.

'What, then?' I say. 'You want to do some business? Maybe I can expand my clientele. You want to buy some pills? They're good ones.'

'You ain't got nothing you can sell me,' says Chacks.

'No?' I say. 'How 'bout some green? Some white?'

'My man thinks he's a joker,' says Ram. 'My man thinks he's funny, blud. You think you'll be funny with a bullet in your head, Jay?' He makes a gun with his fingers and prods my forehead. I let him do it. 'You think you can come in here like it's nothing?'

'How 'bout some red?' I say. 'Some yellow?'

'What you talking about, red?' says K2. 'The only red you got will be over your shirt when I fucking shank you, blud.'

'Hey! Hey!' shouts the man behind the counter, wearing a red and white uniform and the Hot Chick! logo on the chest of his apron. 'I don't want no trouble in here! You cause trouble, you get out!'

'I don't want any trouble!' I say, over the wall of shoulders in front of me. 'I just want to buy my lunch! You can't handle the hard shit?' I take the Milky Way out of my pocket, stretch the wrapper in my fingers. 'How 'bout a Milky Way? You want to buy a Milky Way?'

K2 goes to smack it out of my hand but I pull it away just in time. 'Now, now, K,' I say. 'No need to be rude, bruv. I'll just go and take a look at the menu. I'll be out of your way soon, you get me?'

I try and step past him but he stands firm.

'What kind of a name is K2, anyway?' I say.

'It's a mountain,' he says. 'It's the most dangerous mountain in the world, blud.'

'It's not the biggest, though, is it? You want to show more ambition, bruv. That's typical Yoot, innit? You want to aim a bit higher.'

'My man's got a fucking death wish,' says Ram.

'What?' I say. 'Is the food that bad in here?' I make a point of trying to walk slowly around the wall of Yoot. Dollar, on the end of the line, moves to his side and blocks my way.

'You should let me through, man,' I say. 'Sounds like I'll be giving your restaurant valuable business.'

'I ain't letting you do nothing,' says Dollar.

'You can take that outside!' the man shouts again. 'I said no trouble! Any trouble, you're all barred! I don't want you disturbing my customers!'

'Customers?' says Ram. 'Without us you wouldn't have any customers, bruv!'

'I mean it!' he says. 'Any trouble, I bar you!'

'You heard the man,' I say.

Dollar looks from me to the counter and back again. Chacks grabs his arm and pulls him to the side.

I get to the counter and scan the menu. And I'm thinking, No, it's not a death wish: it's a life wish. But they're easy to mix up if you don't look closely enough.

I order a box of spicy wings and chips, and a can of

Coke. While I'm waiting I lean against the counter and drum my fingers.

Dollar comes up and orders a drink and stands against the counter side-on, facing me. But he doesn't say anything, just tries to burn holes in the side of my head with his eyes.

Conversation starts up behind me but it's about something else, not about me. And I can't believe how easy it is. Dollar can stare as much as he wants; I can take that all day. They can talk, make their bad boy threats. I don't care. It *is* nothing. Some lines you cross, and the world changes . . . *you* change. Others, and the world stays the same – it's just suddenly it looks bigger.

I pay for my box and make sure my thank you is loud enough for my good manners to be heard by the whole restaurant. I straighten up on the walk back to the door; take it slow and calm. Ram and K2 block the way.

'First you didn't want me to come in, now you don't want me to go,' I say. 'Make up your mind, bruv.'

'What you doing, Jay?' says Ram. 'Is this some new Boyz orders? Is this the best you can do? We're taking your customers, taking your turf. You can buy your lunch in

217

here, man, but who's doing what matters? The Yoot are taking *over*. You lot ain't worth shit, blud.'

I pick up a chip and casually take a bite. 'Have you finished?' I say, pointing the chip at him.

'Barred!' the man shouts again.

The two of them make a small gap and I have to push through to get to the door. 'Thank you,' I say. 'It's been a pleasure, you get me?'

I step outside and try to disguise the breath that deflates my whole body. I should have brought a flag to plant. Maybe I should've left the Milky Way. But I want it with me. I need the protection. Maybe I should buy a whole box, get a whole team together.

Milk watches me walk back to the bench, his mouth open, like I'm a ghost. 'What the fuck was that?' he says.

'I thought trying something different might give me my appetite back,' I say. 'Chip?'

'Keep that shit away from me,' he says, shuffling along.

I shrug and stick some chips in my mouth, and realize my hand is shaking. I'm still not hungry, though, and I have to force the chips down with a mouthful of Coke. My stomach starts getting angry straight away and I can't eat any more. I make a point of dramatically throwing the uneaten box of spicy wings and chips into the bin; clapping my hands and rubbing them together.

Taking it minute by minute: I'm still here. I bought a Milky Way: I'm still here. I bought my lunch in Hot Chick!: I'm still here. It's progress. And why stop now? Why stop? I can go anywhere. I can even go *away*.

SIXTEEN

The Boyz don't know about it, but I've got some money saved up. Every time me and Milk did something 'extra-curricular' I'd save some of the cash; not much, but it's enough for a train fare and maybe to live off for a couple of weeks. I've got some relatives up in Nottingham: my dad's brother and his family. We used to see a lot of him when my parents were together but I haven't seen him since they split up. I don't think my dad has either but we always got on well. I'm hoping he'll remember that, and be able to offer me at least a sofa. I'm not kidding myself: I know my chances are slim, but I've got to try. What are my other options? The bodies are piling up behind me, and if I stay here, either I shank Ram or I don't. If I don't . . . well . . . there isn't a *don't*, remember? I've got to think of something else, and the only something else I can think of is going away. Why do I have to just accept it? At the moment I'd go anywhere just for a decent night's sleep.

Marsha was out at some church meeting last night and that gave me the chance to go to bed early. The darker it got, the more the whole idea of going to bed got scarier, almost like the sun was actually being blotted out by a huge, blood-stained demon mattress. I thought if I prepared myself early, if I respected the night, if I did it all while there were enough people up and about in the world to take the heat off me, then it would leave me alone.

And I did it. It worked. I was in bed by half eight and I fell asleep! But then Marsha got in at about half nine and woke me up. It ruined everything; all that careful planning went out the window and fell eighteen storeys to the ground. Suddenly I'd never felt more awake in my entire life. And it stayed like that. It stayed like that until I felt like I was the only person left awake on the entire planet and there was a satellite somewhere monitoring me. A light beeping on some screen in the spirit-world control room, showing exactly where I was and the reasons why I was awake. And of course they had their spies, their cameras;

they had the place bugged. If I don't get some sleep soon I'm going to crumble into dust.

'You look happy,' says Marsha when I shuffle through to the kitchen. She's sitting at the table reading a leather-bound book of prayers.

'Don't you ever get bored of praying?' I say. My voice sounds like an electric razor that's running low on power. I take the orange juice out of the fridge and pour myself a glass.

'Don't you ever get bored of being cheeky? And no . . . I don't get bored of praying. You can't get bored of the Lord. That's like asking if you get bored of breathing or eating. It's a basic human need. A need too many people go without and suffer because of it. Like you.'

I hold the cool glass against my forehead. 'I'm fine without it,' I say.

'You look it.'

'I'm not sure I can stay in that room any more, Marsh.'

'What do you mean?'

'It's those statues . . . and the pictures. They make me nervous. I can't sleep.'

'They only make you nervous because you have something to hide.'

'No I don't!' I say, and I swing my arm away from my head, forgetting about the glass and sending juice down my side and across the floor.

'*No I don't!*' she says in a high-pitched voice. 'There you go. You've proved my point: something to hide. You're staying where you are. And clean that up.'

'It's not fair.' I put the glass down on the worktop, wipe my hand on my dressing gown, take the roll of kitchen towel and begin mopping up the juice. When I bend down my brain rattles hard against my skull.

'I made a promise to your mum and I don't think that promise has been fulfilled. In fact, when I hear you whine like that I *know* it's not been fulfilled.'

'But what are you trying to do to me? What's with the new statue?'

'I thought he would do you good.'

'Where do you get them from? You got a secret stash somewhere? Does God beam them down just when you need them?'

'I have friends, Jaylon. Good friends.'

223

'They're statues, Marsh.'

'I'm not talking about the statues.'

The intercom goes and Marsha's up on her feet quickly and past me into the hall. She answers, sounding bright and cheerful. I hear her open the front door, leave it ajar, and she comes back to the kitchen.

'That's Hannah,' she says. 'She's on her way up.'

'*Now?*' I say. 'What's she coming up *now* for?'

'She was at the meeting with her parents last night. I told her your brain would be at its best early on, so we agreed she'd come round when you'd be most receptive to some education.'

Hannah's coming round to help me with my homework because I'm so out of practice, but I don't like the fact that Marsha's been involving her in her plans. There's something not right about your girlfriend being friendly with your family, especially behind your back.

'What time is it?' I say.

'Just coming up to nine o'clock.'

'*Nine?*'

'You really should try and keep that whine in check. And I'd put some presentable clothes on too.' Marsha smiles, eyes glinting. I don't like it. My girlfriend and my aunt in cahoots: it's not right.

I swear I used to know what I was doing with maths, but now, looking at a page of letters and numbers, my head's swimming and it's got nothing to cling onto, nothing to keep it afloat. When it comes to maths I've been like one of those football teams that get into the Premiership, get a taste of the big time, but then get relegated at the end of the season. And once they're relegated they lose all their confidence, finances, support, and they sink like a stone down the divisions. I was in the top class when I started secondary school but now I'm in the bottom class . . . at the bottom of the bottom class. And I've forgotten how it all works. I can't even remember the basics.

'No . . . look,' says Hannah, and she takes the book away from me. I can tell she's getting exasperated.

'I'm going down to the church,' says Marsha, poking her head into the kitchen.

'You're going again?' I say.

'Yes. You have a problem with that?'

'No,' I say.

'How's he doing?' says Marsha.

'Yeah . . . *OK*,' says Hannah.

'I'm doing fine. Bye, Marsh!'

Marsha waves and leaves the flat. At least when Hannah's around, Marsha's never going to turn into the Deadly Lampshade. In fact she's her total *alter ego*, but it's weird – that makes it all seem worse somehow.

'Do you want to take a break?' I say.

'We haven't even started!' says Hannah.

'We could charge up our batteries, you get me? Lie down for a bit.'

'*Charge up our batteries?* What kind of a line is that?' She turns to her side, crosses her legs and folds her arms. 'I'm definitely not doing anything if you say it like that. I'm not a machine.'

I sit back in a huff. 'Why don't you go down to the church as well, then? You'd probably have a better time, anyway.'

'What does that mean?'

'It means, you seem like you have a better time with my aunt than with me. It doesn't make a man feel good about himself.'

'That's stupid.'

'Is it? Maths is fucking stupid. Words and numbers don't mix.'

'They're called equations.'

'I don't care what they're called.' I sweep my arm across the table and send the books flying like a re-run of the Chinese takeaway incident.

'What did you do that for?' Hannah looks more shocked than I was expecting, and seeing my school books lying on the floor like shot birds, I'm realizing again how near to the surface that darkness is, like some oily river flowing beneath my feet.

I sit forward and rub my hands over my face. 'It doesn't matter, anyway,' I say.

'It *does* matter! You can pass these exams if you put your mind to it.'

'I'm not going to pass.'

'How do you know that?'

'I just do,' I say. I take one of my hands away from my face, move it across the table, and without looking try and find Hannah's hand even though she's still got her arms folded. Eventually she gives up and puts her hand down on top of mine. I work my fingers in between hers. She squeezes.

'I'm leaving school,' I say.

'What are you talking about?'

'I'm going to leave. I'm going to leave the estate. I'm going to leave Hackney. I'm going to leave London.' Just saying it seems to increase the amount of oxygen in the air. I feel like I've got St Michael's wings on my back. I could go through to the balcony, jump off and flap all the way to Nottingham.

Hannah pulls her hand away. 'You're leaving? What do you mean you're leaving?'

I come back to earth. 'I just have to go away for a bit. The Boyz . . . they want me to do something that I don't want to do. They're not . . . Shads isn't the sort of person to take no for an answer.'

'I really don't like the sound of that . . . any of it.' Her arms are folded again.

'No, neither do I. That's why I'm going away.'

'You're choosing your *gang* over me?'

'I'm not choosing them over you: that's the point. I'm choosing me over them. Why don't you come with me?'

'Come with you? Where are you going to go?'

I suddenly don't think I can tell her. And if I don't think I can even tell her where I'm going, what *can* I tell her? I can't tell her why I'm going, I can't tell her where I'm going. I didn't realize it was that much of a mess. Not me and Hannah. I thought that was the *good* bit.

There's silence.

'OK,' she says. 'Why are you going to go?'

'I can't tell you.'

'Was I supposed to be able to hear that?'

'I said: I can't tell you.'

More silence.

'You can't just go away now,' she says. 'What about what happened last week? You can't just do that and then disappear. That was supposed to mean something.'

I don't want to talk now, especially about stuff that's easy to break, easy to ruin.

'It did mean something,' I mumble. But I think because I don't want to talk about it, it sounds unconvincing. I sound unconvincing. Hannah stands up, starts picking up the books and packing her bag.

'Where are you going?' I say.

'I thought you said you were going to tell me stuff?'

'I did . . . I am.'

'But you're not. If it's so bad that you can't even tell me . . . if it's so bad that you have to leave school, leave me, your family, and your so-called *friends* . . . then . . . then it makes me wonder if we should even be together.'

'You want to split up?'

'No, I'm not saying that. What I'm saying is we might not have a choice. I can't be with someone who can't be honest with me.'

'I am honest with you!'

'No you're not. You just said you couldn't tell me what's been going on.'

'Yeah, that's me being honest!'

'That doesn't even make sense. If you're going to leave school, then there's no point in me helping you. And if you can't tell me about something that's *so important* that you have to run away, then there's no point in me being here at all.'

'Can't you just, like . . . can't you just trust me? Give me a chance?'

'How many chances do you want?'

That's a hard question to answer. I'm not sure how many chances I'm going to need. I don't want to sell myself short. 'I'm not that bad,' I say, directing it at my feet.

'You know what that sounds like? That sounds like you're trying to persuade yourself. You know why I like going to church? Because it makes me face up to things. I know I can't hide. I know I can't fool myself. And it sounds like you're just fooling yourself.'

She's standing in the kitchen doorway, her bag on her shoulder.

'Run away if you want to,' she says. 'But I'm not going with you, and it's not even because I want to finish school, to make something of myself. It's not even because I wouldn't leave *my* friends and *my* family to stay with you. It's because if you run away you're just going to keep fooling yourself. And I don't want to be a part of that.'

The truth is building up inside and I want to let it all out. I want to tell her everything. But if I tell her everything she'd never speak to me again. She'd probably even phone the police. That's not a good sign, is it? And . . . even if she changed her mind and said yes . . . if she did come with me and I got caught, what then? She'd be caught up in it all too. And I don't want that either.

'You've got a lot of thinking to do,' she says.

'I'm sick of thinking. My brain can't take much more thinking.'

'Yeah, well . . . maybe you're not doing the right kind of thinking. I'll see you at church tomorrow. Don't forget dinner. And don't even think about not coming or making up an excuse. I'm not going to take no for an answer, either.'

Hannah goes, taking all the air and life and colour with her. It's weird . . . I feel like I've told her too much, but really I haven't told her anything at all.

SEVENTEEN

I was going to keep my head down for the day, try and get some sleep while it's daytime and I haven't got the heat on, but I got a text from Diggy telling me he needed to talk. I don't like the sound of that.

The Boyz are spread out between two benches on the edge of the Downs, just across from the estate. They're arranged pretty much by age: the Youngers on one bench, the Olders on the other, and some mingling in the middle.

I go and find Diggy straight away.

'What's up, Digs?'

'Let's walk,' he says.

He waits till we're out of earshot of the Boyz. 'What was that shit yesterday?' he says.

'What shit?'

'That eating Yoot chicken shit?'

'I don't know . . . I just wanted to try it.'

'You shouldn't be causing trouble. You're meant to be staying *clear* of trouble. It doesn't look good, bruv. You feel me? It looks like you're *defecting*.'

'Defecting? What do you mean?'

'Slippin' on Yoot turf . . . It looks like you *want* to be on Yoot turf. It looks like you got Yoot sympathies. We got these rules for a reason, yeah? We need to know where we stand. You think you're being all clever. But that ain't clever, bruv. That's causing trouble. It's . . . reckless.'

'Is it?' I'm genuinely surprised by this information.

'Yeah . . . I heard what happened on the bus . . . and now with that, and yesterday, Shads is worried you ain't gonna do it.'

'Ain't gonna do what?'

'That you ain't gonna do Ram.'

'Course I'm gonna do it, bruv!' I can't help my voice going high-pitched again. Marsha's right: I really do have to keep it in check.

'Yeah, well,' says Diggy. He doesn't look convinced.

'Shads didn't get where he is without being . . . *thorough*; without paying attention to details.'

'What do you mean?'

'I mean, Shads thinks you need some extra incentive.'

I'm feeling cold. 'Like what?'

'Like if you don't do it he might turn his attention to your girl.'

'Turn his attention? What do you mean, *turn his attention*?'

'There, you see . . . you're reacting like you ain't gonna do it.'

'I am! Course I am! I just . . . I just don't want her involved.'

'Well, the way to make sure she ain't is by shanking Ram, innit? This ain't me, bruv. You know that, yeah? This is Shads. I'm only the messenger. He just wants you to know he's got issues after the other night. He needs to know he can trust you.'

'So . . . what? He's threatening my girlfriend?'

'No . . . but he might, that's all I'm saying. He mentioned your family too.'

'*My family?*'

'Yeah.' Diggy puts his hands out, trying to calm me

235

down. 'But like I said: it's only if you let him down. You know what Shads is like: he's black and white. There ain't no middle ground. If you do Ram you'll be his main boy again. He'll forget all about the other night. That's the thing with him; it's not personal, you get me? He doesn't let feelings get in the way. Shit, he doesn't *have* feelings, bruv. That's what makes people scared of him.'

Diggy puts his hand on my shoulder. We've walked a distance from the Boyz and I look back over. This seems to be about as far as I'm going to get; as far as I'm going to be *allowed* to get. Shads is seeing to that. He's covering every angle. He's not just holding me by the balls; now he's holding me to ransom.

It's a risk even mentioning this to Diggy, but I've got to do it. 'Let's just say, yeah, Digs? Let's just say I didn't do it, yeah? What would happen?'

'What would happen? If Shads gets an idea in his head, that's it. You get me? He wants a job done; he's chosen you to do it. In a way, you should be pleased. Most of the Boyz, especially the Youngers, they'd love that sort of responsibility. The way Shads sees it, he's given you an opportunity. And he's got ways of making you accept it. It's not personal

236

with him, but he can make sure *you* take it personally. You, your girl . . . or your family.

'But, look . . . there's a way out, man. Just shank Ram. Get it over with. And stop worrying. Shit, bruv . . . you can tell you're around just in the air at the moment. You need to relax.'

'Relax, Digs? Relax? Do you know what's been happening to me these last few days?'

'I know, bruv, but look . . . in a couple more it'll be over.'

'It won't be over. Will it? How's it going to be over? You think I'm going to shank Ram, turn up to the fireworks on Friday with my girl and be, like, *Ooh yeah, life's fucking great! Ram? Ram who?* I've seen two people killed in the last *week*. I don't like it, Digs. Maybe I'm telling you too much, but I don't care. You're telling me I should be pleased? You're telling me this is an opportunity? It's a bit of a fucking give-away, bruv, when you get told: *Take the opportunity I've given you otherwise I'll hurt your family.* Yeah, thanks, Shads. I feel touched; you shouldn't have, really . . .'

I shake my head, and suddenly I have to grip the bridge of my nose tight. There's a welling up and I definitely wouldn't get away with that.

'Have you finished?' says Diggy.

I breathe deep, concentrate on the grass.

'I'm going to keep this conversation between us,' he says. 'You're making it worse for yourself. We've set it up for Tuesday – just concentrate on that. What happens after that, worry about it then. Take it one step at a time.'

I feel like saying, *It's not steps, Digs: it's bodies. That's the problem. There's a big, big difference.*

It should help talking to Diggy, but the problem is nothing ruffles him. It's like he's so tall, he doesn't have his head in the clouds, his head's *above* the clouds.

He's been in the Boyz longer than anyone, and I don't think he can remember a time when he wasn't. That's the thing with Digs – he's got standards, morals, but because he's been in the Boyz so long, they're all Boyz' morals. This is all normal to him; it's just the way the world is.

He never does the boasting or the bragging like the other Boyz, and the truth is I don't know if he's ever had to do what I'm being asked to do – or what I've done. I guess he must have, but he never talks about it.

I wonder what the Boyz would be like if Diggy took

238

over? He's not got that same fire as Shads, not got that same need for trouble. Maybe deep down he thinks it doesn't have to be like this. I want to ask him, I want to ask questions. But I think I'm out of questions. I've used them up.

When we get back over to the Boyz it looks like I'm going to be forced to relax. Most of them are gathered together now over at the Olders bench and there's a couple of joints being passed around. I take a drag when one comes my way. It's strong and I feel it straight away, and maybe that's what I need to do – smoke myself into a coma. I draw it in deep, hold it, let it light up my insides and breathe it out again in a long stream. I take another long drag, close my eyes, and I start to feel like I'm reversing inside my own body, shrinking away inside myself like a Russian doll.

I always thought being in the Boyz was a good thing. I always thought it was a bonus. I thought I was seeing life from the side where it looked its best. Yeah, all right, I didn't grow up with money, with privileges. But when you grow up surrounded by concrete and struggling, you've got to take what you can. I took it. And this is the payback. And I thought I was prepared. But I'm not prepared at all. I feel like Shads is pulling me along, dragging me along, and there's nothing I can do. I look around at the Boyz. Their laughing sounds hollow, it doesn't sound real, because they're being dragged along too and they don't even know. Well, either they don't know or they don't care. Maybe they think it's worth it. The price. The payback. Worth it for what, though? Take it one step at a time. *Tuesday*. I don't see a step after that. I don't see one.

I take a few more drags, the cords that were holding me tight start to snap and there's no escaping the fact that I'm tired and I'm hungry. Take it one step at a time. All right then, I'll focus in on that. *Food and sleep, food and sleep*. I take another toke and there's a tug on my sleeve. I open my eyes. Bubs, one of the Olders, is looking at me, angry. 'You gonna share that round or what?' he says loudly.

'Yeah, yeah . . . sorry, bruv,' I say. The words echo round inside my head. When I hand him the joint my arm feels unsteady, like it's the jib of a crane and I'm stuck in the cramped little cab but there's no levers or buttons, and I can only move it by force.

Thinking that sets the ground moving beneath me – I should sit down, but everyone's standing up and I don't want to draw attention to myself – they might see the doubt in my face. Maybe I am defecting, but not to the Yoot, somewhere else . . . defecting to *me*. There's a new Jay, a different Jay. But what do I do with him? I can't get a handle on him. The ground tips again, stronger this time. I need some purchase, some anchor. I step towards Milk; he's talking loudly away to my left. I edge closer, try and listen in.

'It was after football, yeah?' he says. 'None of us had had a drink or nothing. Everyone's thirsty, you get me? We're all getting changed and Samuels pulls this big bottle of Coke out of his bag. Everyone wants some but Big Paolo is standing right next to him, and he's begging for some Coke, yeah? He's got a lot of weight to drag around, you get me? And Samuels, I didn't think he was gonna do it, but Samuels gives him some, but he's like, you're only allowed three gulps. But soon as Paolo's got the bottle to his lips he can't *help* himself, bruv! He's necking the whole thing, like it's instinct or something. He can't stop himself! So Samuels fucking drills him right in the fucking guts, man!' Milk does a demonstration of Samuels's punching technique. 'And Paolo sends this spray of Coke all over Samuels's stuff, bruv! Fucking bag, uniform, coat, everything!'

There's a lot of laughing. 'What happened?' says Slick.

'Samuels went *mad*, bruv. Fucking battered him! My man's never going to drink Coke again!'

I try and join in the laughing but I don't seem to get the timing or the tone right and it sticks out like I'm hitting the wrong notes.

Smiles, one of the Youngers, arrives back with some boxes of chicken and chips. A box waves past me, the sweet, tangy smell shoots straight up my nose and sets my whole face twitching. I follow the box, my eyes wide, and almost make a grab for it.

'My man looks hungry!' says Bubs.

'You sure you want some, Jay?' says Smiles, making sure he broadcasts it around. He's only thirteen but he's got a mouth that more than compensates. 'It ain't Yoot chicken, you know that, innit?'

The Boyz in earshot find this hilarious, a lot funnier than it really is, but the green is intensifying everything, taking away the brakes.

'Yeah, man. I'm not sure you should be allowed any, Jay,'

says Milk. 'Now you've eaten all that Yoot chicken, you might be infected, you get me? Fucking diseased, bruv!'

'I didn't eat any!' I say, but my voice sounds like it belongs to someone else and I start wondering if I even spoke at all.

'I saw you yum down the whole box!' says Milk. 'You couldn't get enough of that shit!'

There's more laughing.

'I didn't . . .' I say, but it tails off because I'm trying to figure out what actually did happen. Maybe I *did* eat it. I don't know. It's all a blur.

'Go on then,' says Smiles, holding out the box. I reach for a piece. 'Not that one, bruv. That one's reserved.'

'Shut up, Smiles,' I say and I start to pick up the leg I was aiming for.

'He ain't lying,' says Slick. 'That's my piece; I'm just saving it.'

I go to pick up another. 'That's reserved too,' says Smiles.

'What about that one?'

'Yeah, that too.'

'Shut up, man!' I say, and again I go to take a piece but Smiles swings the box away.

'I don't remember you putting any money in, Jay,' says Bubs.

I don't know what to do now. I feel like I've come too far, made too much of a point to not get a piece. I notice a bare wing bone, already eaten but with a little meat left on it and I pick it up. 'How 'bout this one?' I say. 'Is that free?'

Smiles laughs. 'Yeah . . . you can have that one if you want, Jay. Have my leftovers, bruv!'

'There's some meat on there!' I say.

'It's a bone!' says Bubs. 'My man's gnawing on a bone! I always said the Yoot were animals, you get me?'

'There's some meat on there,' I mumble, and I nibble what I thought was a bit of meat but on closer inspection turns out to be skin and gristle. I stand holding the wing, feeling stupid, feeling the size of the Statue of Liberty holding the wing like a torch. I don't know what to do and I've got all the Boyz cackling, holding their sides, bent over, almost crying. I swear it shouldn't be that funny.

'I'm going to get some of my own,' I manage to say, and it takes all my energy to drag myself away, the special extra-strong Boyz gravity sucking me back in. I walk back towards the estate.

'Westhall's the other way!' Milk calls after me.

The laughing gets louder, seems to follow after me, bouncing back off the blocks. I'm not going to get anything to eat. I'm going to go and lie down.

Marsha's not back when I get in and I go straight through to the shrine. I collapse on the bed, bury my head under the pillow, press it in at the sides, clamping it tight. I lie still, but my brain's off on some fairground ride, leaving me like a worried parent wringing my hands on the sidelines. We're that far apart. Gradually I manage to put the brakes on – deep breathing, concentration. The ride slows down, comes to a rest and we're reunited. But getting a small window where I feel together just reminds me of all the eyes in the room, all watching me. I twist and turn and tie myself in knots. In the end I have to take the duvet through to the living room. But the hologram Jesus is there, casting his green glow over the room, making it his. I'm on the alive side. I stare up at him and feel the world shrink away, like it did when I shot Sugar Ray. It's just the two of us, and that makes me feel like I do at night, all exposed, no one else to dilute the guilt, no one else to deflect the attention.

He shimmers in the fading light, moves, his expression changing like he's thinking; thinking a million different thoughts, the thoughts of all the world, the burden of everyone's prayers overloading him. Well, he asked for it. He offered.

I get up and walk over. 'I bet you couldn't handle mine, could you? They'd be too heavy. Too fucking heavy.'

I watch him without blinking, the light in the room turning to a murky blue, the dark closing in, and Jesus spreads out his green, turns it up to compensate.

'Where is it?' I say. 'Where's my salvation? I've been trying! Can't you see I've been trying?'

I close my eyes and listen. The wind squeals at the balcony doors. The fridge clicks and begins to whine like a mosquito. Just me and you, Jesus.

'You know you cannot hide,' a voice says.

My eyes snap open and I step away. He's staring right back.

'What?' I say.

That was someone else's voice. I know it. I don't know where it came from; it was everywhere.

'There's nowhere for you to go. Not now.' He doesn't move his lips. The voice is in my head, but it's not mine.

'Even if you run,' it says, 'the mark would remain. The mark *is* you.'

'But I've been trying to make it better!' I say out loud.

'Have you? What have you done?' His voice echoes around my head. It must be him. And he's right, isn't he? What have I done? I've gone from following orders to trying to save my skin. How is that making anything better?

'The stain grows,' he says. 'I know the cost.'

'What is it?' I say.

'The killing has not ended. You know that, don't you?'

'I don't want anyone else to die!'

'When has it ever been about what you want? You don't even know what you want. You've never known. And now it's too late.'

'It can't be too late! Why is it too late?'

'Someone else will die,' he says. He sounds disconnected, uninterested. Stating facts. I thought he was supposed to care, supposed to be compassionate.

'Who is it going to be?' I whisper.

I wait for him to answer, but he's quiet. Keeping me guessing.

'Say something!'

247

'You like Ram, don't you?' he says, quick now, cutting me off. 'You think he's funny. Funnier than Milk. Milk is your best friend. But you don't trust him.'

I want to know how he knows, but it's like Hannah said – he's watching, always watching.

'And Shads, what of him? Your *friend*? Do you love him *so much*?'

'I don't love him!'

'Then why give him your life?'

I start to say I'm not, but it doesn't even form on my tongue.

'You must choose,' he says. 'Running away is not a choice.'

'But I don't have a choice! It's like you – changing from one thing to another with nothing in between. Nowhere to move. Then you die. Love and hate don't even come into it. There's no room.'

'Death is only the beginning,' says a different voice – harsher, more strained, a voice barely clinging on.

The room is suddenly feeling crowded. I tilt my head, lean over slightly. But it needs more than that, I know it. I have to move, and I do it slowly. I edge to the right. Jesus dies.

248

'Was that you?' I say.

'Death is only the beginning.' It is him – must be – and again it's a voice that fills the inside of my head.

'The beginning of what?'

'I'll show you.' He sounds more urgent, more direct. Maybe you have to be when you're in his state.

'How?' I say.

'Help me down.'

'You want to get down?'

'Help me. Break the cycle and I will show you what lies between.'

I hold the sides of the picture and lift it off the hook. He glows close to my face.

'Break the cycle,' he says.

I tilt the picture and he changes. 'Why give him your life?' the alive Jesus says, not wasting a second.

'I'm not!' I say. 'I'm not!'

'You are,' he says. 'Yes you are.'

I raise the picture up, ready to bring it down hard, but there's a figure in the doorway, Marsha's bag on the floor. And she's standing there, eyes wide.

EIGHTEEN

'I look around the world today and I see a crisis. I'm not talking about war. I'm not talking about poverty or disease. I know . . . I KNOW all these are important. The LORD knows these are important. But you know why? YOU KNOW WHY the Lord lets these things HAPPEN? Because the crisis . . . the REAL crisis, is not out in the WORLD. The crisis is here.' There's the sound of a machine gun as Pastor Burke bangs the microphone rapidly against his chest. 'THE CRISIS IS IN OUR HEARTS,' he screams.

Pastor Burke draws his eyebrows in, turning his eyes into dense black buttons. He patrols the front of the congregation, mic in hand, folds of fat wobbling; sweat sizzling on his bald head, brown and shiny like the end of a sausage.

He manages to turn the church into a ship caught in a raging storm. I'm pitching, rolling; swaying forwards, back, left and right.

'IT STARTS HERE,' he says, pounding his chest again. There's high-pitched feedback. 'In our HEARTS. And our hearts have become WEAK.

'WE HAVE IT TOO EASY. All life is about these days is saving us trouble, saving us effort, saving us *time*. Fine . . . but what do we do with that time? What do we do with that extra bit of energy we've got stored up? WE WASTE IT.

'It's ironic that in this world of convenience, of labour-saving devices, of quick fixes and INSTANT gratification . . . this world that should save us EFFORT . . . it's ironic that we have BECOME SO WEAK. And you know WHY we have BECOME weak? Because we have lost touch with our HEARTS. And our hearts MISS us. Our hearts are sitting there by the phone waiting for us to call. They're sitting worried at the bottom of the stairs staring at the front door, waiting, waiting for us to come HOME.'

Amens and halleluiahs ring out, and I have to hold my head and groan a little bit to keep them away.

'Our hearts want us to come home, because it is in our

hearts that God LIVES. And God has set the table for dinner. He has done the cooking and the food smells SWEET. The food smells TASTY. But where are we when he calls us to share in the food which he has prepared? He's even sent his angels to scour the streets to find us. Yet still we don't come home. WHY NOT?'

Pastor Burke lets that question hang in the air while he dabs at his brow with a white handkerchief.

I don't know how long Marsha was standing in the doorway last night. From her eyes I knew she'd picked up on some of the conversation. And I'm pretty sure she only heard my side of it, but she didn't say. Some things it's better not to talk about. Maybe she even felt partly responsible. She wanted me to get to know the Lord . . . well, that's what I was doing.

I put him back on the wall as casually as I could, didn't look at Marsha as I left the room, and I hid in the shrine until morning. Marsha didn't even check to see if I was all right. I'm guessing she knew what the answer was. It was hours before the green stopped treating my brain like Play-Doh. But even then I was left with the facts, or the facts as I could see them. And they didn't look pretty. I think I'm going crazy.

I always thought insanity wouldn't be that bad – look at Leo: you're in your own little world, no real worries, no responsibilities. But it's not like that. The problem with going crazy is that the craziness is real. I can't take a step back and look at it all cold like it's science. I can't take a step back and laugh at it like it's some comedy circus sideshow, either. My brain is my brain – it's all I've got to work with, and it's cooking itself in its own juices.

'Let me tell you the story of Elijah,' says Pastor Burke, softer this time. 'You all know it, but let me refresh your memory. Elijah, fresh from doing battle with the pagan Jezebel and her followers, is lost in the desert and he's tired, he's so tired. So tired he lies down and asks the Lord to let him die. What does the Lord do? The Lord sends his angels to bring him food and water, reviving Elijah for the journey ahead.

'We are all lost in the desert. You might look around and say, It doesn't look much like a desert. Perhaps not on the surface. But underneath, where there should be fertile

253

ground nourished by love, by compassion, by honesty, by good manners, by truth . . . that ground is dry, bare, lifeless. A desert. And you're lost there, and you might be thinking, Why isn't the Lord helping *me* out . . . why aren't there any angels bringing *me* food and water? Now I've got something to tell you, something you might not be comfortable with . . . THEY ARE.'

That's it, he's off again . . . break over.

'They're bringing you food and water ALL THE TIME. And that food and water is just the starter, the hors d'oeuvres for the main course that the LORD HAS PREPARED HERE.' There's more rapid machine-gun chest-pounding. 'But you IGNORE IT. Why do you ignore it? Because you look at the menu, and you think, this doesn't look like the starter to the Heavenly feast I was expecting. That can't possibly be what it is. But if you stopped for ONE MOMENT, if you had the strength and the courage to ENGAGE with your HEART, to go home, turn the key and OPEN THE DOOR, you would have the most GLORIOUS welcome. You can't decide how the Lord comes. You can't decide what meal he cooks for you in the kitchen of your own heart, but once you have tasted it you will realize you never needed to taste anything else.

'So . . . go on home. Go on home to your heart. Stop it from worrying, and together, be revived and NOURISHED by the feast that GOD HAS LAID for you there!'

A wave of amens and halleluiahs swells up from the front of the church, sweeps through the congregation and comes crashing down on my head. I peer out through my fingers until the wave disperses and everyone settles down again.

The church isn't actually that much of a church; it's just a small bare hall with rows of plastic chairs instead of wooden benches, rough blue carpet on the floor and a table with a shiny, bright green cover over it for the altar. In fact Marsha's flat looks more like a church than this place. There are no candles, no pictures or statues. There isn't even a hologram Jesus.

The choir all sit to the right of the altar, facing the congregation. Pastor Burke dabs at his head again with his handkerchief. He hands the microphone to Ash, the choir leader, and looks ready to lie down.

Ash closes his eyes, frowns and starts singing.

It's a song I've heard before, one of Hannah's favourites. All about falling down and getting back up.

I reckon the getting up depends on what made you fall down in the first place.

There are chords on the keyboard and the choir joins in, singing the first line a few more times. Ash moves on, singing out over the top.

More amens ring out, and almost as one the whole congregation stands up. All except me. This is usually the only bit I actually pay much attention to, but right now I'm feeling like it's all being put on just to taunt me. I know that sounds self-centred, but it's hard not to be thinking about myself. I need thinking about.

All the congregation's singing now about getting back up, getting back up. I'm not getting up anywhere.

'Are you going to get up?' a voice says to my right. It makes me jump because I didn't even realize anyone was in the seat. It's a woman, her face obscured by an orange shawl over her head and shoulders. She's standing, facing the front.

'Who you talking to?' I say, even though I know she was talking to me. She doesn't reply. I let out a deep breath and fold my arms tight.

256

The song moves on, speeds up. The whole church soaring.

'Get up,' the woman says again, more powerfully this time. I look at her and can't help the gasping noise I make. She's facing me and her eyes are totally white, completely blank, but the way her head's inclined it's like she can see. 'Get up,' she says again, and this time she holds her hand out. I don't take it, but I follow orders.

'You see her,' she says, nodding towards the front. I know she means Hannah.

Through the congregation, bodies swaying like trees, I watch her, eyes tight closed, her hand in the air. She looks so good I can't help smiling.

'She is beautiful,' the woman says. 'You don't have to leave her.'

'I'm not going anywhere,' I say.

The woman squeezes my hand and a jolt of electricity shoots up my arm. I pull it away and there's no one there. She's vanished. The seat's empty. I look around like I've lost something, and the old couple on my left have stopped singing and are looking at me suspiciously. I try and smile at them but it crumbles away, and I edge past them out into the aisle and towards the doors. Pastor Burke has joined in

257

now, and his ad-libbed screeching is threatening to drown out the rest of the church. I get the door closed behind me and I'm down the steps and out into the car park.

I head to Leo's wall but he's not there. Instead I take his place, sitting down and lighting a cigarette. My hand shakes as I put it to my mouth. I'm seeing things. The green could still be in my system, but it's more than that. I flex my arm – it tingles, feels like it does in the middle of the night when you wake up after sleeping on it and you've got to let all the blood flow back in. It feels real enough. Yeah, I am seeing things. I'm seeing things all the time. It's called life. But what part's real and what part isn't, I don't know any more.

I take a long, long drag on the cigarette and close my eyes as I exhale. I hear the song come to an end and Pastor Burke start up his motor again. When I open my eyes I half expect to see the building rocking from side to side.

There's a flash of orange at the corner of my eye and I turn to see a figure disappear quickly behind the wall of the community centre. I'm immediately up on my feet and round the corner, and I see the flash of orange pass behind the corrugated iron that covers the entrance.

Going inside a derelict building to follow a scary-looking woman who's just sent electric shocks through my body and vanished in front of my eyes seems to make about as much sense as going down to the basement in a horror film, but that's what I'm doing.

The state of the community centre sums up a lot. It stands unsteady, crumbling and sick, in a tight cage of scaffolding. Plaster has crumbled off the walls, exposing the bricks like it's got some mangy skin disease. The centre for the community, and it's not even safe to go inside. Most of the windows across its two floors are either smashed or boarded over. The sheet of iron across the doorway isn't totally secure and stands at an angle, leaving a gap wide enough to squeeze through. Not that the woman I'm following looked like she did much squeezing.

There's something spooky about derelict buildings, like if people don't use them they become as mindless and dangerous as zombies; faint memories inside still echoing off the walls but all distorted, not making sense.

But then people are using this one. Crazy people like Leo and a strange old vanishing woman. And now crazy people like me too.

Even with the gap, I still have to pull at the iron and turn to the side, making myself as thin as possible. The iron scrapes and squeals and the wind whistles through the doorway, scattering leaves across the dusty corridor.

The air's stale, musty, damp, but there's a charge to it. It's hard to explain. I feel like I'm on a stage – I can't see anyone but I know they're there. The smaller leaves, almost like confetti, whisper across the ground. My muscles are tight. I feel like I've got to keep tense; it feels like part of the bargain. If I relax, if I loosen up, I'll be disrespecting whatever's inside. Even saying anything feels too much.

My feet crunch on the leaves and I wonder if that's allowed – but I've got no choice, there's too many of them. *Get up.* I see her eyes in my head, hear her voice.

The corridor opens out into a T-shape. To the right there's a set of doors, and through the reinforced glass I can make out stairs to the next floor. To the left there are single doors on either side, with glass windows again, but it's too dark to see where they lead. On the wall are notice boards with old schedules and flyers stuck up: photos, pieces of paper, torn and curling at the corners. The corridor ends with a set of double doors. The hall.

The floor inside is covered in leaves and debris, and it all looks like it's been spread out from a large mound in the centre of the room, deliberately arranged. I push at the door; it's heavy but opens easily enough. All over the floor are twisting, spiralling rows of leaves, seeds, shells, bark, acorns, conkers, stones; all branching out from a straight wide row at the centre. The colours all arranged: greens turn into browns, browns into yellows, yellows into reds. The thickest part looks like the trunk of a tree, and branches twist off from there, leading to smaller and smaller branches. Wind hums through the broken windows, leaves stir, giving the effect of falling from the tree, but not being affected by gravity, drifting off to settle on other branches. I step carefully in the gaps towards the centre of the hall, the top of the trunk, which is a mass of piled leaves, but hollowed out and compressed slightly in the middle, like a big nest.

'WHAT ARE YOU DOING HERE?'

I stumble, nearly lose my balance, stick out my arms like I'm on a tightrope. It's Leo.

He's standing over by the doors, his arms full, cradling a mass of dead leaves. He doesn't look happy.

'Did they ask you to come?' he says, walking confidently towards the centre of the hall, missing every branch without looking down or breaking his stride, like he knows the shape off by heart.

'Who?'

'You tell me,' he says. He reaches me and opens his arms, letting all the leaves fall onto the nest.

'No one asked me. I saw a woman come in here. An old woman . . . white eyes.'

Leo leans his head to one side. 'Interesting,' he says. He crouches down and begins examining the new additions to his collection.

'Do you know her?' I say. 'She came in here, bruv. I need to find her.'

'Why?'

'I need . . . I need to know she's real.'

'What is real, my brother?'

'That's what I'm trying to figure out! Don't it bother you that some strange woman might be walking around your . . . your, like, house, bruv?'

'Look at this one!' he says. He holds up a wide green sycamore leaf, examining it against the light and putting it to one side. One by one he checks the new leaves; some he picks out and makes a separate pile.

I sigh and squeeze the bridge of my nose. I don't have the energy to argue with Leo. He doesn't give me anything to work with.

'Did you do all this?' I say.

'All this what?' he says.

'The pattern . . . the tree thing.'

'Yes,' he says. He picks up a handful of the new leaves, holds them like cards, and purses his lips as he looks around.

'Why?'

'It is a tree of life,' he says. He hops up and begins scouting across the hall, carefully adding the leaves to branches. 'It is a tree of life for the community. I have made it here. At the centre. At the heart.'

'No one's going to see it though, man.'

'Yes they will,' he says. 'Yes they will.'

He walks back over to the nest, sits down and takes a half-smoked joint out of his parka pocket. He lights it. 'Don't you want to sit down?' he says.

'Yeah, all right.' I sit facing him, hugging my knees, just inside the innermost branch.

'So, what brings you here, brother?' he says, relaxing

now, like his work is done. Smoke billows out and rises to the ceiling.

'I told you: I saw ... I thought I saw an old woman come in here. She was in church. She grabbed my hand and gave me an electric shock.' I rub at my arm. It still tingles.

'Interesting,' he says again. 'Yes.'

'I don't know, man. I don't know what's going on any more. I can't sleep, I think I'm seeing things ... hallucinating ... hearing voices. I'm feeling close to the edge, bruv. It doesn't help that I'm staying in a room surrounded by statues and pictures. It's like trying to sleep in a church.'

'I sleep in a church every day.'

'I thought you slept in here.'

'I do.'

'The church is next door, man.'

'The church is here. The church is wherever I say it is.'

'Anyway, bruv, I'm surrounded by all this stuff and I can't sleep.'

'Did the leaves not help?'

'What leaves?'

'The ones I gave you.'

'I don't know. I don't know where they are.'

'You don't know where they are? I give you valuable pieces of the puzzle – sparks from the eternal fire – and you don't know where they are? I have no sympathy!'

'What are you talking about, man? They were only leaves!'

A breeze sweeps across the hall, leaves scatter from the tree, join other branches.

Leo arches an eyebrow. 'You want to say that again?'

'No,' I say, and my skin crawls like there are fingers inching up my back. I shiver and rub at my neck and have to check over my shoulder. There's no one there.

Over in the church another song begins. It's muffled from here but it's faster and louder than the last one; the service is coming to an end, finishing on a high. It's weird: not being able to hear it properly gives it more character, like me and Leo have got a soundtrack.

'You know the last time I saw you, I told you I was in an impossible situation?'

Leo nods slowly, the smoke getting thicker around him, almost like he's fading in and out.

'Well . . . it's got worse. It's now a life-and-death situation.'

'Life and death? I gave you a leaf. A LEAF. One of the very best! And you threw it away! I've spent days gazing at the wonders of a leaf. DAYS.'

'Are you listening to me? I'm dealing with a *life-and-death* situation here, bruv. Not trees.'

'Do trees not also live and die? What makes you any more special?'

'I killed someone, Leo. I know that doesn't make me special but it makes me different from a tree. I've never heard of a tree deliberately killing someone.'

'You'd be surprised,' he says, not reacting at all.

'I didn't want to kill him,' I say. 'But I did . . . It happened . . . I mean, I wanted to kill him for about two seconds and it feels like those two seconds have ruined my whole life. And it keeps getting worse. It happened again on the bus the other night . . . It wasn't me this time, but I was there and whatever I do I can't get away from it. I'm not a bad person, Leo. I really don't think I am. But I'm surrounded by all this *killing*. And it's like I don't have a choice. I've got so little choice it's like life is telling me that this is the way it's supposed to be. That it's supposed to be this . . . *bad*.'

I meet Leo's eyes. Still no reaction. Two jets of smoke fire from his nose. He lies back, flips up his hood and starts humming.

'And in a couple of days I'm meant to do it again.' I'm losing him, but I'm going to keep going. 'I'm meant to do it again . . . I got asked yesterday if I loved someone so much that I'd kill if they asked me to. I'd never thought of it like that before. I've got to kill someone I don't hate for someone I don't love. And the people I do love don't even know what's going on. That doesn't make sense, does it, Leo? LEO? Shit, man! Are you even fucking listening to me?'

No response.

'Fuck you *and* your leaves,' I say under my breath.

He starts slightly, clears his throat and taps the joint at his side. 'They're not my leaves,' he whispers. He brings the joint up to his mouth again. Smoke mushrooms out and rises. Apart from the distant singing it's all quiet.

'The testimony is in the beat,' says Leo. 'And the beat has budded. It will bear its fruit. I am Mister Music, I am the gate of the gods! Make your supplication. Make your plea. It shall be heard! For they listen and they see. We are the ties in the net! Connected . . . all connected . . . all the same. I see no divide! I see no divide, for there is none.'

He takes a long drag and stabs the joint out on the arm of his parka. I can't see his face from where I'm sitting. I lean forward, peer over the mound of leaves. He has his eyes closed, his eyebrows raised, constant little changes in his expression.

'Wrap up warm, my brother!' he says. 'There's a cold wind blowing! Let them be your scarf and gloves. Bring me your burnt offerings. Draw water for my camels. Together we will find our Zion. Where others stand on lily pads, we will stand on the palms of the eternal ones!

'I will need nothing once I walk on the palms of the eternal ones. Though it be a journey of a thousand years! What is time, my brother Jaylon? What is time?'

I jump when Leo says my name. Even if he's not listening to me at least he knows I'm there, and I barely even know that about myself at the moment.

'Again I will play the psaltery. I will play them all; for I am for ever and I am Mister Music! There are patterns but we see only shapes! Open your eyes, my brother; let them lift the veil!'

He spreads his arms out.

'I have planted vines in the earth and the vines will hold strong. They will bear our weight. And we will see, from the palms of the eternal ones, where the view is fine and good: we will see the glorious majesty! With strong hands and strong hearts, and garments made from the vines, we will sing a new song, a song that will last for ever, and the beat will be Mister Music's, the beat will be the beat of the heart and the heart will be the everything!

'Bless this covenant. Bless the scarf and the glove. Be the uttermost and I will extol thee! Let us travel the palms of the eternal ones! They will carry us. They have told me. For I am the gate of the gods, I am Mister Music and I will play on! That is my vow, that is my word!'

His arms flop and his whole body sinks further into the nest, and I can feel it – he's gone, disappeared out of his body somewhere. I sit back. The singing has stopped.

'Leo?' I say. No answer. 'Leo?'

You see? Leo's a good kind of crazy. He can live in a crumbling-down old building and call it a church. He can spout a load of rubbish and disappear off to some other place and leave his body behind. And now he's gone, I realize I don't want to be here on my own. I don't want to see that woman with those blank eyes again. I get up and step carefully across the hall in the gaps between the branches and reach the door.

'LOOK!' Leo's voice booms across the hall. I jump again and turn quickly. He's sitting upright, fixing me with a crazy stare. 'The universe is exploding and we are dancing sparks in the fire!'

He's scary from this distance, sitting up in his nest, framed by the messy, empty hall and the tree twisting and bending around him. I don't answer him. I open the door and step into the corridor.

'All the bushes are burning, Jaylon! See them! All the bushes are *burning*! See the sparks on the wind! See them fall!' The door closes behind me and I'm turning the corner and heading out.

I edge through the gap in the doorway, but stop quickly and step back behind the corrugated iron. People are gathering at the bottom of the steps outside the church, the service over. I stay half hidden; my eyes dart across them, looking for any sign of the old woman, but there's nothing.

I step away from the doorway and I notice down on the ground a leaf standing out from the rest: a deep-red star. I try to grab it but the wind takes it away from me. I go after it but it keeps moving, cart-wheeling along the ground towards the car park. It comes to rest and I creep up on it slowly. I bend down to grab it but it sets off again towards the church and in between legs. Again I feel like it's personal, like the leaf's being vindictive. I stay low to the ground, following it, and it's stopped by a small, clumpy black shoe. A shoe I recognize. It's Hannah's.

'What are you doing?' she says as I take the stem, peel it off her shoe and stand up straight.

'I had to get this leaf.'

'OK . . .' Her arms are folded tight, her lips pursed. Her eyes don't look angry, though – too wide, sort of worried.

'Have you been crying?' she says.

'No, I'm tired. I haven't been sleeping.'

She looks at me closely; sighs. 'Are you still coming tonight?'

'Tonight?'

'Dinner.'

'Yeah . . . yeah . . . of course.'

Hannah's parents are standing behind her, talking to Pastor Burke. Her dad glances at me, his eyes shifting from my head to my toes, his lip upturned, sneering. Dinner with Hannah's parents: that's just what I need.

NINETEEN

'You're almost late,' she says.

'You mean on time,' I say, trying to smile. She doesn't smile back; only grabs the cap off my head.

'Shoes,' she says. She leaves me to take them off and disappears into the kitchen.

I hate this whole shoes thing. I swear it's just to make visitors feel uncomfortable, inferior. I'm about to face Hannah's family – I want more than socks on my feet. I hate socks; they're rubbish – they can't even work alone, they got to be in pairs. I know shoes have got to be in pairs too, but at least they're solid. I want shoes, chunky steel-capped boots, armour, a tank. I wore the cap for extra protection and now even that's gone.

★ ★ ★

I tried to be brave over the afternoon and look my craziness in the eye; in its hypnotic, swirly cartoon eye. I tried to stare at it cold like science. I tried to be methodical. I tried to come up with a *hypothesis*. You see, I have paid attention in some lessons. Basically I tried to figure out what the *fuck's been going on*.

I know for a fact that I didn't imagine the bin-bag Rasta, and he *knew*. He knew about the old guy. Well, maybe not specifically the old guy, but he knew I'd done something bad, something really bad. I don't know for a fact that anyone else saw the woman in church today. And I don't know if I was really having a three-way conversation with Jesus and another Jesus.

I didn't know whether I really saw a scruffy woman gardening in the exact spot where I killed the old guy either. So . . . I went back to check. I went back to the side-street. And . . . there was nothing there. No plants, no flowers, no sign that there ever had been. I know she said that they wouldn't last long, but I can't believe she meant they'd disappear that quickly.

I had to grip onto my head hard. I had visions of wrapping it in industrial tape, pulling it tight, covering myself like a mummy. I ran back over it: the things she said, her hands on my face, the smell of the flowers. *She took some of my cigarettes*. I couldn't imagine all that, could I?

I nearly went and bought some tape right then.

I realized I've got to *keep* going. Whether I'm crazy or not I've got to keep going. This isn't the army. Shads isn't going to make any special dispensations. I've got to stop picking at something that could come apart. I could come apart. And I can't let that happen. There are certain things I've just got to accept as facts. Like time: time is ticking way too quickly. I can't stop the flow, can't make it go backwards. I got to keep going. I got to face my demons . . . or in this case, the Redmonds, but it's close enough.

I stand in the kitchen doorway and Hannah has to practically drag me into the room. I want my cap on. My head feels like a bare 500-watt light bulb. I could light the whole of Hackney with this thing. If I stood outside I'd attract moths, planes, UFOs.

Luckily it's just her mum who's there. She turns to me and she's smiling, which helps. She takes off an oven glove to shake my hand.

'Hello, Jaylon,' she says. 'Good to see you.'

'Hello, Mrs Redmond,' I say.

'Please . . . call me Sandra. Can I get you a drink?'

I don't know how to answer that question. I realize it's a simple yes or no, but I mean, I don't want to cause trouble, not this early on.

'No, I'm fine thanks.'

'You sure? Glass of Coke?'

'No.'

'Juice?'

'No,' I say, louder this time.

'Water?'

'No!'

Her smile disappears. 'Well, at least make yourself comfortable,' she says and turns back to the cooker. I look at Hannah; she looks down.

The kitchen's clean and shiny, the round dining table set like a restaurant. I wonder whether I should sit down but I don't want to sit down before anyone else has.

There are footsteps on the stairs; a slow, deliberate clumping. A pair of legs comes into view and, despite the tartan slippers on the end of them, they look serious. It's Hannah's dad.

'What's your dad's name?' I whisper to Hannah as he takes the last few steps, heavy as Frankenstein.

'Michael,' she whispers back. She starts to say something else but her dad is in the doorway now, the same disapproving upturned lip, the same cold look in his eyes. He's not tall, a little taller than me, but he seems to fill the whole doorframe. He's dressed smart – neat shirt and trousers – and it's weird: the tartan slippers make him even more intimidating. Like, if he can carry these off, what would he be like with proper shoes on? It makes me wish I had a pair of my own, and for a second I think about asking if he has any spares.

He looks slowly around the kitchen, taking it in, sniffing, as if he's inspecting it for the first time, then finally he looks at me. He acts cool, like we're about to do business but not important business, something insignificant, almost a waste of his time.

'Jaylon.' He states it, firm but weary, and holds out his hand.

I've shaken his hand before and it's a handshake that could crush cars, so I prepare myself to give as good as I get.

'Michael,' I say, tensing up.

'Call me Mr Redmond, please.' And he tricks me: he barely touches my hand, just glides his palm across mine, leaves me grabbing air, and he turns his head away, doesn't even look me in the eye.

'Thanks for inviting me round,' I say.

'It was Hannah's idea,' he says.

I've never met a girlfriend's parents before, not officially like this. Shouldn't he want us to bond over man-stuff? Show me his car? His dog? His new set of tools? No . . . it doesn't look like it. My head's burning and I wonder if somehow word's got back to him about the kind of boyfriend Hannah's really got. I see my life leaking like a sieve, letting all its secrets out over the kitchen floor.

'I'll show you round,' says Hannah, and it's clear if Mr Redmond was going to show me anything it would be the door.

Hannah's not much more encouraging than her dad. We haven't sorted out anything from yesterday and we can't talk about it now, not here. It would be bad enough if things were fine between us. Hannah's way of dealing with it seems to be to get in role and play the girlfriend part, just

278

without any feeling, like she's just walking it through, saying her lines.

I get a full guided tour of the house. The whole place feels as ordered as an art gallery or museum. Every surface gleaming. Pictures and photographs all neat and polished, ornaments in perfect rows. I'm surprised I haven't been given a guidebook or a headset to explain it all.

Hannah takes me upstairs. Her parents' room is out of bounds but her sister's door is open a few inches. Hannah knocks and immediately starts opening the door.

'Don't come in!' squeals a voice from inside.

'Why not?' says Hannah, pushing at the door, which is now being held from the other side.

'I'm getting ready!'

Hannah shrugs. 'OK,' she says.

'Can you knock next time!' the voice says again.

'I did knock!'

'Knocking when you're already opening the door is not knocking!'

Hannah makes a blah-blah face. 'She's getting dressed up . . . going to a Halloween party,' she says flatly.

Hannah shows me her room like I haven't seen it before.

I see an opportunity to try and repair some of the damage, even if just for the evening. I go to pull her in close but she shrugs away.

'I just wanted to show you around,' she hisses.

'Yeah, but I've been in here before.'

She shushes me. 'But they don't know that!'

I can't help thinking that's only an excuse, and after pointing out where the bathroom is she leads me back downstairs.

I really wish I had my cap on. I could pull it down low over my eyes; pretend none of this is happening, like an ostrich. My head really does feel like an over-heated light bulb. I could cover it with one of Marsha's flowery lamp-shade skirts; wrap it over myself like some psychedelic burkha, make a little gap for my fork to go through while we're eating.

Sandra's dishing up when we get back to the kitchen: juicy-looking steak with a thick red sauce, ackee and mushrooms; and a big bowl of chips in the middle of the table that I get the feeling is there because of me. Mr Redmond's already sitting down, looking like an inter-viewer – back straight, taking rapid and serious sips from a glass of water, elbow on the table, other hand on his hip.

'She not ready yet?' he says.

'Doesn't sound like it,' says Hannah.

'At this rate she could've eaten with us,' he says.

'She's eating at the party,' says Sandra.

For some reason, the idea of taking the place of Hannah's sister at dinner makes me feel under even more pressure, but the food looks good and I haven't had a proper meal in days.

To be polite I wait till Sandra's sitting down, then I start digging into the steak.

Mr Redmond clears his throat. 'We say grace in this house first, Jaylon.'

He looks at me like I'm some kind of savage. But I've already taken a big mouthful of steak and I have to wait until my mouth's empty enough to say sorry and put my cutlery back down again.

Mr Redmond joins his hands and leads us in a rambling thanks for the food, and because he's doing it freestyle, and maybe showing off for my benefit, it goes on a lot longer than seems necessary. It's like he wants to carry on until he manages to say something poetic and meaningful but he can't quite find the right words, and eventually Sandra helps him by saying an abrupt 'Amen,' and Mr Redmond's got no choice but to add an amen of his own and we can all start eating.

'So how are your studies going, Jaylon?' he says.

There we go – it's the same old question, isn't it? He's dressed it up a bit but it still amounts to the same thing.

'Yeah, all right.'

'What are your plans for when you leave school?'

'Er . . . I'm not sure. I want to get the actual leaving bit out of the way first, you get me?'

Mr Redmond grunts and concentrates on sawing at a piece of steak. I look over at Hannah for support but she's looking down, shuffling food round her plate.

'So no plans for the future?' says Mr Redmond.

I don't think he realizes but that's the most difficult question I've ever been asked. Like . . . what do you mean by 'future', Mr Redmond? I'm still only fifteen, and in two days I'm supposed to kill a kid that I've known since I was eleven – a kid in my class at school. I've got to deal with the fact that I've already killed someone and somehow live a normal life. I've got to deal with the fact that I've been an accessory to another murder which was probably recorded on CCTV and might be being watched as we speak. And on top of that I'm seeing people appear and disappear, having conversations with pictures, not sleeping, not eating. And now I've got to get through an evening with my girlfriend's parents when she's got no idea about any of this. That's about as much of the future as I can handle at the moment, thanks very much, Mr Redmond. Any more questions?

'No plans, no,' I say quietly, glancing at Hannah, who's still looking down – I'm worried she's going to get some kind of neck injury she's doing that so much.

Mr Redmond sneers, but on the plus side I could say I was going to be an astronaut, Prime Minister and find a cure for cancer by the time I'm twenty-one; then kick back for a couple of years helping the poor and needy, before tackling global warming, world peace and the meaning of life itself – and I'm sure he'd still be sneering.

'This is great, Mrs Redmond . . . Sandra . . . thanks.' I smile at her. Mr Redmond not giving me a chance is suddenly making me more confident, like I've got nothing to lose.

'I'm glad you're enjoying it,' she says, smiling back.

There's silence apart from the sound of clinking cutlery. I accidentally scrape my knife on my plate and Mr Redmond tuts at me.

I feel like telling him I've done a lot worse with knives recently but I don't want to start wearing it as a badge. It's funny – *sort of*: before you've actually done anything really bad you always want to wear it like a badge; now I *have* done it, I want to hide it. Hide it from everyone.

'As long as you're working hard,' says Mr Redmond. He sighs it out, like he's forcing himself to make an effort. 'Hard work is crucial if you want to get anywhere in life, Jaylon. The Redmonds have always worked hard. My grandmother worked all through her pregnancy with my father, gave birth in her lunch hour and then got straight back to work. She had a maternity leave of one hour!' He laughs, a rapid 'HA-HA-HA-HA!' all enunciated and proper.

'In all seriousness,' he says. And I'm thinking, giving birth in your lunch hour sounds pretty serious to me. 'In all seriousness, this world will reward you if you put the effort in. Were you listening to Pastor Burke's sermon today?'

'Yeah, yeah . . . I think so . . . most of it. He's not easy to blot out, you get me?'

'Yes, well . . . the point is, you will be rewarded if you work hard but you're not meant to be doing it alone. Don't think you can do it alone. That's why so many people are in crisis – they try, they fail and they ignore God's message. Those unfortunate souls are doomed. Doomed because they don't recognize the Lord's voice. The Lord might not come in fire or earthquakes or a mighty wind. He might appear like he did to Elijah – in the form of a gentle breeze.'

'What?' I say it through a mouthful of steak and Mr Redmond sneers again. My stomach is starting to panic. It hasn't come into contact with this much food in ages, and proper steak is really putting it to the test. I'm having to chew very slowly.

'I said he may not come in earthquakes and—'

'No, the breeze bit.'

'Well . . .' says Mr Redmond, clearly not impressed with my table manners. 'You would've heard if you had managed to stay for the whole service, but the Lord came to Elijah in the form of a gentle breeze and—'

'Like in the community centre!'

'Yes . . . I thought I saw you coming out of there this afternoon,' says Mr Redmond. 'You should be careful – it's not structurally sound. I don't know why Pastor Burke doesn't see about getting it razed to the ground.'

'It's because it's haunted, Daddy,' says Hannah, managing to lift her head for a second.

'Haunted?' I say. My belly's doing somersaults.

'Well, I don't know about that,' says Mr Redmond. 'But yes, it was tragic, what happened in there, but all the more reason for a fresh start.'

'What?' I say. My eyes are sticking out on stalks. 'What happened?'

'Pastor Francis?' says Sandra, like I should know what she's talking about. I shake my head. 'I'm surprised Marsha hasn't spoken about it . . . about him. But they were very close – maybe it's still too upsetting . . .' She tails off and looks down at her plate.

'If you ask me, it has a lot to do with the second commandment,' says Mr Redmond.

'Don't be ridiculous, Michael!' says Sandra.

'Are you familiar with it, Jaylon?' he says, ignoring his wife and turning to me. I shake my head again.

286

'No,' he says. 'It seems your aunt isn't, either.'

'Michael!' says Sandra, banging her cutlery.

Mr Redmond clears his throat: 'Thou shalt not make unto thee any graven image, or any likeness of any thing that is in heaven above, or that is in the earth beneath, or that is in the water under the earth.' He looks at me like that should explain all I need to know, but I clearly need help joining the dots.

'Pastor Francis was hanging a picture of the Holy Spirit up in the community centre hall. The ladder gave way and he hit his head. He seemed OK at first, but there was bleeding on the brain and a short while later he collapsed and died. If you ask me, he shouldn't have been hanging a picture up at all.'

'Do we have to talk about it over dinner?' says Hannah.

'You're not saying the two things are linked!' says Sandra.

'The Lord does move in mysterious ways,' says Mr Redmond. Sandra gasps and bangs her cutlery again.

'Like with Leo!' I say.

'Exactly,' says Mr Redmond with a smug smile. 'But I thought you said you didn't know him?'

'Who?'

'Pastor Francis.'

'I don't.'

'Leo, Leo Francis. Pastor Francis. Are we talking about the same person?'

'I – I don't know,' I say. 'But – but – the guy in the car park? The guy who sits in the car park? Is that . . . ?' But I can't finish the sentence. The steak is turning back into a cow in my belly. The three of them are looking at me, waiting for more – or less, I'm not sure which. Sweat is running down my head. I dig my knife and fork into the steak harder than I mean to and it spurts blood at me.

'It was a tragedy – he was a good preacher,' says Sandra quietly. 'And what Marsha does is her own business,' she says, directing it at Mr Redmond. 'As she says herself, she needs all the help she can get. Sorry, Jaylon, I don't mean that you . . . er . . . sorry.'

'Don't worry about it,' I say. 'Can I use your bathroom?'

'Of course,' says Sandra, her face strained by an overly reassuring smile.

On the way up the stairs I hear them exchange a few bad-tempered whispers.

I put down the lid of the toilet and sit heavily, with my

hands over my face. My stomach groans. It feels like the cow's going for a ride in the Corsa. It turns a corner, accelerates, bounces over speed bumps.

A Pastor Francis died in the community centre. *Leo* Francis. You got to be joking. What kind of a ghost smokes and collects dead leaves? But I'm ready to believe anything right now. Anything at all. I manage to get up and walk to the basin, wash my hands and face and pat them dry. I look at myself in the mirror and take a few deep breaths – my eyes have grown, they're bigger than ever. I couldn't cover them up if I tried. Big swirly hypnotic cartoon eyes. I thought I had it back under control. But the craziness is like the darkness: always there, bubbling away, and it only takes a pinprick to set it exploding like a fountain.

I take a few more deep breaths, bend over and cool my forehead against the edge of the basin. Then I open the bathroom door and my heart practically explodes. I scream. It's a scream up from my guts, ripping at my throat. There's a body on the landing. Blood all over its chest, skin lifeless. Hannah's sister.

'What's going on up there?' booms Mr Redmond.

'Are you OK?' calls Sandra.

I'm frozen, clinging to the doorway. 'No, no, no,' I say. My lips smack, my mouth's dry. I hear movement downstairs, frantic talking.

How did I not see her? What happened? I don't understand how it could've happened . . . and they'll blame me and find out everything. I see my life melting away. All gone.

They're coming up the stairs. For a second I think of moving the body into one of the bedrooms, hiding it away, but it's too late for that. I should say something, warn them, tell them they shouldn't see it. I go to block off the stairs. That brings me closer to the body and I get jolted by another scream as the body raises its head, eyes fixed on me, teeth bared in an evil grin. And it laughs.

'That was amazing!' it says.

Mr Redmond reaches the top of the stairs, followed by Sandra and then Hannah, the three of them running into each other. And it takes too long, way too long, for me to realize . . . the corpse isn't coming alive; she was never dead.

'You're pathetic,' she says to me, standing up, adjusting her costume.

'What's going on?' says Mr Redmond.

'I was just messing around,' she says. 'I didn't think he'd react like *that*.'

TWENTY

That was the end of that. I told them I was ill, that I'd just been sick. And after my reaction outside the bathroom they seemed happy to go along with it and get me out of the house. Sandra looked embarrassed, Mr Redmond looked smug, Hannah kept looking down, and her sister . . . well, I didn't want to look at her at all.

Once I was outside, some cold air in my lungs, drying me off, cooling me down, I realized: I was sick – the craziness, the darkness, reacting like I did when I saw Hannah's sister – they're signs, symptoms of something worse. A disease. We've all got a disease and none of us know the cure. And when you don't know the cure, the only way to stop the epidemic spreading is death. That's what we're surrounded by. Like the hologram Jesus said:

Someone else has to die. They're the stakes. There's a disease, and if someone's got to die, it should be the person most responsible for the spread. I've got to kill the carrier. I've got to kill Shads. That's the only cure, the only way I'm going to get my life back. *I've got to kill the carrier.* I'm going to get my life back by taking someone else's. *Sorry, Shads, but I need it, bruv.*

What? You think killing Shads is a bad idea? Well, I don't care what you think. I don't care what anyone thinks any more. I'm taking it a body at a time.

I wanted to go and get the shank right then. I wanted to feel it tight in my grip, take it round to Shads's flat and feel, for once, what it was like to hurt someone who deserved it. I wanted to strike while the idea was fresh and new and bouncing around in my head; before there was the chance for any doubts to creep in. I phoned him, told him I wanted to go through a few things about the initiation. I wanted to be extra-prepared. *Thorough*, just like he is.

But he wasn't in. He was out with his new girlfriend, but we arranged for me to go round on Monday evening, when we could talk undisturbed. That's tonight. Tonight, tonight, tonight. And we're nearly there.

After I left, I got as far as mine and Hannah's bench. I didn't want to go back to Marsha's. I didn't want to have to deal with the Deadly Lampshade, or the hologram Jesus – any of them. It was cold and I buried myself inside my coat. I had my cap back on, pulled low; I kept as little of myself exposed as possible and I stretched out. I lost consciousness pretty quickly, but just as quick I found it again when a squeaky voice started repeating 'Trick or treat?' over and over into my ear. I woke up faced with a mini-vampire, on my eye-level, giving me a fang-toothed smile. I told him to go and knock on doors and do it – picking on people out in the open was breaking the rules – but he didn't listen and was soon joined by a whole gang of little vampires, were-wolves, ghosts and devils, making it their Halloween mission to torment me. I felt like telling them that they were wasting their time; my soul was tormented enough as it was. Apart from keeping me awake there was nothing they could do to me. But that, as it turned out, *was* enough, and I had to escape even them. I ended up back at Marsha's the way you always end up alone in the dark scary house in a bad dream. It just happens. It pulls you in.

But having a new focus made me calmer. I had a plan. If

any of my roommates wanted to start kicking off, I had an offer to put on the table: a patent for Shads's Soul Stain Removal. This could be it, this could clean me up, and I went to bed feeling almost relaxed.

The problem is, my body's got so used to not sleeping, it can't let me do it for more than five minutes at a time without panicking, without jolting me awake, thinking maybe it's shutting down for good. So I had a night of seesawing in and out of consciousness, up and down, up and down, which weirdly turned out to be even more tiring than not sleeping at all. But on the plus side, I found out I was too tired to care. Even if my new business proposition was turned down and my roommates decided to quietly tie my feet together, open the gates of hell and drag me on through, I wasn't bothered. Do it. Go on, *do it!*

What do you want to know about my day? For a start, I don't think Milk is talking to me. Well . . . he's not not talking to me, but he's not talking-talking to me either, if that makes sense? We met up before school as usual but he didn't even lift his head from his phone when I got there, just sort of looked to his side, made sure they were my feet, and started walking. Like it was all just a duty thing. I stopped at Bill's, bought a Milky Way, and he didn't even wait. He kept walking. Not fast – more of a shuffle – and he let me almost catch up before he started going at standard walking pace again, but he was making it clear there was a problem, something had changed. I could've asked him, but I didn't. I don't know why. It felt like a big barrier had been built up, and with every passing second of silence it was getting more and more fortified. By the time we got to school it had turrets, barbed wire and armed guards patrolling. It was serious.

It was a bright morning. In assembly Mr Wallace was lit up even more than usual; my blurry eyes making the reflection from the mic-stand spread out into what looked like a pair of wide golden wings. I blinked to make them go away but that made it look like they were moving. So I blinked faster: the wings flapped. I blinked even faster: the whole stage started soaring.

'You having a fit?' said Milk. It was the first thing he'd said to me all morning.

Our first lesson was maths. Another lesson with Ram, and

this time K2 as well, and I managed to meet Ram at the doorway on our way in.

'You wanna put those eyes *away*, blud,' he said.

'You wanna put your mum away, Ram,' said Milk from behind me. The air came out of him like a burst balloon. It was clear he'd been finding the silence a struggle. 'Lock her in a cage,' he said. 'I'm sick of her coming round my house in the middle of the night, blud. I'm fucking *tired* of her, you get me? She's wearing me out.'

'What you talking about *house*, man?' said Ram. 'Since when did you have a house? Where are the fucking houses on your estate?'

'I got stairs where I live. That means it's a house. Stairs weren't even *invented* when Westhall was built, blud.'

'What are you talking about, man? How do you get five-storey blocks without stairs? You should think about what you're saying before you open your mouth – you just sound stupid.'

In maths the seating's more freestyle and there's always a rush on to get the best places. The desks are arranged in an angled U-shape facing Miss Radcliffe's desk at the front. Milk cleared a way to the far side, by the window. Ram and

K2 hung back, all calm, and sat opposite. It was a sit-down stand-off.

'I ain't never been close enough to Westhall to find out,' said Milk. 'I might catch something, bruv. I thought you just built tunnels with your hands over there.'

'The only tunnel I been in recently is the one between your mum's legs,' said Ram. 'Could walk up there, blud. It's almost as big as her head.'

'I'm finding this conversation very offensive, boys,' said Miss Radcliffe, wearing a long dress and rattling beads. 'Can you be quiet and take out your homework, please?'

I didn't have anything to show, and instead sat back and closed my eyes, which was a mistake. The classroom was hot and stuffy and it wasn't long before my eyes were clamped shut and impossible to open. Suddenly I was on a slab, an operating table, surrounded by surgeons and nurses with masks and aprons on. They leaned over me, talking amongst themselves; it was muffled, though – I couldn't make it out, could just see the anxiety in their eyes. They stepped back. There was pain across my skin, like when you've got the flu and all your skin hurts, but it was more intense, more focused. I felt pushing from inside. At points my skin stretched outwards, like there were fingers pushing it up from underneath. I heard a voice say my name. Thick hairs broke the surface; as they came through, the pain got sharper but then faded, and I realized they weren't hairs; they were plant shoots. They unfurled into tiny trees, like bonsais. More and more of them sprouted up. I heard my name louder and louder. The trees were covering me and my name was shouted. I heard laughing too, and I was being shaken, and somehow I wasn't on the operating table any more; I was in school, in a maths lesson, my skin covered only in my school uniform, and the whole class staring at me.

'I'm pleased you've started turning up to my lessons, Jaylon. But I don't want you sleeping through them.' Miss Radcliffe was standing in front of me. Her perfume was tangy, like incense, and it made my nose itch. 'Where's your homework?'

'I haven't got it,' I said, pinching my sinuses.

'You look a mess – take your stuff and stand outside. I'll see you out there when I've collected the work; work that everyone else, it seems, has managed to find the time to get done.'

Out of habit I looked to Milk for support but he was

concentrating hard on a scribble at the top corner of his exercise book, digging his pen into it.

When I was out in the corridor, I noticed further along a decorator up on a stepladder adding a fresh coat of white paint to the wall. There was something familiar about him. I moved closer and realized it was the same man Muzza nearly crashed into, wearing the same white overalls. He was up on the top step, slapping on paint with long rhythmic brushstrokes. Gold bars of diagonal sunlight were streaming in through the windows, highlighting swirls of dust. I was going to speak to him, ask him if he remembered what happened, ask him what he had said to Muzza, but as I got closer the wet paint began to look watery, wavy in the light, and I could see through the wall like it was a window. The decorator didn't seem to notice – either me or the window. I stepped nearer. Through the wall I could see a dark sky hanging over a frozen lake lined with trees and surrounded by a giant horseshoe of cliffs. Long icicles hung from the branches of the trees and from the overhanging rocks. I saw millions of them, hanging from every twig, every branch, every piece of stone. On the other side of the lake a sun began to rise. I could feel the heat from it. The rays hit the icicles and they started to explode, making the sound of knives against glass, the pitch higher or lower depending on their size. The explosions created bursts of light and rainbows, until it all rang with the chinks of exploding ice, and the air was filled with light, and the light seemed to come out of the wall, spread around me, spread through me, lift me up. I felt myself disappearing into it and I wanted to keep going, keep disappearing. But just as I was leaving the ground, something snapped and it was gone. I was staring at the blank corridor wall. There was no decorator, no ladder. The walls were dry.

I looked both ways. The corridor was empty. I shook my head hard from side to side, like a dog shaking off water. I wanted to make sure I wasn't still sleeping through the lesson, wasn't still on a park bench, wasn't in the shrine, a mental hospital, sitting with a weed-smoking ghost in a rundown community centre.

I was as sure as I could be – which isn't all that sure, to be honest – that I really *was* in the corridor. I was looking at a blank wall. But like the feel of the flower woman's hands on my face, or when the blank-eyed woman squeezed my hand – I could still feel the sun, I could hear the exploding ice. I put my hand to the wall, moved my palm over the dry paintwork. I pressed my finger into it, half expecting it to ripple or even break. It didn't do either. It's inside me that the walls are coming down. The joins, the edges, the bits in between . . . they're blurring. Life/death, the blade in/the blade out.

I suddenly remembered Miss Radcliffe. I didn't want her to see me. I didn't want to have to explain why I hadn't done my homework, why I was sleeping in her class, or why I was pressing the corridor wall with my finger like some confused caveman. I couldn't spare the energy. I didn't wait around and I clung hard to the rail down the stairs, taking each step carefully, in case they decided to ripple too. In case they turned to water and fell away.

So I'm outside Shads's flat, a new-build block on the edge of the estate. This is his castle, his palace. And it's all his. It's enough that he lives by himself, got his own place. He's made it already in Blake Street eyes – his own flat, his own car . . . his own gun. *Don't think about that last bit right now, Jay.*

Shads has lived on his own as long as I've lived on the

302

estate. His life before that is all stories, and which ones are true and which are made up isn't really clear.

When Shads got kicked out of school, he stayed out. When he got kicked out of home, he went back until he got kicked out again. His parents had a reputation that gave their whole *block* a reputation; the balconies and stairwells would echo to the sound of them fighting and shouting. The noise would travel across the car parks and playgrounds, until the sound of the fighting got drowned out by the sound of the sirens arriving.

If it was as bad as people say, I don't know why Shads kept going back, but one day going back wasn't an option – the whole place went up in flames, the flat totally gutted. Shads didn't get in any trouble for it, at least not with anyone outside his family. And maybe it was an accident, but the story is that Shads tried to cook his family while they slept. They left the estate after that, leaving Shads behind. He was only in the Youngers then, but he moved into a flat with some of the Olders and never looked back. The Boyz became all the family he needed.

I don't think anyone ever expected him to be the boss. He was too unpredictable, too crazy. But going inside

303

changed . . . not all, but certainly some of that.

When he got sent down it could've been for anything. I had visions of the judge sitting there with a list of offences in front of him, his eyes closed, waving his finger around and eventually going, That one! And that one was GBH. He was in there for eighteen months. And it changed him. He came out a reformed character. He decided to take the Boyz *seriously* after that. He'd made contacts, learned all sorts of new tricks. He learned how to take the Boyz to the next level. And when the old boss, Rizz, went inside, Shads had all the right credentials to take his place.

That all seems like a long, long time ago now. Time moves fast when you're in the Boyz. Too fast. It feels like Shads has been in charge for ever. I'm trying to change history.

What am I expecting? I don't know. I feel like I'm doing the world a favour and I'm hoping that will carry me through, count for something. Diggy can take over the Boyz, I can get my life back. I know the chances are slim, but what choice have I got? Like I said, these are the stakes. It's not my fault it's come to this. At least . . . not totally.

I flex the shank in my fingers. I can do this. I've done it before. It takes a second, that's all. One second and he'll be down and I can finish the job. I'll be quick – like nature, like fate. That's what this is: I'm not even the main event. It's just cause and effect: live by the sword, die by the sword. I'm the sun rising. That door's going to open onto a new world. I ring the bell.

I hear him, taking his time. 'Yeah?' he says from the other side.

'It's Jay,' I say.

The door unlocks and opens. Shads stands there in white vest and tracksuit bottoms. He holds the door and door-frame, both arms up high, like an eagle swooping down. I can smell the sweat from under his arms. I tense up when our eyes meet, grind my teeth together and hold my fists tight and ready inside my coat.

His eyes scan me up and down. He seems to spend longer on my hands and I shuffle them slightly. Then he's back to my face, my eyes. 'Are you gonna kill me?' he says. My eyes snap wide.

'I don't believe it, bruv!' He laughs. 'Get inside!' He's shaking with laughter, corkscrewing away down the hall. 'You came to fucking kill me!'

He's one step ahead, and now I want him to be quiet

305

more than anything else. I want him to stop making it true, taking it over. This was mine. But I'm stepping into the hall and closing the door behind me, the same way I leaned forward and *covered his mouth*. I can go against gravity but my muscles still can't go against Shads. The moment the door shuts, the laughing stops, Shads has his gun out from the back of his tracksuit bottoms and is pointing it at my chest.

'Give me it,' he says. He's serious now, deadly. I should've thought about that bit. I should've thought.

'What?' I say.

'Whatever you were gonna use. Give me it.'

'I ain't got nothing, bruv.' It's not convincing.

'I'll put a bullet in you right now, Jay. Give me it.'

I try and bend the blade shut in my pocket without him noticing.

'Now!' he says.

I take it out, the blade half in, and hold it out.

'On the floor,' he says.

I start to crouch down.

'Not you, you prick! The fucking shank!'

I drop it at his feet and straighten up.

'Anything else?' he says. I shake my head.

306

He steps forward, gun high and ready. He grabs my neck and forces me against the wall; the other hand sticks the barrel deep into my cheek, bunching it up against my eye. His eyes are so close I can see my own reflection. I clench all my muscles tight. I've learned that much.

'You think you can kill me? You think you can come to my house and fucking *kill me*?' He spits it in my face. 'You can't touch me, you prick. I'm your owner. You're mine.' He flexes his hand on the gun, grinds the barrel deeper into my cheek, the other hand gripping tighter at my neck.

I'm choking, can't speak. But I couldn't anyway. There's a hand at my throat and a gun at my head. There isn't room for anything else.

'Do better than that tomorrow night,' he spits in my ear. 'Or you're a dead . . . I was gonna say *man*. But you ain't no man. You're nothing. You're a kid. A little kid who pisses himself at the first fucking sign of trouble. I'm not even sure you shanked anyone. Look at you! You ain't no *killer*. You're a pussy. You come here, you don't know what the *fuck* you're doing.' The barrel moves, finds its way to my temple. He presses it in.

'You'd better shank Ram good. You'd better carve that

307

little prick up. Because if you don't I'm gonna carve you up. I'm gonna rip your fucking throat out. You and your frumpy church bitch.

'I should shoot you right now. But I want to see you work for me. I want to make sure you know your *fucking* place. Who the fuck do you think you are?' He flexes his hand, the gun grinds in.

He steps away, holds the gun high, pointing it down on me. I'm feeling as small as that reflection in his eye. I'm feeling like that's where I am really. It's me who's reflecting back.

'Pick that up,' he says, giving a sharp nod towards the shank. I do as I'm told.

'You're nothing, bruv! Nothing. Shank Ram, you might still have a chance. Don't . . .' He tails off, shaking his head, face like Mr Redmond. But with a gun.

Without moving the gun or his eyes from me, Shads opens the door; he switches hands, and with his free hand shoves my head towards the gap in the doorway. And I can't believe I'm going. I want to try again. Run through it again. I know now, I know what to do.

'Get the fuck out of my house,' he says. 'I better see you

tomorrow. Try anything stupid, you're dead. Fuck it up, you're dead.'

The door slams shut.

I feel like I've been sucked up and spat out. I didn't taste nice. I was undercooked. Underprepared and undercooked. Sloppy.

I walk back through the estate feeling like I'm on a tightrope, feeling so edgy I'm putting one foot after the other on a wire stretched from the Earth to the Moon. That was it; that was my chance, and if you take chances like that you better make sure you take them right. The estate feels different, it looks different. The blocks stand out dark against a dirty red sky. The lights in the windows like evil eyes. This place isn't mine any more.

Don't think about the gun, Jay? *Yeah, good planning, bruv, really good.* A big part of me wants to cry, let it all go, but if I do that I'm going to fall, and I can't fall yet. I've got to keep taking it a step at a time; wrap my toes round the wire. Keep going until I'm away and clear. And I am going away, aren't I? Somehow that's it. That's going to be it. That's the end.

TWENTY-ONE

Lloyd comes to the door. Same old Lloyd; if he had his arms outstretched, drooling, with his head lolling on one side, it wouldn't surprise me.

'All right?' I say. He turns slowly and staggers back towards the bedroom. He doesn't answer. I follow him into the room, open the wardrobe and take out the shoebox. Lloyd doesn't notice; he's focused on the Xbox. By the time he's my age he'll have thumbs the size of yams.

My mum's in her usual place on the sofa, the TV screen the only light. I flick the main light switch. Nothing. She's looking even more like a ghost than usual.

It's like both of them don't know that Halloween's over, like they're on a two-day, two-person party. A ghost, a zombie . . . and then me. What am I? What does it matter?

'All right, Mum?' I say.

The ghost turns her head and looks me up and down. 'Taking the whole box with you, are you? Must be important.'

'What?' I say. My fingers clench on the box; I tighten up. 'I'm just getting some films, Mum.'

She nods sharply and turns back to the TV. 'I know what you keep in there,' she says. 'I'm not stupid.'

I back into the door and close it shut behind me. 'What you talking about, Mum?'

'Using your little brother's bedroom as a storeroom,' she says.

I shake my head at her. 'You're crazy,' I say. 'You need help.'

'Don't say things like that to me,' she hisses. 'I know you sell drugs! I could call the police right now and all you do is insult me!'

'There's nothing in there,' I mumble.

'Then show it to me! Show me what's inside!'

My fingers hurt I'm gripping it so tight, and I wonder if every time I've come back it's been that obvious. It seems so stupid now leaving it here, leaving it within easy reach.

What was I thinking? I was thinking it would make it harder for me to get caught, that's what I was thinking. Me. Some brother I am; some son too.

Shads, the shoebox . . . I spend all this time thinking, so much time with my head down, thinking, I'm missing all the important stuff leaping around behind my back.

'Why didn't you do anything?' I say.

'You think I didn't want to?' Her voice breaks as she says it. She turns back to the TV, breathes out heavily through her mouth. She concentrates on the screen like it's the only thing keeping her from floating away.

'I didn't know what to do,' she says. 'I tried so hard with you. So hard. Whenever I got paid, the first thing, *the first thing* I did was buy you books . . . try and make sure you got an education. And you were so clever . . . but you acted like you were ashamed of it. Ashamed to have a brain. Then you get mixed up with those kids on the estate and I lose you altogether.'

Her chest heaves, she shakes, and tears start flowing. She doesn't try and stop them.

'I don't want that to happen to Lloyd but I didn't know what to do. I knew you kept stuff here. *Drugs*. Every night

I go to bed expecting to be woken up by the police at five in the morning . . . Lloyd's bedroom raided . . . But I think if I get rid of it, throw it away, what will happen to *you*? I know what goes on out there, and it's worse than anything the police could do. I thought I was protecting you . . . it sounds so stupid. I didn't know what to do . . . I never know what to do. I thought I did the right thing, and look what happened to you.'

She starts clawing at the tears. 'I tried so hard to do the right thing, and it doesn't work. Nothing works.'

She leans forward, puts her elbows on her knees, palms against her eyes.

I didn't know. I didn't know she was even there, not properly. And she knows. She knows it all. She doesn't even have to move. I feel like I'm looking at her for the first time.

I put the box down on the armchair and go and sit next to her. I put my arm on her shoulder and she leans in to me, head against my chest, crying, sobbing.

'It'll be all right, Mum,' I say.

We stay like that, my mind blank now, and I keep repeating it. 'It'll be all right.' Soon I realize the door's open and Lloyd's standing there. My family.

'It'll be all right,' I say. 'I'll make sure, Mum. It'll be all right.'

I look at the TV. I swear I can feel the static from it, the suction, the pull; like a vacuum cleaner for your soul, sucking it in, sucking it up – your life disappearing inside, but tricking you into thinking that's where it belongs, that's where it's happening, that's where it wants to be. But real life is here, suffering and feeling cheated, but too hungry to even be able to tell you.

'It'll be all right, Mum.' It's like a prayer now; if I repeat it enough it'll come true.

'It won't,' she says. 'I thought I could do this on my own but I can't. Where's your dad? Where is he?'

'I don't know, Mum. He's just . . . I don't know . . . confused or something.'

'Confused? That's no excuse! This is too important to be confused. You and Lloyd are too important.' She gasps and moves away from me. 'Get that thing out of here, then. Get it out!'

I get up, don't say anything else – whatever goes through my head feels wrong. Lloyd watches me pick up the box and walk past.

'Look after Mum,' I say quietly. 'One of us has to.'

I rub the top of his head. My little brother. I get to the front door and lean my forehead against it. I breathe hard. One step at a time. I feel pretty high up already. I can't look down.

Hannah doesn't ask any questions. I think the tone of my voice is enough – it's like a big bell ringing out, something serious. It's the same deal as before: I have to wait for a text to tell me it's safe. In the meantime I head back to Marsha's. I'm doing the rounds.

Marsha's in the living room when I get in, sitting in an armchair near the balcony doors, looking up at the dead side of the hologram. There are the remains of some radioactive substance on a plate on her lap.

I stand in the doorway. We've switched places. 'You got different sides for different moods, Marsh?' I say.

'Yes, I do, actually. Do you?'

'Yeah, I guess so.'

She gives a quick, thin smile, maybe wondering what mood it was that made me want to pick him up and split him apart.

'What's wrong?' she says.

'Nothing.'

'It doesn't look like nothing.'

It must be my eyes again. For the next twenty-four hours I should probably wear sunglasses. 'I just had a conversation with my mum. She spoke.'

'Well, that's good.'

Marsha sounds weary, troubled, and I'm thinking of what Hannah's parents said about her being close to Pastor Francis. I'm wondering if they're *still* close.

'What do you know about Pastor Francis, Marsh?'

Her eyes go wide when I say his name. 'What about him?' she says.

'It's just something Hannah's parents said last night. They said you were close.'

'Did they?' She shakes her head. 'They like to gossip, those two. I don't think they ever actually liked him. They certainly never saw eye to eye. Pastor Francis had . . . unusual methods.' Marsha stands up, avoiding eye contact. 'But yes, we were close.' She walks past me into the kitchen.

'Do you believe in ghosts, Marsh?' I say to her back, and it straightens up and freezes. She doesn't turn round. I wait for her to reply but it looks like I'm going to have to push

316

it, spell it out. Maybe I can say my goodbyes to the Deadly Lampshade too. 'Hannah said the community centre was haunted by Pastor Francis.'

'Rubbish,' she says under her breath. She walks to the sink, washes her plate and bangs it down hard on the draining board.

'Do you believe in ghosts?' I say again.

'No I don't,' she says, keeping her back to me.

'But what about Jesus? Isn't he like a ghost?'

She turns round. Yep, there we go: the Deadly Lampshade is putting in an appearance. 'Just because Jesus died and came back does not mean he's a ghost. And just because when you pray you talk to him does not mean you should be having conversations out loud with pictures!' She breathes out heavily and softens slightly. 'But you know what? That would be just like Leo. He put so much effort into that community centre. He really tried to make it work. It would be just like him to want to keep on trying. Even now. That's the thing: you two are actually very alike. You both have a talent for taking things too far.'

She turns to the pot on the cooker. 'There's some dinner left if you're hungry.'

'No, I'm good, Marsh.'

'Yes, I thought that's what you'd say.'

'I'm going out, anyway.'

'You've just got in!'

'Yeah, but I've got a lot to do.' I breathe deep. I'm feeling edgier than a cut diamond. 'Thanks, Marsh,' I say, my voice breaking a bit.

'For what?'

'For lots of stuff. Thanks.'

I let it hang in the air. Maybe for once I'm not taking it far enough, but like I said, I've got to keep going. If I stop for a second I stop for good.

Next is my dad's pentagon. I look all around it, but for some reason the Brown Cow is my last stop, even though it's the most likely place for him to be – and there he is. I don't go inside; instead just look through the window. And stay looking.

He's sitting at the same table with the same friends as before; looking like some beached whale, all fat and bloated on hot air and fermenting juices.

With my mum I felt like I let some light in. It wasn't

much but there was a chink, a little thin ray. I don't see that with my dad. I don't think I can talk to him. I don't think he'd be ready. I could tell him exactly what's been going on and he'd look at me like I was talking some new language. I don't see any light, not any real light. It's like his pentagon's some weird inverted prism. No real reflection, just pretending. I haven't got time for pretending.

I don't see the bin-bag Rasta either, and he's someone I do want to speak to. I want to ask him about the mark, if it's still there, still growing. I want to ask him about the sacrifice – if I've done it yet, how close I am, what he even meant.

But there are always going to be questions. There are always going to be loose ends. And maybe that's what people like my dad are doing. Maybe you can live with questions that don't get answered if you don't even ask them in the first place. You can pretend it's not happening. But it *is* happening, it's happening all the time. Open your eyes. You see? It's right there in front of you. Whether you like it or not.

It's another good walk round Hackney before I get the text telling me I can go to Hannah's. She lets me in and we find our way up to her bedroom and onto her bed without saying anything – no whispers, not even any hand signals. She keeps the light off and we just lie there in the dark. I'm on my back and she lies on her side, her head on my chest.

She knows I'm going away. I don't think she knows where or how, but she knows I'm going somewhere.

I thought maybe I should warn her, tell her what Shads said. But I still think I can solve it. I still think there'll be a way out. A way out of that one, at least.

I have stopped now; I can't help myself – tears are forming in my eyes. I don't stop them from overflowing and slipping down my cheeks. I must shuffle, shake maybe, make some noise, because Hannah puts her hand on my face, feels it's wet.

'Are you crying?' she says, lifting her head up. Her eyes are shining. 'What are you crying for?'

'I don't know . . . I'm just happy, you get me?'

She sits up and looks at me seriously.

'Give me some love,' I say. 'I need some love.'

She wipes at my cheek with the cuff of her pyjamas, then leans over and kisses it instead. She kisses me all over my face and finally lands on my lips. She pries them apart with

320

her tongue and works her tongue in between my top lip and my teeth.

She knows, but I don't tell her anything. I just kiss her back, and keep kissing. I fill my lungs with her smell, remember how she feels, how she tastes. I'm going to take her with me. I'll bring her along, and we're going together now, and I hope she knows how I feel; can pick it up through my hands, through my lips, through rhythms and pressures.

We move together, take our clothes off without saying anything. And I hold her against me, her cool skin all over. It's like before when we used to kiss each other. It was so good there wasn't room for anything else. I'd take anything right now. Anything could happen. If this is it, if this is the deal, I'll take it. I'll take it.

I'm inside her but it doesn't even feel like I am. I feel like we're just the same. This is where there's no gap, no join. All and everything together. And we're moving faster, getting closer.

'Hannah? Are you OK in there?' It's her mum outside the door, and we both land back on her bed.

'Yeah . . . yeah, I'm fine. I was just having a bad dream.'

'You sure you're OK?'

'Yeah, yeah, fine.'

We wait, not moving, and listen to her mum go to the bathroom and back and close her bedroom door again.

'You were having a *bad* dream?' I say. 'What do you mean, *bad*?'

She shushes me. 'I couldn't tell her it was a good dream, could I?'

Hannah moves and gets on top of me. She looks sort of serious, concentrating. She starts slowly, maybe nervous. In the dark I can see her biting her lip, frowning. Gradually she speeds up. We cling onto each other. Every movement she's changing the world, pulling me free, showing me where I belong. All my nerves lit up and alive. We're going clear, and we keep going, keep going.

My whole body ripples. It starts to surge and flood. And I'm gone. Blank and disappeared. No one, no name, nothing. Peace. I'd take anything you could hit me with. She falls on top of me. She covers me with the dark, pulls it over me. Like a sheet over a dead man.

TWENTY-TWO

I'm watching smouldering clouds and fluorescent trails in a burning sky. The atmosphere lit up like exploding lava. It says it in the Bible: I read it. There's going to be a firestorm at the end of time, the day of judgement. But it's cheating. There's a firestorm every day. Every day is a day of judgement.

I'm up on the roof of Blake Point with a clear view. I stand up and balance myself against the bars. Why is no one watching this? Crowds of people should be out on the streets, on the Downs, arms raised. No one's seeing it. No one's looking up. They're focused on the pavement, their feet, their shadows, their problems.

I never realized before how much I like sunsets. Why's no one else watching? Because there'll be another one? Not for everyone there won't.

I stay standing, barely moving, barely blinking. I watch the clouds cool and stretch; get longer, darker, flatter. I watch the pinks change to purples, watch the light fade.

I'm going to kill Ram. I'm going to kill him. What choice have I got?

I smell the smoke from the top of Shads's path. My heart drops to my belly. It's ominous; it makes me expect an ambush. The second that door opens I'm expecting to be ripped apart by hot metal. The green can make you focus, make you appreciate deeper levels, sophistication, make you a connoisseur. Even though I'm one of their own, I can see the Boyz loving it.

I'm losing the energy. I was solar-powered while the sun was up. Now the sky's as black as a body bag. Zipped up and airless. All I got are my reserves, and they're running into the red; low and spluttering. I need to draw them in, make them dense, powerful, like a black hole. No escape.

I stop and listen as my hand reaches the bell. I can hear talking inside, laughing, action. I ring and there's a hush but nothing else happens. I ring again, keeping my finger on for longer.

Eventually the door opens and it's Diggy. He gives me a nod, but his expression isn't clear, and while I'm trying to decipher it he turns away and walks back down the hall. There's a sheet of smoke hanging low over the living room, wavering slowly, spooky like a graveyard. The room's crowded, but there's no sign of Shads. Most of the Boyz are sitting on or standing behind the L-shaped sofa, watching the game of *Mario Kart* being played on the huge TV. There's so many of the Boyz crammed in it's not even clear who's playing. But they're too stoned to notice me. Or maybe I'm being too charitable. Maybe I'm being ignored. I don't care. What could I talk about anyway? Tonight I'm speaking that new language. I've learned it quick.

'Shads wants to see you,' says Diggy. 'He's down in his room.'

A shout goes up around the sofa. It's the end of a round. And I can't tell. I can't tell whether life's too much like a game or not enough. And maybe the Boyz can't tell either, maybe they're mixing it all up.

Jay's killing someone, blud, so he can join the Olders. No he ain't; he's just rubbish at Mario Kart − *that's his punishment. Ram is shit at* Mario Kart − *that's why he's getting shanked. No,*

325

man, look, Jay's going to meet Ram on the Downs to play Mario Kart — *one of us has got to jook someone. Nah, man, they've turned the whole of the Downs into a racetrack, Jay's going out there to race Ram — he's got to beat him otherwise he won't join the Olders.*

Standing outside Shads's room I feel like I've reached the end of a level. That's what all doors are feeling like. It's like every closed door is the beginning and the end. When I knock I'm one step closer. When I open it I'm one step closer. And after that? Who knows?

Knock. Knock.

'Yeah?'

He's still alive. I was hoping somehow he wouldn't be; like somehow he'd choked between giving Diggy the message and me getting to his door. He'd stood up, tripped and shot himself through the heart. I wait a few seconds to shorten the odds; my dad would be proud. You never know. I take hold of the door handle but I lose control of it because it's pulled from the inside, and I'm expecting the hot metal again, but in my face is a scowling Muzza. He swings the door wide and lets me through the gap between him and the doorframe. He looks fully recovered.

Shads is sitting at a desk against the far wall with his back to me. He's hunched over, busy. Muzza closes the door behind me and I move into the centre of the room, trying to position myself as far away from them both as possible.

Shads's bedroom isn't much. It's small and bare. There's a double bed with another big TV at the end of it; a wardrobe, completely fronted by mirrors; and the desk, which Shads is in no hurry to move from. He's counting under his breath, quickly flicking notes, and I wonder if he's testing me. Sitting there, exposed, not even looking. I came to kill him last night, and now he doesn't even have to face me. He can let Muzza get his hands dirty if it comes to that, but Shads can stay clean, uninvolved, and admire himself in his mirrors afterwards.

I think about saying something, saying his name, but it's a word that feels too dirty, so instead I clear my throat. He stops for a second, but only a second, and he keeps going until he's filled a shoebox with notes. He puts the lid on and swivels on his chair.

He's wearing a tight white T-shirt, thick silver chain at his neck. His forehead's glistening with sweat; he rubs at it and pulls at his nose.

327

'Look at all this,' he says, pointing at the piles of notes on the desk. 'It's a hassle. I need more outlets; more avenues to stream the shit. Why do you think I've got that little runabout? Had to pay for it all in cash. If there's one thing this game teaches you, it's patience.'

He's keeping it all on the surface, keeping what happened last night to himself, only going to bring it out when it suits him. He's staying in control, owning it, still trying to own me. He stands up, hops over, and I shrink away by reflex.

'Take this,' he says. He hands me a cheap mobile. 'It's Shaky's phone. We've arranged with Ram for half-eleven, first underpass on the Downs; that's *our* side. He's keen, so he'll be there, but don't expect him to be on time. You know what dealers are like; they run different schedules, even small-fry like Ram. So give him time to show. Do the business then head back this way. Go on a detour first though, yeah? We don't want you leaving no obvious trails.

'The phone's for emergencies only, or if Ram tries to contact you. I don't see a problem, though. At that age dealers love it. Fucking meeting in an underpass in the middle of the night, pretending like they're in some film or some shit . . . He won't be able to help himself.'

Here goes. 'I was thinking, bruv.'

Shads tilts his head. 'Yeah? What about?' He says it like it's a dangerous pastime.

'I want to make sure I do this right, you get me? I was thinking a shank might not be enough.'

Shads raises his eyes to Muzza.

'It'll be cold,' I say. 'Ram's got this big coat. I want to make sure I can get through. I want to use more than a shank.'

Shads rubs his jaw. 'Do you?' he says.

'Yeah . . . I was thinking . . . maybe I could use your gun.' And I feel like I've just shot one by saying it.

'Use my gun?' He swings away. 'You hear that, Muzz? My man wants to use a piece.'

'I know what it feels like,' I say. 'I shot Sugar Ray. I know I can do it. With a shank, I don't know, man. There's too many things that can go wrong and I got some making up to do, innit?'

Shads steps in close, his eyes working me over. 'There's more that can go wrong if you're using a gat, but I appreciate your ambition. And yeah, you have got making

329

up to do. What do you think, Muzz? You think we can trust a man who tried to kill me?'

Muzza grunts.

'It'll sound like fireworks,' I say.

We stare at each other. I'm not folding this time. He can trust me – on this. Not on much any more, but he can trust that I'm not going crumble. I'm learning.

'All right,' he says. 'You're lucky I got spares.'

He turns to his bed, lifts a corner of the mattress and takes from underneath the same gun that I had pressed against my head last night. I sense Muzza step forward, not taking any chances.

Shads gives me a short introductory lesson, wipes the gun clean, and hands it to me. Muzza is right over my shoulder now, but he doesn't have to worry: I slot it into the back of my jeans, just like Shads.

'I can't believe a pussy like you has caused me so much trouble,' he says. 'But do this right, you stand a chance. We all act crazy now and again.'

'OK,' I say, breathing it out. 'I know.'

He looks me over, a hint of a smile turning up his mouth. 'I want that little prick dead,' he says.

'Now, leave me alone. I've got to finish my accounts.'

Muzza follows me out and sticks close. I stop in the hallway and he almost shunts into the back of me, like he's in traffic again. I've got a question.

'What did that van guy say to you, Muzz?'

Muzza stares past me to the living room, like I'm wasting his time.

'Help me out here, Muzz. Come on. I ain't got long.'

'I told you. He said, Slow down.'

'That it?'

Muzza flexes his arms, his eyes stony. We stare at each other and in my mind I fire back wrecking balls. We stay like that, I don't back down, and eventually his eyes shift and he ushers me further along the hall. 'There was a woman on the traffic island,' he says, only a little above a whisper. 'She was wheeling a buggy. She'd been crossing the road. That's why he stopped the van in front of us. He said we would've gone right through her.'

'And you believed him?'

'It was more than that. I could see it happen. In his eyes . . . could feel it.' Muzza's face suddenly looks haunted, like a soldier reliving the front line. 'He said, *You see? I saved your life too, didn't I?'* He shudders, rubs his arms. 'I couldn't drive after that.'

'Then why come back?'

'Look what happened when I weren't there. I'm supposed to look out for Shads. But maybe that ain't the way round it's meant to be. Maybe I'm meant to be like that van . . . parked right in front of him.'

'He needs more than that, bruv,' I say.

'Yeah, maybe. But it's a start.'

'And what about tonight? Why ain't you stopping this?'

Muzza checks over his shoulder. 'You tried to kill him last night. That makes it complicated.'

'Yeah . . . I know.'

'It was a good idea to ask for the piece. If I was you I'd keep it. You've got more of a chance that way. And I ain't even talking about Ram.'

'Muzz?' It's Shads, his head poking round the bedroom door. 'Jesus, man! What's got into you? What you doing?'

'I'm just giving him a little pep talk,' says Muzza.

'A pep *talk*?' says Shads. 'A pep *talk*? What you *talking* for? We got work to do!'

With a nod Muzza points me towards the living room.

332

'Good chatting to you, Muzz,' I say.

He grunts and ambles back down the hall. 'Sorry, boss,' he says to an earful of grumbling.

The only space in the living room is behind the sofa. A joint gets passed my way but I turn it down. The *Mario Kart* marathon moves on and the controller gets passed my way too, but again I turn it down. I want to keep my head clear, and I'm rubbish at *Mario Kart* – I don't want it affecting my confidence. Milk is sitting on the sofa in front of me, cosily tucked in, and when I refuse the game he turns and smiles at me. It's a stoned smile, disjointed, but sort of spiteful too, and I wonder if he'd mind if I didn't make it back tonight; if I just cleared the way for him. There's been a crack forming between us ever since I started getting more attention from Shads. But Milk doesn't understand. Look where it's got me: the end of the whole fucking line.

I can just see Milk later: *Nah, man, I always knew Jay was a pussy. I tried my best wiv him, you get me, bruv? But what can you do? He ain't a gangster, not like me, innit? He can't even play* Mario Kart.

He didn't meet me before school at all today. And I never realized before how much I relied on him there. I felt lost, no purchase. He's used to me not going in, barely making it over the start line or disappearing halfway. I realized Milk goes in every day. He can cope, he's got reserves – inside and outside. I had to look around the playground, search out my own planets to orbit. The universe has turned upside down.

After a couple more rounds Diggy pats my shoulder. 'It's time,' he whispers, and I skulk behind him to the front door. He opens it and we both stand out on the path.

'Digs,' I say. 'If this doesn't work out the way it's supposed to, and I don't come back . . . between you and Muzza . . . make sure that's enough for Shads. He doesn't need to take it out on anyone else. Not if he's got me, yeah?'

'What you sayin', bruv?'

'I'm just covering myself, that's all. My family, my girl, they've got nothing to do with this. It's just me. Make sure that's enough, that's all I'm saying.'

'Yeah . . . OK. I'll try. But this is Shads we're talking about, yeah?'

'Yeah, man, I know, but . . . just try, that's all I'm asking.'

'Course, bruv.'

'Thanks, Digs.'

'Good luck, man.'

Diggy clasps my hand, pulls me close, and too quick the door bangs shut and I'm standing alone. The next level.

No more preparation, no more instructions. I feel like I've missed something – some meeting where Diggy and Muzza are all moving models of the Yoot and the Boyz around a big map of the Downs with long sticks, and Shads is standing on a platform high above barking instructions. But no, it ain't like that. This is it. It's too simple, too easy. All you got to do, really, is want to do it, get the ability, the resources, then you're done. Point yourself in the right direction and go. I pat the gat in the back of my jeans, turn away from Shads's door and towards the Downs. And I can almost feel the world itself turning under my feet, like I'm a clown on a ball. The future's rushing at me so fast my cheeks should be drawn back by the g-forces, exposing my gums, my eye sockets.

I'm coming, Ram, I'm coming.

Out from under the cover of the estate and I begin skirt-ing the Downs. I hear the *pap-pap-pap* of fireworks, the whine of rockets. I smell them on the air – gunpowder, sulphur, smoke. I head to the path that runs along the railway line. Trees hang overhead, waving and hissing in the wind; the branches lit from underneath by orange streetlights. They make me think of Leo's tree spread out on the community centre floor. And I wonder if he's here some-where now, watching me. Leo the *ghost*. I still can't believe it.

A train rumbles and screeches past on the tracks up to my right. A long goods train. The sound of it swamps everything and makes me slow down, like I need all my senses clear, need to be able to focus with sight, sound, touch, everything.

I can see the underpass up ahead, its white walls lit up. It looks like the entrance to a cave but in negative: it's dark outside, light inside. My breathing gets shallow as I edge closer, my steps getting smaller and smaller. The train passes, the sound fades, but the wind picks up and rushes through the branches above me. Every sound is getting involved, making it personal. The underpass opens out. I'm early and Ram will probably be late but I can't help think-ing of him there. Not even that – I'm thinking of blood spattered over the white walls, like I've leaped through time, jumped up, let the ball turn, and I'll land and get a glimpse of the future.

But it's empty. Bright strip lights light it all the way down to where it ends and the path rises and skirts off round to join a quiet backstreet. Now what? It's too bright. It feels too clinical, like an operating theatre. I can't wait here. I walk to the end, where it opens out, creating an angle which I can tuck myself into, but even that's too exposed. I've got to get Ram where I want him. I can't let him get away.

I'm feeling the nerves now, coming in waves. I walk quickly back to the opening. There's dense bushes along the verge, and it's dark in there. If I crouch down tucked up against the wall, and Ram comes, he'll be in the underpass before he sees me. I need him in there first.

I push through the bushes and get down on my haunches, resting my back against the wall. My view of the path is patchy but the entrance to the underpass is clear to my left. If anyone comes, any doubt, I'll see them there. And the walk through is clear – I can keep it quick and quiet. But now I'm settled, the waves are getting bigger and at the top of each one I don't feel like I can do it; it passes and I'm calmer, but then there's another wave and the same thing happens. I just hope Ram turns up in between waves.

The last couple of weeks are rushing over me:

SHADS: Guns draw attention and I'd be worried you wouldn't have a clue what to do with one.

DIGGY: Shads thinks you need some extra incentive.

SHADS: All you got to worry about is turning up, and when Ram shows: *blam!*

MILK: Even if you get caught, so what? You go inside for a few years. Everyone will think you're a *bad boy*.

DIGGY: He might turn his attention to your girl . . . and your family.

BIN-BAG RASTA: You got a mark on you . . . a stain . . . on your sooooooul.

SHADS: You'd better carve that little prick up. Because if you don't I'm gonna carve you up. I'm gonna rip your fucking throat out. You and your frumpy church bitch.

The waves are getting bigger and bigger and I don't think I can do it. I've got a plan. I want my wings. But it's all getting jumbled up in my head. I take the piece out, feel it tight, point it, practise. But it's like it's got a life of its own now. I check the safety's on. Check it again. Point it. Then there's a sound, scuffing footsteps, and I freeze. There's someone coming up the path to my right, the direction of Westhall. I grip the gat hard, hold myself steady and focus on the dark shape moving on the other side of the bushes. He turns into the underpass. It's not Ram.

It's a youngish white guy, not walking straight, drunk maybe – you'd have to be to be walking up here at this time. I listen to his footsteps echo along the underpass and then he's gone.

The seas have settled, like that was the last big wave and it's crashed onto the beach and drawn away. That's what I needed: a dress rehearsal. I wish I could've had one of those last night. My muscles know what to do now. And I think back over last night. I'm not letting that happen again. Ram comes, I'm quick and I'm definite. No mistake.

It's gone eleven-thirty. I settle back into position against the wall. There's been no text from Ram, which hopefully means we're on schedule. Now I just got to wait till the drug dealer rulebook tells him he's free to go.

Five minutes. Another train rumbles past and my eyes burn through the bushes to compensate for the sound. It passes and I'm counting – ten minutes, eleven, twelve. And there's another set of footsteps, coming from the same direction. I freeze again. And all it takes is one split second in between the bushes to know it's him.

He turns into the underpass and stops. From here he could see me. I didn't think of that. I didn't think it could be two-way. *Good one, Jay.* I slowly move the gun, get it ready. All he would have to do is turn his head to the left and the game changes. But he doesn't. He steps forward into the underpass. I hear him mutter under his breath. He might not hang around if he thinks Shaky's let him down. I move quick along the wall and turn into the underpass.

Ram is halfway down, facing the other way. I run up behind him; he turns when he hears me but the turn of his head gives me more to aim at and I crack the handle of the gun across his jaw. It knocks him off his feet. He groans, tries to scramble up but can only get onto all fours and I kick upwards into his ribs, to turn him over as much as anything. Lying on his back, I step over him and put my foot down hard on his chest and point the barrel at his head.

He rolls like a beetle, his arms up. He gets a glimpse of me. He groans. It sounds like my name.

'I got to kill someone to join the Olders, Ram.' My

voice echoes, multiplies off the walls. 'I'm choosing you. Congratulations, bruv!'

'What – what – where's Shaky?' He holds his jaw, swelling up already. He's only half there.

'I set you up. You're dead.'

He tries to say something but he gasps and his head lolls to the side.

'We haven't got long, Ram.' I grind my foot into his chest to get his attention. 'Before I kill you I want to ask you some questions. Do you want to live? Answer me, you prick! I said: do you want to live!'

'What are you talking about?'

'Answer my question!'

'Just do it if you're going to do it!'

'ANSWER MY FUCKING QUESTION.'

'Yeah, yeah, I want to live,' he says, the words tumbling out onto the ground.

'Why?'

'What?'

'WHY?'

'I don't know – I don't know why.'

'Think about it!'

'I don't know . . . I just do.'

'What's the worst thing you've ever done?'

'What?'

I kneel down on his chest and grab his jaw. I turn his face so he can see me. He gasps at the pain. I say it slow, like I'm talking to a baby. 'Before I kill you, I want you to tell me what the worst thing you've ever done is.'

'Why?'

'Just do it!'

He tries to move his head away but I grip it tight. He closes his eyes and breathes hard and unsteady.

'When my granddad was losing it,' he says, his voice thick. 'I used to take some of his money. Not much, but I used to pretend to him like he must be losing it more than he realized. I kind of got used to taking it, and I always sort of meant to give it back, but then he died.'

'That's the worst thing you've done? You act all tough like a gangster, and that's the worst thing?'

'That's all I can think of. Shit!'

'I know it's hard to think with a gun at your head. Who are you going to miss most?'

He tries to wrestle me off so I put the barrel between his

eyes and press more of my weight down. 'Answer my question, Ram.'

His head rolls. He mumbles something.

'I can't hear you, bruv!'

'My mum. I'm going to miss my mum!'

'Why?'

'I don't know! 'Cos she's my fucking mum, that's why!'

'What did you want to be when you grew up?'

'What?'

'What did you want to be when you grew up?'

'I don't know . . . I don't know . . .'

'Think about it, Ram!'

'Why?'

'Because now it's too late! You could've been anything you wanted. But you think this is more important. You think dealing in the middle of the night makes you special. You think slippin' on Boyz turf makes you special. You think being in some crew that doesn't really give a fuck about you makes you special. And now it's too late. You could've been whatever you *wanted*! I want you to know that before I kill you. I want you to know!'

'Do it, then! Just do it!'

'Why? Why do you want me to do it? Because you're too much of a pussy to actually *live*, to properly *live*? Go on, cry, you pussy! Cry for your mum. Cry for yourself! Cry for the life you're losing!'

'You're sick, man. You're fucking sick.'

'What's your favourite thing?'

He almost laughs, and I stick the barrel against his nostrils and press upwards.

'Tell me! What's your favourite thing?'

'My bed! I like my bed!'

'Why do you like it?'

'It's comfortable. I've got loads of pillows. I like sleeping. Shit, why does it matter?'

'I like sleeping too, Ram. But I haven't fucking done it in weeks! I'm so tired, bruv. So tired. I want to sleep but I can't. It's like life is all pressing in, the colours are too bright, the sounds are too loud. And it's because I know it all matters, Ram! All of it! But you never pay any fucking attention! And I want you to think about that. I want you to think about it! I want you to think about what you're going to miss in your last few seconds!'

'I did think about it!'

344

'No you didn't! If you did you wouldn't be here now! You got a girlfriend?'

'Yes.'

'Do you love her?'

'Shut up, man!'

'Don't tell a man who's holding a gun to your head to shut up, Ram. That's fucking stupid! Do you love her?'

'I don't know; it's only just started.'

'Yeah, well, now it's finished. Now it's too late.'

'You're sick,' he says again.

'That's right. I am. But so are you. So's all of us. Say goodnight.'

I get up and wedge my foot firmly into his breastbone. I point the barrel at his head, holding with both hands. He shakes, turns his head away and squints, crying now. His hands are up. Surrender.

I flex my fingers, holding tight. 'Night-night, Ram.'

And I fire.

TWENTY-THREE

My arm kicks badly but I get three shots off, filling the underpass, a noise so loud I wonder if the Boyz are going to pause their game of *Mario Kart* and ask each other what that sound was.

I take my foot off Ram's chest and step away. For a minute I just watch him, my ears ringing. I feel deaf and I'm glad of it. And I'm glad it's over. It all feels so messy – the screams, the shouts, the blood, the pain. It must be like being born.

'You gonna lie there all night?' I say, sounding underwater to my own ears.

He shakes in front of me, same position. 'What are you doing?' he says, his voice sticky, asthmatic.

'I missed,' I say. 'You got another chance.'

346

His arms and legs twitch. Eventually he lifts his head; gasps as he moves his jaw. He gets up awkwardly and stumbles backwards into the wall.

'How does it feel?' I say.

He lurches, holds the wall and looks at me, eyes a red hate.

'Where there's an end, there's a beginning,' I say.

'You're crazy,' he says, but he's shaking too much to say any more.

'What? And you're not? Look at us. You telling me fighting over lines drawn up by people who don't care if we even exist . . . what? That's not crazy? Wake the fuck up!

'I'm making a deal. I'm dead, you're alive. I want you to remember that. I chose you over me. Not because I care about you, but because for some reason I can't figure out, I care about life and if I can't have it, I want you to have it. But I can't give it to you if you don't appreciate it. I've seen a lot of dying over the last few days, and that's enough. That's more than enough. I was meant to kill you. I could've killed you, but I didn't. I've got a mark I want to get rid of. I haven't got another chance, but you have.'

I've realized second chances do exist if you want them

to, but only if you give them to someone else; you can't make them for yourself.

Ram uses the wall for support and edges back out to the Downs, his eyes on me.

'I could've done it, Ram. Don't forget that. I still can.'

I point the gun at him again and he bolts, out into the darkness and away.

'This is a new life for you, Ram. You hear me! I've given you a new life!'

Is that going to work? Probably not. But what else could I do? I didn't exactly have many options. I'd like to see you do any better. But whatever happens, Ram isn't my problem any more. I tried. Now it's up to him.

I take out Shaky's mobile and dial Shads's number. This *is* an emergency. It rings out and goes to voicemail.

'I did it, Shads,' I say. 'But I did it my own way. My way, Ram died and came back to life. It was a miracle, bruv. You should've seen it. But I know you won't believe me. That's why I'm taking my own way out as well. You don't own me; you don't own nothing.

'You're a coward. And deep down you're scared. I know

348

you are. You're not at war with the world; you're *scared* of the world, bruv. That's why you're trying so hard to get caught. You want to get caught. Stabbing someone on the bus . . . shit, man, that's just snitching *yourself*. I'm right, aren't I? But you're probably so scared you won't even admit it.'

I hang up and look at the gun in my hand. This was going to be the end; this was how I saw it – shank or piece, killing myself in the underpass. But now I can't do it. I've got too much energy in my system. Life is clinging on too tight, clamped on my ankle like a bear trap. I'm feeling righteous, and righteous men don't commit suicide. And if I kill myself, I'm saying Shads is right – and he's not, he's not right.

A shout surges through me, turns into a scream, comes up from a place I never knew existed till a few days ago. It fills the underpass, rebounding and multiplying off the walls. It's so loud it kills the sound of the gunshots, takes on a life of its own, breaks out, flies away, and I wonder if the Boyz will hear that too. And it makes me think: Shads isn't going to sit around waiting; he's going to send the Boyz out to look for me. And there's someone else I need to see. A ghost.

I walk out of the underpass into a hard wind. Branches swaying, all hissing and whispering. Leaves fall and join others that are blowing in circles like mini tornadoes. It's all too unsettled and I wonder if I've messed with something I shouldn't have messed with. I didn't think this far ahead, and now I'm wondering if I was even supposed to. I walk across the Downs expecting to see trees floating high in the air and clouds upright growing from the ground. Everything upside down. I've got this weird feeling that I wasn't meant to see past this point. Now all bets are off.

I pull at the corrugated iron and it grinds loud on the ground. I step past it and into a darkness so total it feels solid, feels like it's squeezing the air out of my lungs and I can only breathe in short breaths. I edge along the corridor, and without anything to train my eyes on, my mind starts racing. I'm seeing the bin-bag Rasta, I'm seeing the old guy, the plant woman, the woman in church with those blank eyes. And I'm seeing Leo, the way he was on Sunday, sitting up in the nest. And maybe he's so protective of the community centre he won't like me coming at night, trespassing. And ghosts are different at night – they're nastier, more powerful. Just after midnight too; this is ghost peak-time.

'Fear has no place here,' a voice says from nowhere. I almost shout again, but there's a hand over my mouth. It stays there until I start to settle and it lets me go. It's Leo.

'I'm not scared,' I say. I put my hands out, wave them about in front of me, but I only feel air.

'You look scared,' he says.

'How can you—?' But I stop because there's a grab at my sleeve and I'm pulled down the corridor.

We turn left, the dark diluted by a dim orange glow, and I recognize the hall doors up ahead. Leo becomes visible in front of me; his parka; the silhouette of his overgrown hair, pieces of leaf sticking out.

He opens the door, stands to one side and ushers me through. The security light outside gives the inside of the hall some faint definition. I can see Leo's been busy. The pattern has grown, the whole floor of the hall covered in intricate lines and spirals. From the left-hand wall it seems to grow from roots, joins the thick trunk all the way to the nest, which spreads out into a tumbling mass of branches and twigs and stems that cover the rest of the

351

floor. A breeze blows through the open doorway, displacing some of the leaves, sending them tumbling into other rows.

I stand still and wait. Leo shuts the door and I let him lead the way to the nest. It's harder to navigate this time, not as much floor space. He sits down in one of the compressions and motions for me to do the same. He takes a new joint out of the inside pocket of his parka and lights it.

'So . . .' he says.

'What?' I say.

'You have come.'

'Yeah. I'm dead, bruv.'

Leo raises his eyebrows. 'Are you?' he says. 'You don't look it.'

'Yeah, I am, pretty much.' I sit down on the edge of the nest and draw my knees up. 'Remember when you gave me that leaf,' I say. 'You said: *You can hear them*. Who were you talking about?'

Leo clicks his fingers. 'Give something a name, the truth disappears.'

'Don't give me a name, then. Tell me what you were talking about.'

'I have been! I told you: I am the gate of the gods!'

This isn't going to be easy, is it? 'Are you a ghost?'

Leo prickles. 'Do I look like a ghost?'

'I don't know, bruv. Not really, to be honest.'

'People watch a few films, read a few books and they think they know everything! Good research!'

'Did you used to be a preacher? I got told a preacher called Leo died in here.'

'I didn't die! The Spirit came for me, caught me, and rested me on the palms of the eternal ones. There's a big difference. However . . . I was returned. My work was not finished.'

'But you are, like, dead. I mean, really.'

'In your terminology I suppose that would be the definition. But as I told you – give something a name, the truth disappears.'

'I don't understand.'

'No, but that's not important. Understanding is over-rated. Complete understanding is unattainable, partial understanding is misleading. Much better to appreciate.'

'So who were you talking about?'

'You should know: you've met them.'

'What? What do you mean?'

'I asked them to provide you with guidance. And they agreed. I am the gate!'

'Guidance? What guidance? I don't think you should've bothered, bruv. Look where it's got me.'

'It has brought you here. You have set yourself free.'

'Free?'

'Yes . . . do you not agree?'

'I wouldn't call it free.'

'What would you call it?'

'I'd call it fucked, bruv.'

'You see? Give it a name, the truth disappears. And as I know a wise man once told you: truth is the final destination.'

'You know him?'

'Of course.'

'Who is he?'

Leo looks at me like I'm stupid. But it's all right, I know the answer.

'How come people can't see you?' I say.

'They could if they wanted to, but how many people really see anything?'

'But what about my aunt, Marsha? It sounds like she'd want to see you.'

'No. No, she doesn't. And a good thing too. She'd order me to have a bath and put on some clean clothes. I used to like that about her, but now it's not that simple.'

'Don't you get to choose? If you're, like, a gh— a gate or whatever?'

'I appear as I need to appear.'

I'm not used to Leo being this straight-talking. I'm wondering why he hasn't been like this before.

'Why are you telling me all this now?' I say.

He waves his arm. 'Because it is almost finished.'

I look around. 'What? The tree?'

'Yes. Time is short. The Spirit comes. Hold fast, my brother. Hold strong!' Leo takes a long drag, cloaking himself in smoke.

'What . . . What do you mean?'

'I mean the time is *now*. Listen!' He holds his hand up, points it to the ceiling.

There's silence. I hear a car in the distance, the wind blowing, but nothing else. I'm about to tell Leo I don't hear anything different, but then there's a scuffing in the car park. Footsteps.

I spin to face the windows and crouch down into the

nest. Leo doesn't move. I see a shape move past the windows and walk in the direction of the main door. My skin is on fire. I thought I was prepared – again I thought I was prepared, this time for anything. But life is always a step ahead. I listen hard. There's the sound of metal scraping against concrete.

'They're coming in!' I whisper. Leo sits motionless, his hands together, the joint out now.

In my mind I follow the footsteps up the corridor, follow them as they decide what way to go, and then turn towards the orange glow.

I swallow hard, my mouth dry and sticky, my eyes stuck to the hall doors. I watch for what feels like ages, zoning in. There's a change in the shadow at the doors, like someone walking past. I go to reach for the gat in the back of my jeans, but just that movement reminds me – reminds me where I am, what I'm doing. I'm trying to survive again, but this is a different kind of survival; a survival that breaks borders. It's not shooting and staying alive; it's making myself clean and keeping myself clean.

The hall doors open slowly, both of them together. A figure walks through into the hall. I grip at the leaves beneath me. It's Milk.

He looks around, notices the pattern and follows it with his eyes. He only sees me when I stand up.

'Jay?' he says.

'Yeah.' I state it. It's not a question. I don't want to know what the answer might be.

'What are you doing in here, bruv?'

'Are you the Spirit?'

Milk takes a few steps into the hall. He kicks through a couple of branches, then stops, checks his footing and looks around. 'What you talking about, man? Everyone's out looking for you. What you doing in here?'

I turn to Leo. 'Help me out, bruv,' I say, but he doesn't move. He's sunk into the leaves and looks like he's disappeared off inside himself again. 'Leo? For fuck's sake, Leo?' I'm not having him disappearing now. I step towards him. 'Leo?' I go to grab at his shoulder, to shake him, but all I grab is a handful of leaves, and he crumbles away, mingling with the nest. A pile of leaves. Nothing else. I look at the leaves in my fist and let them fall.

'Who are you talking to?' says Milk.

I jump because in those few seconds he's come close, too close. I turn quickly and step away.

I can see it now. I can see it. It's him, it's all of us.

'I'm glad you're here,' I say.

'Why?'

'I didn't want to do this on my own.'

'Do what?'

I don't answer him. I can't. I know what's coming. Milk steps closer.

I turn to my side, stand still and look away. I don't want to see. There's movement; I stand firm, try hard not to react, and Milk swings his fist and connects with my ribs. It's harder than it looks and it's enough to knock me off my feet and onto the nest. I'm wondering how it could, when Milk stands over me and I realize it wasn't just his fist; I see the metal. He swings again. I put up my hand but it's half-hearted and he avoids it easily. I feel the jolt, and this time the pain, but not sharp like the blade; it's dull, an ache deep and wide. And I feel cold there, wet and cold, and it spreads.

'Sorry, bruv,' he says. 'You're my ticket. I want to be in the Olders. It's nothing personal, you get me?'

'Nothing personal?' I say. 'How is this not personal? You want to explain what personal would be? You're supposed to be my best friend!'

'The Boyz is more important than that. The Boyz is all there is. You should've killed Ram, man. You should've done it.'

'I did kill him. He just came back to life.'

'Yeah, well . . . I got to make sure that don't happen to you.' His voice tenses at the end as he swings again, and it's a blow hard enough to knock me flat. I sink down. But all that goes through my mind is: it's not that bad. It's not as bad as I thought it would be. I thought it would hurt more, I thought I'd panic. And I think, This is so much easier. Compared to Ram. It's so much easier to kill someone than it is to give them life. I wonder why that is? I wonder if it adds up, if there's some equation that explains it. But then you'd have to explain the equation. Letters and numbers don't mix. I breathe out heavily; my head's swirling. I'm getting tired – tired enough to sleep.

Milk crouches down and our eyes meet for a second. I see him swallow, go to speak, but then he starts digging into the leaves and patting at my sides, looking for something. He doesn't find it. 'Have you got Shads's piece, bruv?' he whispers.

I roll onto my side and feel the wetness spread up my

chest, soaking now. The aching grips, clamps and squeezes. 'Back of my jeans,' I say, my voice getting caught. I have to cough, but that cough sets off a whole stream of coughs.

Milk takes the gun. 'Thanks, bruv,' he says, standing up. He says it kind of gentle, like he's genuinely grateful. Maybe he is.

There's a breeze across the floor; it rustles leaves, and I swear they speak, whisper. 'Get out,' they say. Or was that me? I don't know. I'm getting really tired, fading in and out.

Milk starts to speak, I try and focus in on what he's saying but he stops. He doesn't say anything else, and I listen to his footsteps across the hall. The door opens, bangs shut. For a second I'm scared to be left alone, but only a second. It's OK. I force myself onto my back, my body nearly too heavy. I wonder if Leo's going to come back. I wonder if I'm lying on top of him. It's his fault if I am.

'I hope I'm squashing you, bruv,' I say, my voice sounding distant, not even mine.

I look down and see leaves on my chest, moving with my breathing, which is harder and faster than it feels. I take one of them; an old sycamore leaf, curled and gnarly. I'm careful with it, holding it up. I'd want a better-looking one to take with me, but I don't mind if this is it. I tuck it into my grip, hold it like a hand. I don't mind about anything. I don't mind. I don't mind where I go. If I go down, I'll fight my way back up. I'll climb every step. And if I don't go down, I've got a lot of questions. I'm going to ask why make it so hard? Why not give us chances when we can take them? Before it's too late? But maybe it's not just about one person. And maybe Milk's right in one way. Maybe it isn't personal. Maybe the picture's bigger than that.

And I guess soon I'm going to find out how big. And I'll see if I can come back somehow like Leo, see Hannah again. Even if I'm only a breeze against her face. Even if she has to peel me off her shoe. I'll be the best-looking leaf she's ever seen. She can put me in the corner of her room, and I'll look after her, watch over her. Whisper in her ear. It's OK. *It's going to be OK.* And it is, isn't it? Whatever happens. It might hurt. It might hurt a lot. It might hurt for a long time. But it's always going to be OK.

ACKNOWLEDGMENTS

The Lucas family, especially my mother Sylvia and brother David; and my nephews Joe and Luke Fisher. My agent Ajda Vucicevic and Luigi Bonomi at LBA. Parul Bavishi, Annie Eaton and all the team at RHCB.

A very big thank you to you all!

Turn the page for

TROUBLE

a short story featuring characters from

TURF

ONE

What happened was this . . .

To begin with it just looked like a really busy afternoon. But as Carl's eyes started to take it in, he could see it had been twisted, cranked up. On Mare Street they weren't shopping. JD Sports had been broken into and people surged inside, ran out cradling trainers and tracksuits. A chant went up around the watchers: 'JD . . . JD . . . JD.' Traffic was gridlocked, the sounding horns pointless, and the air was thick with sirens and the whirring rotor blades of helicopters hovering low above. Crowds filled the pavement and the street – some getting trouble, some wanting trouble, some just watching everyone else, drinking in the spectacle, filming it with phones high above their heads. Further up the road under the railway bridge, a zigzag of police cars was parked across the street, one smashed up. A line of riot police were stood there. They weren't moving, seemed content to leave everyone to it, only responding when anyone came too close, to goad them or throw missiles. They were letting people break what they wanted, steal what they wanted, do what they wanted. Even the buses stuck in traffic were set upon, their windows broken. A van had its back forced open and crates and planks of wood were being taken out, carried off.

Carl looked up at the helicopters, three of them there; their steady sound only adding to the unreal atmosphere, feeding it, recycling it; sending it back down hotter and denser. A group of kids came through on bikes; Carl thought he recognized them. But then they all looked the same, hoods up, faces covered. One mass, one energy.

Carl watched them go and a voice rang out clear in his head: *There's catching up to do.* He followed them up the street, past the bystanders, the rubberneckers. Carl wasn't interested in watching from the sidelines, not any more. He wanted a piece of it. He wanted to *take* a piece of it. He'd tried playing the game; he'd tried following the rules. The rules didn't work. Just look around: the rules *definitely* didn't work.

Up ahead a kid picked up a metal bin that had found its way into the middle of the street. He carried it over to the pavement, raised it high and, speeding up, slammed it into a shop window. A cheer went up, whistles. Another followed, this time with a shopping trolley. Others came with planks of wood, chairs, whatever they could get their hands on. They were carrying the fight, spreading the fight. They took it in turns, hitting the same spot on the window, and it started to weaken, the glass patterned like a web.

Carl saw a thin metal pole in the gutter, tight up against the kerb. He picked it up, and for a second he questioned himself. But there was no confusion. His head was clear, pinpointed. Something had to give, that was all; something *was* giving. Something had to be *done*. This was doing, this was *now*. There wasn't any *now* in the life he'd been living. He'd grown to realize there wasn't even a *later*. With cheers at his back he joined the assault on the window, swinging the pole hard.

A kid, his hood up, red bandana covering his face, joined Carl, holding a bike frame high – no wheels, no seat – and hit the window with it, same place. 'Yes, mate!' he shouted.

366

'That yours?' said Carl.

'Yeah,' he laughed. 'It is now, innit?'

Carl and the kid took it in turns, hitting the window again and again. Carl *was* catching up. He could feel it. Nearly two year's worth.

Once the window had gone, the kid dumped the bike frame on the ground and reached in to get what he could. Others joined him, but Carl moved on. He followed the road up. All around, shop windows were getting smashed. Bins were dragged into the middle of the road and set alight.

The riot police began to mobilize, coming forward in a steady blue line. People picked up bottles scattered across the street from upturned bins. They ran towards the police and hurled the bottles at them, the air ringing with breaking glass. The ones that hit were swatted away, but it kept them slow. Others arrived with fireworks, shooting whining rockets at the advancing line.

Down a side street a car was being set upon, kids attacking it from all sides. Carl was running to join in before he even knew it. It didn't matter where they were from – what estate, what school, nothing. All that was set aside. It was like a game. It was like a game, but at the same time felt more real than anything ever had before, like this was the way it was always supposed to be, if no one got involved – no authorities, no police, no laws.

A brick went through the car's passenger window. A kid arrived holding a breeze block above his head and smashed it through the windscreen. One young kid, only about eleven or twelve, climbed up on the roof, started jumping up and down on it. With his pole, Carl got to work on the taillights, smashing them with ease. There wasn't much space left around the car, and one older kid, his grey hood pulled tight around his face, just had the driver's door to focus on. He opened it, slammed it shut, opened it, slammed it shut. After a few goes he wasn't making much headway, so he walked off, took a run-up and fly-kicked it instead. He disappeared and came back with a plank of wood that he sent through the driver's window. Carl moved round to the side, swung his pole like a baseball bat into the back door, making deep dents with a satisfying crunch. A flaming bottle was tossed in through the open windscreen and it landed on the driver's seat.

Carl paused to watch the seat begin to burn. He caught sight of himself in the back-door window. He didn't want to look at first, scared of what he'd see. But there he was. His eyes wide, his jaw set, his shoulders set. Standing tall. His heart hit hard inside his chest, beat like it was meant to. *At last*. His head whirred like rotor blades, thoughts and feelings all churned up. And his reflection saw him; told him the news just by looking: he was back.

TWO

What happened was this . . .

'So you wanna . . . just . . . leave?'

'Yeah.'

'Just like that?'

'Yeah.'

'Where you gonna go?'

'I dunno. Nowhere.'

Bells laughed a spluttering laugh and kicked back in his chair. 'You wanna leave and go nowhere?'

'Yeah.' Any other time Carl would've thought that was weak, not enough. But this wasn't any other time. The night before, he'd had a gun pointed at his head, shots were fired, he didn't know how, but they'd missed. It had changed things.

Bells' tone went cold. He stared hard at Carl. 'I can't have people thinking they can just walk away. What do you think this is? Some holiday camp? Some job or hobby or some shit?'

'I know what it is, Bells. I've been doing it long enough.'

'Yeah ... so you should know what to expect. You should know what you're asking. Take some time. Go away and take some time. I've been shot at myself. I know what it's like. It gets you thinking. Gets you thinking all kinds of shit. It gets you thinking, but that's all it does. It doesn't change anything. The world's still the world. You understand? The estate's still the estate. Hackney's still Hackney.'

'It's not, though, Bells. I saw it. It was different. *I* was different.'

'What? What did you see?'

Carl looked down at his feet, his trainers nestled deep in Bells' cream-coloured carpet. Up until then he had been rising fast. Rising so fast he was on course for the top, maybe even taking Bells' place one day. Now he'd come to see him, the boss, the big boss, the man who ran things on the estate, to tell him that he was leaving the crew. It wasn't a decision you took lightly; it wasn't a decision you were

371

supposed to take at all. But Carl *had* changed. That night had changed him in the blink of an eye, the click of a trigger, and he had found himself somewhere down the dark barrel of a gun.

Carl told Bells what had happened.

'You realize if you ain't with us . . .' said Bells, speaking into the silence that followed. He held up his fist and looked closely at the scar across his knuckles. 'If you ain't with us . . . I ain't gonna say you're against us, but . . . no one's gonna look out for you, you understand?' He paused to pinch the scar between his fingers. 'You get in trouble: you deal with it. You get hurt: that's your business. Ain't no one gonna help. Ain't no one probably even gonna *speak* to you. You understand? You prepared for that?'

Bells raised his eyes. Carl nodded.

'I'm gonna have to tell people you gone crazy, that you're a liability. That way it looks like we're doing ourselves a favour by getting rid of you. And that means you keep your head down, you lay low. And you stick with what I say. No mistakes.'

'Whatever you say, Bells.'

Bells rocked forward. 'Yeah . . . that's right,' he said. 'It is whatever I say. It's always whatever I say. Remember that. But I'll give you a chance. Take some time. You got a day.'

Carl knew he'd already said too much. Even if he went back the next day and told Bells that he'd reconsidered . . . he'd already broken some faith, some trust. There couldn't be any weakness, any *sign* of weakness. But the fact was, he didn't want to go back. Bells was in charge out on the estate, but inside . . . inside, Carl had handed over control to someone else, someone who could not be argued with, who would not be denied, a person who would not take no for an answer: *himself*.

The night before was a sharp night in early November, twenty-one months before those few days in August when the curtain was pulled down, the world caught out, caught napping. That night, Carl had been introduced to the real Carl; the deep-down Carl. The Carl that lived so far inside him that it was barely even a Carl he recognized.

THREE

What happened was this . . .

Carl was sixteen then and he loved trouble. Him and trouble had been *tight*. It was trouble that gave him purpose; that gave him the spring to bounce out of bed in the morning. It was trouble he'd meet at the school gates. Street-level trouble. The kind of trouble you'd bump into coming round a dark corner, or in the shadows of stairwells and alleyways. The kind of trouble that would ring late at night with coded messages and details of covert meetings.

That night trouble called and Carl went out to meet it. But it turned out Carl had been set up. He got jumped from behind – a crack on his jaw and he was down, a gun right in his face, the barrel gaping wide, about to swallow him up, swallow the whole world. The barrel pressed hard against his head, the finger on the trigger, pressing down, pressing down.

'DO YOU WANT TO LIVE?'

'Of course I want to live!' shouted Carl, gasping at the pain in his jaw.

'WHY?'

Why? What kind of a question was that? And how was he supposed to answer? *Why?* The questions kept on coming and the gun kept on pressing down. Carl felt his life being pulled out of him, wrenched out of him like a roll of film. He watched it play out behind his eyes, in front of his eyes, all around. IMAX and surround-sound. There was no hiding place. He watched the moves he'd always made, the parts he'd always played. He watched the posing, the posturing, the pretending, the acting, the trying to be somebody. It was him, a version of him, but it wasn't *him*.

It was a cruel trick to play. Here he was, about to die, and he saw – saw with ice-cold clarity – that he had never even lived. Sure, he'd had air in his lungs, blood pumping in his veins, light in his eyes. But he'd never *lived*.

Lying there, down on the concrete, blood and grit in his

mouth, the black steel against his forehead, Carl knew –
knew it that second – that if he'd had his time over, he
would've been serious. He would've had *serious* fun; he
would've laughed, cried, run, slept, eaten, breathed, washed,
kissed, fought, talked, walked, with a hundred per cent of
everything, with a whole world of commitment, with every
sinew and fibre and muscle and ounce.

It was too late, though. It was all going to end and he'd
learned it too late. The gun fired: BANG-BANG-BANG.

. . . But he was still there . . . he was still there . . . he was
still there. He didn't know how, he didn't know why, but he
was still there. He'd been given another chance. He ran
home. He flew up the steps of his block, slammed his front
door and locked himself in the bathroom. Clinging tight to
the washbasin, he stared at his reflection, the film on constant repeat behind his eyes.

Carl reinvented himself in the bathroom mirror. He
shaved off his hair, he changed his name. He saw a different
future. A future without trouble.

Carl went to see Bells as arranged. Taking the time he'd
suggested had only made Carl more sure, more determined.

Bells made it clear that Carl was cut adrift, that he might as well have been shot and killed. He might carry on living in the same flat, the same block, but as far as the crew was concerned, from then on he wasn't anyone, he wasn't worth anything.

'Anything?' said Carl.

'That's right. You should be prepared to accept anything. In fact, you're lucky if you get anything. There are plenty of people out there who can't even get that.'

'Great,' said Carl. 'Inspirational. Thanks.'

The man behind the desk pushed his glasses up his nose and looked at Carl blankly. 'We're not here to be inspirational. We're here to get you into work. And with your age, your education, I'd advise you to take any work you can get. If you don't want a job that's up to you, but if that's the case, you won't get any benefits.' He smiled a smug, case-closed smile, and joined his hands together.

Carl hadn't said he didn't want a job. That's why he'd come to the job centre: because he *did* want one. He wanted to tell the man how hard he'd worked to get that education he was sneering at; how close he'd come to not even seeing that age; how tough it had been to even find his way into the seat opposite him in the first place. But the man wasn't interested. Carl was just a number, a name, a box to tick. The man handed over a mound of forms and paperwork. Carl was dismissed.

It was the end of the following summer; ten months after Carl's gunpoint revelation, his meeting with Bells, and his decision to turn his back on the crew.

The only way he'd got through it was by keeping himself busy. He did his schoolwork, worked out; played football, basketball; joined a boxing club. Avoiding trouble had kept him busy too. It still hung around – in school, on the estate, on the streets. Carl had to leave the flat early when the coast was clear; he had to walk different routes, come home late, check corners, check shadows. But he'd done it. He took his GCSEs in the spring, and considering he crammed five years of school work into five months, he did well.

When he got his results, it seemed the hard work had paid off. He could have stayed on to do his A-levels but he wanted to get out into the world. He wanted that new life, the life he'd seen for himself that November night.

Carl went to the job centre every week. He searched the touch-screen machines, printing off available jobs, taking them to a desk when his name was called, and was shown how to apply. He did his bit, they gave him a form, he signed his name, he went on his way.

Applying for jobs became a full-time job in itself. It took whole days to do it. Page after page of personal statements, questionnaires, employment and experience histories (even if you didn't have any), evaluations, critiques, essays, personal statements, questionnaires, employment and experience histories . . . It was like he was going for a job at NASA or MI5, not loading boxes at a warehouse.

'Why do I need to write all this?' Carl asked.

'Because there's a lot of competition. They need to make sure they choose the right candidate.'

'I've got arms and legs. I can carry stuff. Ain't that enough?'

It didn't seem like it was enough, no.

If there was one thing Carl quickly learned about the world, it was that it was built on forms, made of forms, stuck together with forms. Stacks and stacks of them. You needed a form to do this, a form to do that. You needed a form for a form that meant you could fill out a form which gave you access to a form that meant you were registered for another form. The world turned on forms. Forget fire, forget the wheel, forget the computer, it was the form that was clearly the height of human achievement.

When Carl sent off an application for a telesales job, didn't hear anything back, and continued to see it advertised, he began to wonder if the jobs he was going for even existed at all; if it wasn't really some conspiracy, some kind of population control – just keep them filling out the forms, the forms, the forms, the forms, keep them quiet, keep them occupied, keep them *out of trouble*.

Eventually a couple of Carl's applications did lead to interviews, but the interviews didn't lead to jobs. Too many of the other applicants had the necessary experience. How much experience you needed to work in a fast-food restaurant or behind a deli counter, Carl wasn't sure. But either way, he didn't have it. He didn't have what it took.

It was Christmas when Carl got his first official job. It was a temporary one, stacking shelves overnight in a cavernous supermarket. The other staff members drifted like ghosts along the aisles, nocturnal eyes wide despite the unforgiving strip lights. The only sounds the squeak of trolley wheels, the rip of packaging, and the occasional whispered bad joke, followed by the echo of a desperate laugh. Carl started to think that maybe his mind had tricked him. Maybe he really *had* died on that November night after all; maybe this was some kind of afterlife, some limbo land he'd been condemned to inhabit in everlasting confusion.

As it turned out, it only lasted a month. The supermarket offered permanent jobs to some of the Christmas staff, but Carl wasn't one of them. He was told he 'didn't have the right attitude to represent the company'. It was the only good thing anyone had said to him the whole time he was there. 'Thanks,' said Carl.

Carl's job seeker's allowance didn't stretch far, and his parents' help only stretched to essentials, so Carl had to give up the gym and the boxing. To keep busy he volunteered at a local community group, the idea being that he'd talk to younger kids about his experiences, about his old life, about how close he'd come to dying, and how it had changed him.

Carl had a story to tell, but his voice was shaky – telling it was different when there was a group of kids staring at you, looking bored, trying not to be interested.

Stephen, a mouthy know-it-all twelve-year-old, put his hand up. 'Why's your life so much better now, then?' he said.

Carl met his eyes. He could tell from the look in them that Stephen was on the edge, on the verge of squeezing trouble for all it was worth.

'Well . . .' he said. He swallowed hard. 'It's just better. I feel better. Inside.'

The kids laughed. Carl looked at Stephen. To begin with he didn't join in with the others – maybe wanted to hear more, wanted to understand – but all too quickly he was laughing along. They didn't want to hear about feelings – they wanted evidence, results. They wanted excitement and action.

On his walk home that evening, Carl realized he hadn't thought it through. He hadn't thought it through because he didn't want to know the answer himself. Of course, it was obvious that risking your life, risking someone else's, risking a life banged up, these were bad. But what was the alternative? What did it look like? Carl was finding it hard to tell. It had all seemed so simple that November night, so clear. But where did it all go now? Where did it fit?

When Carl turned the corner to the stairwell of his block, a big hand hit hard into his chest and pushed him up against the wall. It was Bells. 'What do you think you're doing?' he said, his voice rasping, his face in close.

'What are you talking about, Bells?' Carl's voice was thin; the old bravado rusty.

'Where you been tonight.' It sounded like it should've been a question but it wasn't. 'What was the deal? Can you remember what the deal was?'

Carl's mouth was dry. He couldn't answer.

'No more talking. You understand? No more messing with kids' heads. You understand? What did I tell you about keeping your head down?'

'OK,' said Carl. His breath had gone. Nothing to offer.

'No mistakes, yeah? No *talking*. No causing trouble. You don't want to leave the estate in a bag.' Bells slipped off into the shadows, every other shadow turning deadly in his place.

Carl didn't go back to the community group. At first it was because of Bells. But soon it felt like it was the whole world. Carl found it hard to even get out of bed in the mornings. It was a fight too big. And if he was up against the whole world, then he'd just avoid the world. He started to spend more and more time at home. He played computer games, gave up whole days to them, whole weekends, whole weeks. It felt like he was giving his life away; it was anti-life, a way of forgetting he even existed. But at least in the games he could be somebody; he could make progress, achieve something, even if that something didn't have a place outside his bedroom. In his bedroom he could be the hero. And his bedroom was better than nothing.

He'd have crazy dreams – dreams where he put on massive parties, taking over the whole block, inviting the whole estate, his old crew, Bells. He'd wake up, his cheeks wet with tears, his heart pounding, like it was trying to take over the job itself, start a coup, a mutiny, break away while Carl was unconscious.

The job centre started hassling. They told him if he didn't start applying for more jobs there'd be trouble – he could lose his benefits. *Trouble*. The word chimed, it rang out. Trouble: Carl had missed it. Carl missed that spring in his step, that fire in his belly. He missed his friends who still lived their lives with it up close, entwined.

By that summer Carl felt as formless as a ghost. He surprised himself whenever he saw his own reflection, like it was a trick of the light, a flashback, a hallucination. He didn't want to see it, didn't want to be reminded of who he was. The summer only made matters worse; the contrast of the sun trying hard to get through his closed curtains just made his room all the darker.

He knew what had been happening those few days in August – even if you were like Carl, you couldn't avoid it. The police had shot a man dead in Tottenham. The circumstances were suspicious, hazy. People wanted answers, but they didn't get any, didn't get anything. There'd been a protest. The protest had turned into a disturbance, the disturbance into a riot. And the riot had spread, was getting in people's heads, giving them ideas. It was blowing up.

From his window it looked like the whole estate was out on the streets. He could see smoke rising in the distance, helicopters. Trouble was closing in. Maybe it was looking for Carl. Maybe it was calling him back. It was. It did.

FOUR

What happened was this . . .

Carl's reflection was obscured by the flames taking hold inside the car. He dropped the pole and walked a distance away in case the tank blew. He would've set light to it all if he could, send it all up, burn it all up, rip it all up and start again. Maybe next time they'd get it right. Wasn't this proof, wasn't it all proof that the world didn't work?

He looked at the helicopters again, hovering low: the police, the media. They created their own invisible ceiling, created a hothouse. And maybe that was it: maybe down on the streets they weren't meant to reach any higher. Maybe that had been Carl's mistake: *trying*. Maybe he had to stick with what he had, who he was, who he really was. Like he used to be. Street level. Street-level ambition, street-level hopes, street-level dreams. Street-level trouble.

What cause are you going to fight for when everything, when even just living, is a fight in itself?

Get up in the morning, *win the battle*. Walk straight, *win the battle*. They step out of your way? Good. *You won the battle*. That was as far as it got. There was no time for right and wrong. Right and wrong were luxuries, luxury items. Right was an expensive education and a fat wallet. Right was a bronze tan, a silver spoon, a golden handshake. And wrong was whatever *right* said it was, whatever *right* wanted it to be.

That day there was no right. Right was on holiday. The government was on holiday. It could afford one.

The riot police had cleared a path along the main road now, so Carl went the other way. He saw other groups of kids involved in pitched battles, smashing shops and cars and breaking windows, setting light to bins, or getting hold of whatever they could to take the fight back to the police.

Carl walked the streets. He was surprised how easy it was – first to take part, to cross lines he'd always thought were impossible to cross, then to walk around, be a tourist, watching, taking it in.

When he got back to the estate, battles were still going on with the police. There was a front line further up — it kept changing position as the police charged, retreated, charged, retreated. But for a large area behind, it could have been Carnival time. The streets were crowded, people laughing, drinking. The only difference was the burning smell wasn't grills and barbecues; it was cars and wheelie bins; and there was glass everywhere, crunching underfoot.

As the sun went down there was a lull. Most of the police had moved on, leaving the burning cars to smoulder on into the dusk. But there were still plenty of people who hadn't finished. Carl watched as a local mini-market was broken into. A crowd gathered outside, looking tentative at first, like captive animals who've had their cages opened. They weren't quick like they'd been on Mare Street. They didn't need to be. But once the first person went in and came out cradling bottles of spirits and packs of cigarettes, it didn't take long for others to follow, and soon there was a steady stream helping themselves.

There was a grab at Carl's shoulder. Carl turned and

immediately recognized Bells from the narrow slit between bandana and hood. 'What are you doing here?' said Bells.

In that instant Carl knew the ground between them was flat, level. It was all level that day. He shrugged. 'The same thing everyone else is.'

'It's great, innit?' said Bells, softening, looking around with pride. 'Best day ever.'

'Yeah . . .' said Carl.

Bells patted Carl's shoulder and disappeared into the mini-market.

The best day ever? Carl wasn't so sure. He watched the people walk in and out of the shop, all casual about it now, like it was normal. He saw Bells come out, meet someone he knew at the doorway and share a joke. Then Bells was gone, down the street, sauntering into the crowd, swigging on one of the bottles he'd taken.

Carl wasn't sure if he was there for the same reasons everyone else was, either. There'd been a bomb ticking. That afternoon it had gone off. Carl had known the owners of the mini-market since he was a kid – he didn't remember them ever causing any trouble. They were his own people, part of the community, the *same* community. It was one thing getting angry, one thing blowing up; but it was another letting that bomb go off in your own face.

Carl didn't hang around for much longer, but the damage had been done. A couple of days later he saw Bells again in the car park outside his block.

'You want to be careful,' said Bells.

'Let it go, Bells. I'm finished with all that. Do what you want, man. I don't care any more.'

'I ain't talking about that. Look: I'm saying watch yourself. I saw you walking around. You should've covered yourself up. Those sentences are harsh, bruv. Two of my boys gone down already. No bail. Straight to court, straight inside. And straight inside for *long*. Watch yourself.'

Bells was right. It wasn't long before there was a heavy banging on Carl's front door.

He was taken to the police station and questioned – just a formality, going through the motions. He was put in a cell alone while he waited to be charged. He wasn't expecting anything else. He paced up and down; when he got bored of that he read the fire safety notice. He read the graffiti on the wall; back to the fire safety notice, managed to learn it off by heart. There wasn't much else to do. He lay down on the thin vinyl mattress and concentrated on his breathing. And he surprised himself: he started to laugh.

He'd tried to be good, but the world wasn't designed for people to be good: it was designed for them to be obedient – being on time, filling out forms, staying in line, keeping your head down. On the estate, off the estate, it worked out as the same thing. The crew and the police actually had a lot in common. They should get together, talk it over.

Carl thought back to that November night again. He thought about the whole time in between. He thought about going back to the community group. This time telling his story properly. All of it. What good would it do if he didn't? The world needed to change, but no one ever changed anything by staying in line. Not the crew's line, not the police line, not the dotted line on all the world's forms. Carl had to draw his own line. That was the only line that mattered.

He pictured Stephen again, this time asking him about the riots, asking him about his sentence, what prison was like.

'Well,' said Carl quietly. 'What happened was this . . .'